HARD AS ROCK

Khargals of Duras

STEPHANIE WEST

INTRODUCTION

A thousand years ago, a Khargal scouting party left Duras, only to crash on a planet called Earth.

Injured and outnumbered, the stranded Khargals hid among stone effigies and observed the slow evolution of the planet's primitive inhabitants. With no means of returning to Duras, they watched from their shadowy perches and faded into legend, becoming the mythical gargoyles.

Until today. Long after any hope for rescue had died, the distress signal has finally been answered.

It's time to go home.

HARD AS ROCK

After the loss of her parents, Meline scrapes together the cash to take a once-in-a-lifetime trip. Armed with her great-grand-father's journal, retracing her heritage should be exciting, yet she can't shake the frightening feeling someone's been watching her from the moment she arrived in the old city. Then Roc shows up just when she needs him, offering to help. He's sexy-as-sin, wealthy, and well-connected, but there's something he's hiding.

Roc needs to locate his Khargal sire's lost sigil before all hell breaks loose, and Meline holds a journal with the answers. After centuries of "liberating" art, he's never thought twice about lying or stealing, but when the captivating woman appears at the site where his father's buried, he hesitates. Something about her has gotten underneath his stoney exterior, and he doesn't know what to do.

When a clandestine group hunting the sigil emerges, Roc and Meline must face them together before the sigil turns every-thing to ash. Yet the challenge may not be finding the sigil so much as breaking down the wall guarding Roc's heart.

ROC

Roc smiled to himself as he soared over the tree tops. The job had gone well. He made it into the ridiculously gauche private gallery and retrieved the painting without incident.

"Who puts pieces like that in a hall with a skylight? Don't they know light wreaks havoc on art?" Roc muttered into the wind whipping past him as he flew.

When he laid eyes on the Van Gogh self-portrait, he was tempted to keep it for his own collection. The paint strokes were strikingly bold as only Van Gogh could pull off. But it was the tortured expression on Vincent's face that tempted him to keep it the most. There was something in the man's eyes that made him instantly feel like they were kindred spirits. However, it deserved to go back to its rightful owner, so he'd consoled himself by also liberating a lesser-known work by Klimt before leaving the ostentatious home. He had just the right spot for it in his Montreal estate.

Roc snapped out of his thoughts when his cell phone

pinged. He was nearly on top of the location programmed into it. Roc glanced around at the miles and miles of dense forest, then double checked the GPS.

"This is it," he confirmed with a smirk.

Roc shook his head and did a nose dive, aiming for a barely noticeable swath cut through the trees, leading up the mountain.

"Ah dammit." He batted at the attacking brush as he landed on the gravel road. "I seriously need to remember the *duramna* next time I land at Zaek's," Roc grumbled as he pulled the brambles from his wings, tucked them back, partially shelled in his *duramna*—stony form—before heading up the overgrown road.

The moonlight struggled to pierce the dense woods and light the way, not that he needed it to see the cabin ahead. It just highlighted how far out in the sticks his friend chose to hide himself away.

Zaek's not that unfortunate-looking for a purebred. You wanna talk about a tragic mug, that would be my sire, and hell, he bagged my mum.

Roc paused midstride. It had been a while since he'd thought about his mother, the sweetest, kindest human he'd ever known. A twinge of guilt gripped him for his idle rambling. Theresa loved his sire, Petronus, despite his looks and a heart harder than his *duramna*. And that was saying a lot since she lived in an age when the unexplained was called satanic and the Khargals who showed themselves were hunted. Although the twenty-first century wasn't too different from the fifteenth when it came to prejudice against the unknown.

"But we do have modern amenities. *Lar* dammit, Zaek,"

Roc cursed his friend as he stepped onto the porch and tried the door. "Seriously, why bother locking it?" He looked around incredulously at the forest. "Who's gonna break in, the bears?"

Roc tilted his head and listened, but didn't hear anyone inside, and there wasn't a single light on.

"You gotta be kidding me. That hermit never leaves home," Roc mumbled. *Well, there's no way in Macero I'm waiting out here.* It hadn't been an incredibly long flight, but he was ready to rest his tail and throw back a beer.

A rotten grin twisted Roc's face as he imagined Zaek getting his tail in twist when he found him in his home.

That male really needs to chill.

He opened his mouth and hummed the tune too high for mortal ears to hear. The wolves howling in the distance nearly broke his concentration, making him want to laugh. Apparently, they didn't appreciate his serenade. He concentrated and listened for the innards of the complex lock to fall into place. Eventually everything fell in line like it always did when he used the handy subsonic sounds—the gift of his sire's clan. His ancestors used the talent in defense of Duras, infiltrating the enemy and acquiring the means to defend the home world. At least that's what his sire went on about during the hours and hours of training as a youth. However, here on Earth there wasn't much use for a Khargal's talents or a Khargal at all, so Roc used the clan gift for less noble ventures.

A man has needs, after all. And his conquests had been so much fun.

Roc stepped over the threshold and something zipped past his head, narrowly missing his eye. His hand whipped up and caught the projectile as he jumped back. Roc stared in shock at the dart in his hand. The diamond tip guaranteed the flimsy projectile would easily pierce his stony facade. And if he wasn't mistaken, he scented a powerful sedative.

"Are you fucking kidding me, Zaek?" he bellowed as his gaze swiveled from the fancy dart to the pressure sensitive tile.

He studied the foyer, taking note of the motion sensitive laser array. The thin red beams bisected the entry, shifting in an ever-changing pattern. Even if he flew over the booby-trapped foyer floor, he'd still break the beams and set off the damn tranq darts.

Not even Fort Knox has this kinda shit.

Roc tilted his head and studied the pattern. Everything slowed as his focus honed in on the goal. He hadn't had a challenge like this in a while. Roc's tailed flicked with excitement. He forcibly stilled it and tucked his wings tight against his back. Roc launched himself forward and flipped over the first beam, tucked and rolled beneath the next. He pivoted right to avoid the third but the clawed tip of his wing grazed the roving beam.

"Fuck me!" He dodged the projectiles that shot out from both walls. "Screw it." Roc ran for it, then dove, skidding into the living room. He stood up and smiled. "Now, where's the suspicious bastard's control panel?"

He flanked the wall, knocking on the solid logs as he went. He didn't dare venture further into any of the rooms considering the welcome he'd just received. The place was more stark and somber than he recalled from his friend. Of course it had been a decade, maybe two since they'd seen each other. Zaek hadn't been an extrovert back then either, then again most Khargals weren't, especially purebreds. But it looked like Zaek was really wallowing in his hermitude here in the sticks.

Roc froze in his tracks when he reached the back of the cabin. The hair on the back of his neck stood up like it did when he sensed something odd. His gaze narrowed on an unusual spot on the wall. There was something there, hidden. He felt the ridges on the log, his finger catching on a knot. There was a click and a panel opened revealing a keypad.

"Bingo."

His fingers flew over the controls as he teased out the sequence of numbers. *It would be easier if he knew Zaek's password, but what's the fun in that?*

"That's what I'm talking about!" Roc whooped with a pump of his fist when he finally got it, disengaging the system.

A hidden door slid open, revealing a rocky corridor that appeared to lead into the mountain.

I am so not going into Zaek's secret room. The last thing I need to find is he's into bondage or some shit like that. Although it'd be worse to discover he's hiding a collection of My Little Ponies, Roc snorted as he shut the secret door, then added himself to Zaek's security system just to aggravate the male.

Roc took a little tour of his friend's cabin, grabbed a beer then headed back to the living room and took a seat in the comfortable oversized chair. He propped his feet up on the tree stump turned coffee table and flipped on the TV to pass time.

"Well, Zaek, you're not quite a savage. At least you've got cable. Maybe I should buy a bunch of porn flicks on his pay-per-view." He chuckled, imagining Zaek's face when he discovered the cable bill.

Roc paused on the news when a recognizable building captured his attention. It was Château Frontenac, in Quebec City, the place where he'd grown up. Dread filled him as he watched the story unfold. They were excavating the remains of the old governor's mansion at the foot of the palatial hotel.

"Shit, this isn't good."

It seemed like yesterday when his mother died, but in reality, it had been centuries. Human life spans were a blink of an eye compared to a Khargal's. If Petronus had kept his hands to himself, his mother wouldn't have died trying to give birth to a sibling. His sire couldn't even give her room to breathe, kissing her incessantly as she clung to life. Unable to reconcile his anger, after watching from the shadows as the Jesuits consecrated his mother to the earth, Roc left the city of his youth and set out to see the world. It took a long time for the bitterness to fade, longer than he realized. Eventually he returned to Quebec to discover his sire had retreated into the *duramna* and gone to ground. And the only clue to Petronus' location were senile ramblings about the governor's mansion from the grandson of a long dead human friend.

Snarled curses from the front door drew his attention. Roc smiled seeing the perturbed expression on Zaek's face as he stomped into the living room.

"How's it hanging, sour puss?" Roc waved a tranq dart as he grinned at his friend.

"You are about to be hanging lopsidedly if you do not remove your fucking feet from my furniture," Zaek growled.

"Oh, please. You can just mangle a tree and make another.

It's not like it's a Louis XIVth." Roc thumped his heel on the stump.

Zaek's bark was worse than his bite—most of the time. And if the male's subtle snort was any indication, his antics had the desired effect. Despite his kind's generally brusque demeanor, it was good to see one of his own. It meant he didn't have to hide his wings and tail, or cover up his horns with a hat. Except rather than greeting his friend in what should be a happy reunion, his attention was again pulled toward the TV.

"Your sire is close to that, yes?" Zaek inquired, nodding toward the Quebec hotel featured on the screen.

"Yeah, the stubborn bastard," Roc growled.

"So, you do not plan to move him before they discover him?"

"I still have to *find* him. He's gone so deep into the *duramna*, the stoning, that I can't even sense him. All I know is he's somewhere entombed at the foot of Château Frontenac."

Roc didn't talk much about Petronus, and certainly didn't want to start now. He could hardly recall the last time he tried to reach out to his sire.

A decade? No. Two?

Roc frowned as he tried to recall when he last wandered where the old mansion stood overlooking the river. It was hard to keep trying when in three hundred years he'd yet to hear a single word from his sire or sense him stir. Roc took a sip of his beer to keep from snarling at his friend. His issues with Petronus weren't Zaek's fault.

"Hmm. You may want to get started on that. The beacon

has fallen from orbit and gone active," Zaek replied casually, as if he were talking about the weather.

"Say again?" Roc cleared his throat with another swig of beer. Surely, he misheard.

"The rescue beacon just switched on. We are getting off this miserable fucking rock."

The beacon! It's live?

Roc had been about six when he first learned about the beacon and sigils. He'd been nosing through his sire's cache and discovered the most amazing thing he'd ever seen. It wasn't like the other baubles and coins Petronus amassed, no, it was much more special. The way the ruby medallion shimmered and glowed, he was certain he'd found real treasure. True to form, his sire grumbled something about the home world being lost and shoved the sigil back into the trunk. It was his mother who patiently explained the oblong sigil connected his kind to their true home, a star in the heavens.

"How? Where'd you hear that?" he asked, shocked to hear about the beacon and sigils after all this time.

"I have monitored the frequency since we got here. As we all ought to have been." Zaek cast him a look that clearly said he thought he was a dumbass.

"I just thought that shit was wishful thinking." Roc's sharp brow furrowed. He figured the beacon had drifted off in space, but apparently not. "And I've never been to Duras. Why the fuck should I care?"

"So, you want to stay here, hiding from the Earthians for the rest of your long life?" Zaek asked incredulously, his tail flicking in agitation. "Regardless of whether you were born here, you do not belong on this planet. You know that."

Purebreds spoke of Duras like it was the promised land.

Every Khargal he'd met was so damn miserable, pining for their lost home. They were always shocked to discover he had no interest in going to a planet he'd never set foot on.

"Yeah, 'cause my sire's first family is going to welcome a half-breed with open arms," Roc snarled.

Zaek grunted and kicked Roc's feet off the coffee table, spread his wings wide then plopped down on the couch. Zaek coughed before continuing with the touchy subject, "You are welcome to join me on my land back on Duras."

Roc had several homes here on Earth filled with more than enough beautiful things. Why the hell would he give all that up? And then there was the very fulfilling hobby that brought him to this part of the States, not to mention human women. He shivered recalling the description of Khargal females. They sounded more like males than the fairer sex. No, he much preferred his females soft and round, even if it took some effort to see those soft and round parts.

"Dude, that's a nice offer, but I've got a pretty sweet thing going here." Roc smirked as something occurred to him. "But I know of someone who would go back. If I can wake his ass up."

"Who?" Zaek asked, looking perplexed.

"Petronus, my sire, rocket scientist." Roc shook his head. For being such an intelligent male, his friend really had his bonehead moments. "You know, this just might be the news he needs to snap out of his funk."

Over the centuries, Roc tried to reconcile his frustration with his sire and let it go. It had to be hard crashing on a planet where foreign races, humans, forced them into hiding. Even for him it was trying sometimes, and he'd grown up on Earth and was just human enough to find ways to blend into society. But giving up and retreating into stone, the *duramna*, was just a cop-out. Zaek and other Khargals hadn't taken the chicken shit way out.

Roc's head popped up as he recalled something his sire said. "Wait, wasn't there some doomsday shit connected with the sigils?" The grim expression on Zaek's face confirmed the worst.

When the Khargals crashed a millennia before it hadn't been an issue, the humans weren't advanced enough to pose a problem, but that had changed. The sigils weren't merely a signal telling the rescue ship where to find them, they were a communicator and transporter all wrapped up in one. And in the wrong hands they were dangerous, like on an epic scale. Roc shivered as he pictured nuclear blasts going off all across Earth.

"We need to put out a call. All the sigils must be retrieved immediately. Even your sire's, regardless of whether or not you decide to stay."

"You think?" Roc shook his head at Zaek. As if they could just ignore the threat the sigils posed. "Except my sire, in his ultimate wisdom, didn't wait till I returned from my little walkabout. He passed it off to his human friend and went to ground. The son of a bitch couldn't even say *goodbye, good luck, don't fuck-up and get lynched, Roc.*"

Why Petronus entrusted something so valuable to their human friend, foolishly assuming the mortal would still be alive when Roc returned from his voyage, he would never know. Petronus was well aware of how short a human's life span was.

Because he stopped giving a shit. And like most of his kind, Petronus long ago lost hope of being rescued. Honestly, he couldn't blame them. A millennium was a long time even for a Khargal.

"Fuck," Zaek growled, his expression darkening.

"Believe it or not, I've been looking, but shit is not that easy." Roc stood and started pacing the living room. "My sire's friend was rather…prolific. Do you know how many descendants one human can have, and who's to say they even kept the sigil in the family?" Roc shook his head and snarled. "I should've come back home sooner. If I had known…"

The sigil was one of the reasons he traveled the world collecting art and antiquities. He'd acquired multiple fortunes, yet that one relic eluded him. In the past he wanted it because it was the first beautiful thing he coveted. The desire remained, but now there was added impetus.

"I have been working on a tracker to trace the origin of the frequency the beacon operates on. That's why I was out when you…*arrived*. I needed parts. It may take me a few days to finish, but I am close."

"I don't have a few days, do I? They could find Petronus before then," Roc pointed out, waving at the television even though it was no longer playing the news story.

"Then you need to go. Find your sire, and that sigil."

"And save the world." Roc finished the statement with a cheeky grin.

"You are an idiot," Zaek muttered with an exasperated eye roll.

Roc's grin widened when his friend chuckled under his breath as they headed toward the door. This was serious business, but a bit of comic relief was never a bad thing.

"Be safe. And do not fail." Zaek slapped him on the back as he nodded farewell.

Yeah, don't fail. Roc sighed, partially hardened his skin and leapt into the air.

MELINE

"Yes, sir, the Bora Bora seven-night, all-inclusive, oceanfront bungalow package does include the snorkeling and spa treatments you asked for. I've also reserved your private dinner and catamaran cruise on your anniversary. The price I quoted you is with the first-class airfare and transport from the airport to the resort," she explained to the caller.

Meline tried not to choke when the man used his debit card to pay for the twenty-grand vacation and it actually cleared without a hitch, when half the time she had to check her balance to buy a latte at the café around the corner.

Which I'm now wearing on my blouse. She scowled as she looked down at her stained shirt.

"I hope you enjoy your vacation, Mr. Carter, and again, happy anniversary," she reiterated, then hung up and pulled off her headset.

It was hard to not be jealous of whoever was married to that man. She'd kill for a surprise trip to Tahiti.

Hell, I'd kill for a surprise trip to Albuquerque. But the only way anything that exciting was going to happen to her was if men in ski masks showed up in a blacked-out van. She snorted at the depressing thought then stifled it. *Don't bitch. You're going on your own adventure.*

"When do you leave?" Jennifer asked when she pulled off her headset.

"Tomorrow. At the crack of dawn."

"I can't believe you're driving to Quebec." Jen shook her head.

"I just figured that would be the easiest way to see everything." Meline shrugged.

"I wish I was taking two weeks off to travel," her friend said wistfully.

Meline shut off her computer and looked around the travel agency. She'd gotten a job there hoping she'd get a good deal on trips and see the world, instead she stared at glossy posters of places she still couldn't afford to visit.

"It's not like I'm going on a tour of Europe, Jen."

"No, but I hear that Old Quebec is almost the same."

"Either way it'll be good. I just wish my dad could go." Meline frowned as she thought of her parents.

This was really a trip her mom and dad had planned. Their ancestors were founding families of Quebec, alongside Samuel de Champlain. Supposedly there was even a statue featuring her umpteenth great-grandfather and grandmother.

"Crap, I keep forgetting you're not just going to sight see. I'm sorry."

"Stop apologizing. It's been a year since their wreck," Meline chastised her friend.

The trip felt all the more important now that her parents had joined the ranks of their ancestors. *God rest their souls.*

"You sure there's not enough money left over from selling their house for you to make a jaunt across the Atlantic?" Jennifer wagged her brows.

"Um no." Once she paid for their funerals and settled her parents' estate, there was just enough to take this trip.

At first she debated moving out of her little condo and keeping the house. But without her parents in it, the place just felt weird. It was almost like someone else was there. Occasionally she even thought things had been moved, but that was just crazy. As good a friend as Jennifer was, Meline still wasn't about to admit she thought the house was haunted. Either way, selling it was the smart choice. She couldn't move on with the constant reminder that her parents were no longer there.

"Well, girl, the French accent isn't as sexy as a Scottish one, but it ranks up there. There's still a chance to mark 'torrid affair with a foreign god' off your bucket list."

"Stop!" Meline laughed.

She glanced at her reflection in the computer monitor and groaned at the way her brown hair hung flat over her shoulders and how washed out her complexion was.

Ugh. Yeah, like that's gonna happen.

There was nothing glamorous about her life, from her job in a cubicle and forgettable appearance, right down to her genealogy-inspired vacation. And the saddest thing was that she was actually excited to see where her long-forgotten family had walked the Earth. It was no wonder she hadn't attracted a man, let alone one willing to drop twenty thousand on a trip.

Oh well.

"I better get going. I still need to review my itinerary and finish packing." She smiled and grabbed her purse.

"Send me a postcard," Jen hollered as Meline headed for the elevator.

ROC

"Come on, Petronus, wake up, dammit," Roc hissed as he wandered the dark archaeological site beneath the boardwalk of Chateau Frontenac.

He'd been here every evening since returning from Zaek's, but his sire hadn't made the slightest indication of rousing. And the situation was worse than he imagined. Not only was the park service excavating the old governor's mansion, they'd turned the whole place into a tourist spectacle. Petronus was going to get left behind. Or worse, wind up the prime feature on the nightly news if he didn't wake the fuck up.

"Did you hear me? The beacon is live. It's time for your grumpy tail to go home."

Roc's heightened vision made it easy to see in the dark, yet he couldn't make out where his sire was. He'd canvassed every inch of this place and there wasn't a single Khargal-shaped rocky outcropping. The closest he'd come to finding a promising spot was the section of an exterior wall that still lay half buried. He couldn't be certain why he was drawn to it. Was Petronus entombed somewhere in there, or were his memories as a youth of watching the bustling mansion from afar making him fixate on the location he recognized? 1640 was a long time ago, and yet sometimes it felt like yesterday.

I guess none of it matters if I don't find that sigil. Roc pictured half of Canada going up in a blaze of glory. *Sacrament*, he cursed.

"Wake up and help me find the damn thing before a lot of people get hurt," he growled at the rocky wall.

Voices near the cavern entrance silenced his tirade. The guard should've already locked up the site since it was past dusk. As he crept toward the gate, it seemed like every pebble shifting under his boots echoed off the walls. His heightened hearing made it seem louder than it probably was. Still, he didn't want to alert anyone to his presence. Roc knelt and peered through the bars.

"I'm sorry, the Chateau Saint-Louis excavation is closed for the night," the guard explained to a group of tourists.

"Okay, thanks." One couple walked away.

"Well, shoot. I thought I read that you have extended hours? I was really hoping I'd get here in time," a soft-spoken woman replied, sounding frustrated.

Roc couldn't see much of her besides a white sweater and blue-striped skirt past the guard, but the way her shoulders slumped, she was obviously disappointed.

"The site will open again at nine."

"I guess I'll have to come back. I'll have more time to look around anyway. My family's from Quebec. Louis Hébert was my ancestor," she replied.

Half of Canada is related to that man at this point. Roc

snorted then stifled it and looked wide-eyed at the group, certain he'd betrayed his presence, but no one acted any the wiser.

"Welcome home then, madame," the guard said in a chipper voice that made Roc roll his eyes.

"Thank you," the skirt chuckled, obviously charmed by the man's cheesy reception. "I guess I was overly excited to get the sightseeing started. One of my great grandfathers, Nicolas Peltier, supposedly worked on this building in the 1640s and built the roof of Notre Dame de Quebec. It's kind of exciting getting to see the places he wrote about in his diary."

Roc froze hearing the name from his youth. He was barely a teen when his parents fled France in search of a safer place to raise him. They had arrived in Quebec just as the roof of Notre Dame was being built. The virgin city wasn't nearly as crowded as the Old World. The new cathedral, while a pale comparison to its namesake in Paris, was the tallest monument in the city, so that's where they went late their first day on dry land. Roc recalled the burning resentment and shame as he was relegated to the shadows wearing the cape he always donned to hide his less than normal appearance while his human mother kept watch for locals. Just because there'd been a few mishaps in France as he learned to camouflage himself and take to the skies... How was he supposed to learn? After all, wasn't this why they'd forsaken civilization for the barren New World?

As angry as he was for not being allowed to go with his sire to scout out their new home, he was still in awe as Petronus appeared to meld with the stone then scaled the church wall. Petronus had the broadest wings and could fly for hours carrying him and his mother without getting winded. Roc intently studied the way his sire fearlessly walked along the parapet of the lofty height, his tail swaying like a counterbalance. It was such a simple feat, and yet one he himself couldn't accomplish. His mother claimed his agility would return once he stopped growing and eating everything in sight, and it had, but her kind words had made him feel even more like a babe.

They'd thought all the craftsmen had gone home for the night, but a lone man rounded the half-built spire and came face to face with his sire. The human lost his footing and with arms flailing, tumbled off the precarious ledge. Roc still remembered the feeling of relief when Petronus swooped in, saving the man from certain death. He'd seen enough death when they fled their old home to last a lifetime, most of it by Petronus' hand. To this day Roc wondered why his sire risked exposing them again by rescuing the human. Undoubtedly his mother's influence had softened the Khargal's stony exterior. Luckily from that day on, Nicolas Peltier was a true friend, keeping their secret safe. And he was the only man Petronus would've trusted with his sigil before going to ground.

"That's neat that you traced your family back that far," another tourist commented about the skirt's brief story.

"Thank you. Well, I guess I'll be back," the woman sighed and headed off.

Roc realized he better follow her. She'd mentioned something about Nicolas having a journal, which was news to him. This was the best lead on the sigil he'd had in ages, and couldn't let it slip through his fingers.

Before the moment passed him by, he sprinted to the rear exit and raced up the stairs, emerging on the boardwalk, without bothering to reseal the gate. The brisk evening breeze rolled over the Saint Lawrence River and whipped up the hillside, threatening to blow off his hat and expose his horns as he darted across the deck toward Chateau Frontenac. He flanked the imposing edifice, sticking to the shadows as he neared the other entrance of the excavation site.

Dammit! Where is she?

Roc panned the terrace surrounding the stately hotel. He snarled in frustration when he saw none of the people milling around the statue of Champlain were her. She couldn't have gone that far. He ran alongside the hotel, toward the main road, 'til he caught a wisp of blue and white entering the nearby park.

"It would be so much easier to follow her by air," he grumbled as she disappeared among the trees. The sun had set but this was a popular tourist spot, so flying was far from wise.

He kept to the sidewalk as he skirted the park. His frustration grew when she headed down a narrow cobblestone footpath between a row of shops and a small church. He shook his head as he eyed the old narrow road.

"I can't follow her down there without looking like a grade-A stalker. And even if I don't give her a heart attack, what am I gonna say? Hey, I know I just followed you down this dark alley, but I was eavesdropping on your conversation about your family and wondered if you'd follow me to a bar for a chat," he muttered sarcastically under his breath as he pictured the girl running for her life when she saw him coming down the alley.

But if he went the long way around, he was sure to lose her. She was a brunette, and that was the sum of what he knew about the chance descendent of Nicolas. He hadn't even caught a glimpse of her face yet.

I blame you for this bullshit, he cursed his sire.

Tourist hotspot or not, he really didn't have a choice. Roc glanced up at the metal rooftops on the shops and then around him. Seeing no one nearby, he pulled off his trench coat and tossed it aside. There went another jacket. At least he had sense enough to get his suits tailored for situations like this. He closed his eyes as he released his wings, letting the strange sensation roll over him as they unfurled and swiftly filled with blood. It always felt bizarre when the two large pinions emerged from his back. Surely none of the purebreds had this issue.

Roc launched himself into the air, hugging the stone wall till he reached the rooftop. He skimmed along the peak as he followed his quarry. Roc landed on the far edge and peered down at her as she neared the end of the block. The woman stopped and looked around.

Shit! He froze when she glanced up, shifting his *duramna* to blend in to the shadows.

MELINE

Meline batted her hair from her face as the wind whipped it about. Her hotel was only a few blocks from the archaeological site, but she should've had her head examined for walking alone after dark in a strange city.

When it was still light, she'd been in awe of how much the

historic city looked like Europe, just as Jen said. She'd been absurdly excited when she parked her car and registered at the quaint old hotel situated at the end of a stone rowhouse. The pictures she googled hadn't prepared her for being immersed in a place nothing like Connecticut, surrounded by people speaking another language. It was oddly nostalgic, like a part of her was home, and made her feel continental, as if such a thing could rub off from just visiting a place.

But as she walked back to her hotel, peering down the ancient side streets and up at the dimly lit buildings, the history the city oozed had taken on an ominous air. She could swear she was being watched, like the ghosts of the past were coming out now the sun had gone down.

Why didn't I just wait till tomorrow? Her excitement to start exploring the instant she arrived would be her downfall.

Meline turned her gaze away from the dark rooftop of the nearby building. The shadows played tricks, making it look like someone stood there. She shivered, pulled her sweater tighter and picked up the pace. Her hotel was in sight. Her Mary Jane's struck the pavers in a rapid rhythm, reflecting her breathing, as she hustled down the block. The moment she made it through the heavy red door, she leaned against it and exhaled in relief.

Safe!

By the time she mounted the old wooden staircase to the top floor, entered her room and flipped on the light, the goose-bumps on her arms had gone away. As a woman, she knew better than to walk around alone at night. She never would've at home.

Just because you're on vacation doesn't mean you abandon all rules of common sense, she admonished herself as she locked the door. She'd been way too serious lately and decided to take a little break from herself while on vacation. But that didn't mean being reckless.

The hotel was too cute, with only a few rooms on each level. As small as the inn was, she was pleasantly surprised she had her own bathroom. Many hotels like this shared facilities, not that she had firsthand knowledge. The couple who ran the place had done a great job. Although her room wasn't filled with décor half as old as the building, the art deco furniture and bohemian cabaret painting hanging over the bed made it feel stylish and warm.

"I guess my adventure begins in the morning," she sighed, only slightly put out, as she stared at the sleepy buildings outside the window. From the safety of her room the old city didn't look quite as daunting as it had moments ago.

Meline pulled out the family research she and her father had compiled, and sat down at the dressing table doubling as a desk. She smiled wistfully at her dad's notes then frowned. It had been a year, and only now was it really sinking in her parents were gone. She always pictured them puttering around some retirement community on the coast, bemoaning the early bird selection at the local clam shop. But they hadn't even made it to retirement. And what made it worse was the cops never learned what caused the car accident.

Her gaze went to the translation of her umpteenth great-grandfather's journal.

That's the reason I've got the heebie jeebies.

Nicolas' life story began with a colorful tale of his voyage across the Atlantic. Most days the weather forced him below deck, where it was overcrowded, and dank from the sea, not to mention dark, since they couldn't light a single candle for fear of fire. It sounded absolutely miserable, but fascinating at the same time. Then the story turned positively bizarre once he arrived in Quebec.

My ancestor was insane, she mused, recalling Nicolas relating how he met the devil atop Notre Dame. The thing had two sets of horns, like you'd see on a yearling goat. Its long tail reminded him a cat, though hairless. And its massive wings were leathery like a bat's, equipped with talons that could fell a charging boar in one swipe. It went on and on. Nicolas was so descriptive she honestly believed him, and was a tad frightened.

Come on now, be fair. Her ancestor probably wasn't any crazier than anyone else. He lived in a time when people commonly believed demons and witches walked among them. *Fine, Nicolas was super imaginative and could probably give Mary Shelley a run for her money.*

Meline shook her head as she dismissed her ancestor's ramblings, grabbed her toiletries and a t-shirt then headed for the bathroom. She needed a long, hot shower after driving most of the day.

And since I'm on vacation, I'll use that new body wash I packed and stay in till I get all pruney and the bathroom fills with steam, she decided as she stripped. *Maybe I'll get up early and try that crepe place I saw for breakfast.* Meline did a happy dance, hoping they had blueberry crepes as she waited for the water to heat up.

ROC

From the neighboring rooftop, Roc watched the brunette shut the bathroom door. She'd been in there for several minutes when he decided to get a closer look. He spread his wings and launched into the air. The third-floor dormer window jutted out from the roof, giving him the perfect place to land. He touched down without a sound and crouched to covertly check out her room.

Awesome. Roc smiled, hearing the shower running in the bathroom.

He panned the room and instantly spied a pile of papers on the dressing table. From this distance he saw what looked like old script but couldn't make out what it said. As good as his eyesight was, he needed to get closer. If he was lucky, they'd tell him what Nicolas did with the sigil. There was just one thing standing in his way—he smirked at the window.

"They really are begging me to break in," he scoffed as he examined the shoddy old window latch.

Roc pulled out the pocket knife he kept handy, then slid the blade between the two sashes and lifted the simple drop latch. He swung open the window and froze. The shower was still running, so it wasn't fear of being discovered halting him; it was the waft of lavender nearly bowling him over. It was so strong he was instantly transported to his last night in France, when despite the danger, his sire took his mother to see the lavender fields one last time. There was also something else about the scent filling the room, something he couldn't put his finger on. Roc shook his head and shoved aside the distraction as he crept inside.

As he passed the bed, Roc noticed the woman's purse. He rifled through and pulled out her wallet. Roc bypassed the cash and credit cards. He may have survived and even thrived liberating things from those who thought they owned them, but he wasn't a common thug.

So, who are you, descendant of Nicolas?

He flipped open the flap exposing her driver's license. Roc grimaced as he took in the brunette's picture. Meline Lauber of Connecticut wasn't homely, but she was just, well, nondescript. Not really the kind of broad he tended to go for. Blondes seemed to attract his attention more often than not. The ones with full pouty lips and smoldering smokey eyes. This skirt looked a bit somber, not jovial, like the ladies he attempted to woo in the pubs. Then again, the women he got lucky with were probably giddy because they were smashed. It wasn't like he was a total lech. If he tried, he could coax a sober woman to his bed. Unlike a purebred of his kind, his mug wasn't hopelessly tragic. It was the rest of him, the horns, tail, and wings that complicated matters. And since he wasn't a priest, liquor was the social lubricant assuring he didn't have a perpetual case of blue balls.

Roc shook his head. He hadn't fished out Meline's license to see if she was suitable for his serial monogamy hall of fame. He grabbed his phone and took a shot of her address just in case she got away from him, then moved on to what brought him here in the first place.

"So, Nicolas, what did you have to share with the world?" he quietly mused as he scanned the papers on the vintage dressing table. He never realized the old Frenchman could write, let alone decided to pen the story of his life.

Nicolas' script was on the left-hand side, the English translation penciled on the right. Not that he needed the translation to read it. You didn't live four centuries without picking up a few languages, Khargal included.

His old friend started off his tale lamenting the harrowing voyage over sea. Roc shivered recalling a similar trip as a boy. His was made so much worse since he'd been forced to hide with his sire amongst the farm animals in the dark, smelly hull of the ship. He flipped the page, continued skimming then paused, his eyes widening.

"What the hell?" Roc groaned when he reached Nicolas' frightening description of Petronus. A sense of disappointment filled him as he read further. All this time he considered Nicolas a friend, but the way the man spoke of Petronus, he wasn't so sure now.

Who cares what he thought? Just look for mention of the sigil. He flipped the page and kept reading.

His head popped up when the knob on the bathroom door creaked. He'd gotten so caught up reading Nicolas' tale, he hadn't heard the shower cut off.

Shit!

Roc dropped the page he was reading and leapt for the open window like his tail was on fire. He just made it through the opening when Meline rushed out of the steamy bathroom.

"Oh, no! They're everywhere," he heard her declare.

Roc landed on the roof beside the window and listened to her scramble to collect the papers his flapping wings and hasty departure sent flying.

"You gotta be kidding me. How did this blow open?" she huffed, sounding confused, while fiddling with the window latch before closing and locking it again.

It took a while for her to turn out the lights. When she finally did, he crept around the dormer ledge and peered in at the woman curled up in bed, her back facing the window. He waited forever, watching her breathe, just to be certain she was asleep.

"Let's try this again." He'd only gotten through the first several pages of Nicolas' journal.

Going back in was a risk, but it wasn't like this was the first time he'd snuck into a room while someone slept. His Khargal lineage wasn't good for much, but it had blessed him with some skills. Roc eased the latch up with his knife as he watched Meline for movement. He slowly swung open the sash, retracted his wings and ducked inside.

Son of a bitch, he cursed when he noticed the dressing table was empty. *Of course she put everything away.*

He turned to scowl at her and noticed her shoulder bag propped beside the bed. That had to be where she put the journal. As he crept toward the edge of the bed, her phone pinged on the bedside table. Meline groggily groaned and rolled over. Roc dropped and hugged the floor as she grabbed the cell.

You gotta be fucking kidding me!

He cursed the light the device cast, hoping she didn't glance down at the floor as she tapped on the phone. Khargals had a lot of skills, but disappearing into thin air wasn't one of them. He could change color to blend into the wood floor, but a lot of good that would do since he was wearing pants. What he wouldn't give for a pair of threads that changed to match his skin, like some purebreds owned.

Roc relaxed when Meline sleepily shoved the cell back on the table then closed her eyes and seemed to drift off again. As he studied her peaceful expression, he noticed she wasn't half bad looking, cute really. The photo on her license hadn't done her justice at all. Meline wasn't a buxom blonde, but she also didn't have the kind of manufactured beauty that came from a bottle. She had the thickest eyelashes he'd ever seen. No doubt she was dreaming already the way they fluttered against her pink cheeks. Faint light streamed in, haloing her long brown hair that was tousled on the pillow. The way she still smelled of lavender and that unidentifiable compelling scent added to her gentle allure.

A feeling Roc never felt when breaking into a place crept over him—guilt. Meline was innocent and obviously not pretentiously rich like the people he usually targeted.

It's not like I'm going to steal her journal. I just want a peek. He had to find the sigil. The thing was dangerous.

A problem occurred to Roc as he was arguing with himself. There was a chance Nicolas' journal wouldn't reveal what he done with the family heirloom. He'd never find out all she knew if he just took her briefcase and left. It would be better if he could both see her research and pick her brain.

Roc sighed. This was becoming complicated. He needed to come up with a plan. Roc crept toward the window but paused when Meline shifted. He glanced back to find her eyes still closed.

"Stealth frog," she mumbled.

His hand flew to his mouth to stifle a burst of laughter. *What the hell is she dreaming about?*

"Is that so. Tell me more," Roc whispered, unable to resist. He really had to know.

"Sliced pickles," she dreamily rambled.

Roc snorted before he could repress it. *I gotta get out of here before I wake her up acting a fool.*

He swiftly headed out the window and shot up above the cloud cover where the moon shone bright. It was barely autumn, but in Canada it was chilly at night, especially at this altitude, not that it affected him much. It was actually a nice night, made better by this promising discovery of Meline.

He was still grinning like an idiot at her goofy rambling when he dove toward his penthouse condo and landed on the balcony. Roc shook off the moisture that collected on his wings before retracting them and heading inside.

"Little John," Roc called out as he stepped into the living room.

"Very funny, sir. Your allusion to Robin Hood never gets old," John commented, wearing a dry expression as he entered the room.

John was his butler, but besides taking care of his home, the Englishman researched the antiquities they liberated. Roc considered him a friend and partner in crime, trusting the man with almost everything.

He lured John away from an unappreciative employer while doing a job several decades earlier. Being a proper butler, the loyal-to-a-fault man balked at first. Then again, he probably took exception to the fact Roc had broken in. However, as soon as Roc informed John his employer was into human trafficking, the man was more than willing to shift loyalties. And the rest was history.

"Come on, John, don't be so stiff. You know you like the nickname," Roc teased.

"Indeed, sir. May I take your coat?"

Roc chuckled seeing the slight smile contort John's serious mien. As much as the man tried to repress it, John liked the work they did and the money it made them.

"No. I'm not wearing one," he replied, not the least bit

concerned John might see his wings, tail or horns. John was blind, an attribute that made their friendship easier.

Roc grabbed the brim of his hat and effortlessly flipped it onto the side table by the wall. It landed upright, ready to grab on his way out. Roc glanced in the mirror and smoothed out his bad case of hat head. If it weren't for his damn horns, he wouldn't have the extensive hat collection. Even though he usually kept them cut short, they were still a noticeable nuisance.

Don't bitch. At least you got your mother's looks. He cast his reflection a cocky grin then scowled. *Well, at least you don't look like you've been beat with the ugly stick,* he furrowed his sharp brow.

On good days he was glad to be hybrid. With the right clothes he could go out at night and mix with the fringes of society. But sometimes it chafed, not being Khargal or human, but some aberration in between.

"That museum curator is going to drive me mad. I assured him everything is in order for the gala tomorrow night but he's still hounding me to meet you," John commented with a slight huff, which was about as angry as he got.

With all that happened this evening Roc had forgotten about the benefit. He'd donated a Bosch painting to the Quebec art museum along with a small fortune. However, his motives weren't altogether altruistic.

"I'm sure you've got it handled."

"Indeed, sir. And you are certain you don't want me to look deeper into any of the patrons on the guest list?"

"If you want," Roc chuckled at John's eager and slightly maniacal expression. "If you find anyone who needs to be brought down to size, by all means, add them to our watch list. More than anything I thought this would be a good excuse to get out." And be himself for a change. "But now I'm debating if I have time to fool with it."

"Ah, yes." John grimaced. "Pardon me for prying, but have you had any luck locating your father?"

Roc smiled at his sympathetic old friend. John didn't know all the dirty details, but he'd related how Petronus basically abandoned him and now it was imperative to find his grumpy old sire.

"Don't worry about it. No, I've not heard from good old dad, but I did find a lead. I located the granddaughter of his friend Nicolas."

"That's wonderful, sir."

"Yes." Roc grinned, recalling Meline's sleepy ramblings. "I'm going to meet her tomorrow." Well, he planned to follow her.

"During the day?!" John asked, sounding uncharacteristically surprised.

"Yes," Roc countered with a sarcastic smirk even though John couldn't see it. "I can meet a woman during the day."

"Good for you, sir. Should I give you an afternoon wake up call, so you don't miss the gala?" John gave him a cheeky wag of his bushy brows before taking off for the kitchen.

"It's not like that," Roc hollered after him. This wasn't a booty call. "That's it, I'm not bringing women home ever again. You could pretend your hearing's not heightened because of the whole blind thing." The man's hearing was almost as good as a Khargal's.

"I'd have to be stone deaf not to hear all that screaming," John commented over his shoulder.

"They do get kinda loud." Roc puffed up his chest. The ladies had no complaints at all.

"I was talking about you, sir," John snorted.

"Classically trained butler, my ass," he muttered under his breath.

"I heard that."

3

MELINE

"Thank you for your time. This has all been very interesting," Meline commented to the lead archaeologist as she finished scribbling notes as fast as she could.

She wasn't being sarcastic. As nerdy as it was, she was truly excited seeing the ruins of the building her ancestor built with his own two hands. It made her feel like a part of something larger, not just Meline the travel agent who'd never been anywhere. And yet ever since she woke up she'd been in a weird mood. The harrowing walk back to her hotel after dark and the things in Nicolas' journal had polluted her dreams with shadowy dark figures. It didn't help that when she awoke the damn window had blown open again.

This city's haunted. It has to be. That was the only explanation. She'd made doubly sure the window was latched before going to bed. She even tugged on it and it refused to budge.

"If the damn thing's open when I get back to my hotel,

I'm changing rooms," she mumbled as she left the excavation site then shoved aside her paranoia.

Meline took several pictures of Champlain's monument, then boarded this weird ride called a funicular. It was basically a glass elevator that descended the steep hill to the lower city like an escalator. The view of the river from the glass box was impressive. She got off the fancy elevator and gawked at the old stone buildings and narrow cobblestone streets as she toured the city, making a giant circle.

Halfway back to her hotel, that funny feeling of being watched struck her again. Meline casually pretended to look at the scenery as she attempted to determine who was making the hair on the back of her neck stand on end. There were a handful of couples, a family, and a few lone tourists milling around, but no one seemed to be covertly staring at her. Meline shook her head at herself and continued on.

It was easy imagining what the city was like hundreds of years ago because it seemed barely changed. People probably bustled about the narrow streets much like they did now. Although they didn't have cars. That kinda killed the mood.

She was peering through the window of a shop when she noticed the reflection of a guy with a buzz cut, wearing jeans and a souvenir t-shirt across the street. She couldn't be sure, but she thought he'd been one of the people in the crowd the last time she got the funny feeling. Meline casually walked into the store and pretended to shop. After a few minutes she wandered out, relieved to see the man had moved on.

I really need to get a grip, Meline laughed.

As she continued down the sidewalk, movement captured her attention. It was the creepy tourist again. Meline picked up the pace, heading straight for her hotel. As she turned the corner, she glanced behind her to find him still following her at distance.

Oh shit!

Meline frantically glanced back and forth. Seeing another shop, she quickly darted across the street. She snagged the heavy wooden door as the creepy guy came around the corner, and then she hustled inside. She squinted in the dim light filtering through the windows and gaped at the bookshelves packed into every square inch of the musty old shop. Dusty volumes were stacked in the aisles and bowing the shelves they littered. Meline couldn't find the shopkeeper as she ventured down one crowded row.

He's probably buried under one of these piles.

This was not the refuge she was seeking. If anything, it looked like the perfect setting for the stalker to murder her in.

"You look lost," a deep voice commented from behind her.

Meline screeched and spun around, almost stumbling into the bookcase nearby. She came face to face with the broadest chest she'd ever seen. A wall swathed in a trench coat and black suit had sprung up behind her. Part of her relaxed seeing it wasn't the stalker, but then again, holy fuck this guy was huge. There was hardly enough room for both of them and all the books, with the way he spanned the narrow aisle. No doubt her stalker took one look at the giant entering the store and decided to give up the chase.

She craned her neck up and her jaw dropped open seeing the man attached to the imposing body. He had the chin of a boxer and full thick lips. The features would've overwhelmed his face, making it seem very square if it weren't for his high cheekbones and strong, sharp brow. She drew in an abrupt breath when her gaze met his. The man's eyes were gray, but in the dim light they seemed to glow silver. His expression was assessing, almost penetrating, and she suddenly felt not just short next to his hulking size, but awkward to boot. It didn't help the man's suit probably cost more than her entire wardrobe. The gray pinstriped fedora he wore cocked forward on his head was a tad cliché. Too many men tried to pull that hat off and failed. And yet, somehow, he rocked it. A bit of his black hair peeked out beneath the brim, curling up at the tips. He was a mix of harsh, strangely handsome, and all-around unnerving.

Jesus, Mary and Joseph.

Her instincts were jumbled. Unexpectedly running into this daunting man in an entirely too creepy shop after the odd experience in the street was setting her on edge. On one hand, she wanted to suss out why she found him so compelling despite the circumstances, but on the other she debated making some excuse to flee. Meline saw the smile that started at the corner of his mouth and spread. It was slightly cocky, and she realized he noticed her gaping at him.

Don't just gawk. Stop being a freak and say something, idiot! she shouted at herself, frantically attempting to find her voice.

"Did you see someone out there? No, never mind." Meline fidgeted with her skirt, feeling foolish for being paranoid. Why would someone be following her? "I'm on vacation doing family research and seeing the sites since they were from here. I've never been to Quebec. Never been to Canada at all really. All this history has this strange vibe and it kinda has me jumpy. Do you ever feel that way?" she rambled.

Oh God, just shut up now, she cursed as his grin broadened. Meline repressed smacking her forehead for being such a big dolt. Instead, she quickly clamped her mouth shut and flatly smiled, which undoubtedly looked as pathetic as she felt.

"Well this shop has a lot of good books. If your family is from here, you'll undoubtedly find something about them on one of these shelves," he replied.

She was so fixated on his accent and how deep his voice was that she almost didn't hear what he said.

"No," she swiftly blurted after the awkward pause. Her sudden response was so loud her voice echoed in the old shop. "Um, I mean that would be a good idea if I could read French."

"Oh." His thick brow quirked as he looked down at her bag, and she realized how dumb she looked in a French bookshop but couldn't read French. "If you'd like, I can help you."

"That's not necessary. It's really nice of you to offer, but you don't need to waste your time on me. You came here to do your own thing, and I would need more help than would be polite to saddle you with."

Yeah, you need help, you're babbling again! She stopped abruptly.

"Nonsense. Let's see what they have to offer. My name's Roc, by the way."

Rock, more like mountain.

He held out his hand, and she stared at it, dumbfounded by how large it was. His fingers would easily touch if he wrapped both hands around her waist, and she wasn't a small girl. The image of King Kong on the Empire State Building came to mind till Roc waved his fingers, capturing her attention.

Meline focused and realized he was gesturing toward a desk along the far wall.

Fucking hell. Pay attention, you're staring again!

"Okay, uh, well, thank you, Roc. I'm Meline." She hadn't planned this, but if she learned something new about her family, that would be cool.

Her eyes widened as she followed behind him. Roc had to be a bodybuilder or something. That was the only thing that explained the way he filled out the coat. He was built like a freaking tank.

"Pleased to meet you, Meline."

"So, Roc, what do you do?" she asked, her curiosity getting the best of her as she attempted to relax.

"I'm basically a fine arts dealer. I travel, hunting down antiques."

"Oh." Meline paused. "Really?" She gave him another once over.

"Does that surprise you?" Roc chuckled as he glanced sideways at her.

"Um, yeah, sort of."

"Did you think I was a football player or something?" He raised one brow.

"Well." Meline tucked her head, embarrassed that she'd made a snap judgment based on his size.

That explains the fancy clothes. He's probably here to research some glorious treasure he dug up in a place she could only dream of visiting. She could almost picture the intriguing man canvasing back-market stalls of colorful cities like Morocco or Venice, haggling with merchants.

Smart and built. The combination made him even more daunting.

"I'm just messing with you, doll. It's okay. I know how big I am." Roc cast her a sardonic smile.

Meline had to repress a schoolgirl giggle at the way he called her doll. No one had ever called her that. It reminded her of something they'd say in the fifties.

"What do you do when you're not digging up the past?" he asked.

"I'm a travel agent."

"I bet that's fun."

"Sure." She grimaced, picturing her bland cubicle.

"That didn't sound convincing."

"No, it's fine. It's work." She perused the shelf of books that time forgot.

"Sorry, you're on vacation, you probably don't want to talk about work."

Yeah, that's it. She nodded. Or his job was positively glamorous compared to hers.

"So, are you interested in looking for someone in particular?" he asked with that smooth, deep voice.

"Um, yeah, let's see."

Any other moment and she could've rattled off a dozen of her ancestors' names and details, but now she couldn't think of a one. Meline hefted her shoulder bag. She tugged too hard on the zipper and it unzipped completely, spilling her notebook and research onto the floor.

"Crap!" she said, flustered.

Seriously. Get it together.

Meline bent over to grab the papers that scattered everywhere, just as Roc did.

"Ow," she yelped when her forehead thunked against his.

The man had a seriously hard head. She stumbled back

and fell flat on her ass, her skirt nearly exposing her purple panties. She didn't know whether to rub the spot on her forehead that smarted or to yank down her skirt first.

"Merde! I'm sorry," Roc exclaimed. He straightened his hat with one hand, while extending the other to help her up.

"No. It's my fault." Meline turned bright red as she took his hand then scrambled to get up and not look like a newborn colt attempting to stand for the first time.

Jesus, really?! She wanted to find a hole and climb into it.

"Are you sure you're okay?" His gaze raked over her, landing on her hips.

"Yes." She tried not to squeak, her body overreacting to his casual appraisal.

Don't get all worked up. He wasn't checking you out.

"Let me pick these up," he offered.

"Okay, thank you."

He glanced to where she still gripped his hand.

Oh my god. Let go of the man. She turned redder as she instantly released him. *Seriously, you're acting like you've never been touched by a man.* Well, she hadn't, certainly not a man like Roc. The last time she'd been with someone, it had been a chiropractor she met online that ended in unsatisfying third date sex.

Convincing her stomach to stop doing somersaults as he picked up her papers was near impossible. There was just something about him that made her feel unbalanced, figuratively and literally. Her hand tingled where they'd touched. The man's hands were warm and rough, like he did manual labor, though she doubted it from the way he dressed. Then again, he was so huge he probably hauled the antique furniture he bought all by himself. She could only imagine how ripped he was beneath that high-priced suit.

Not helping! She was just making herself more flustered.

"Thank you for your help but I think I'm going to just chalk up my losses and call it a day," *before I manage to injure you and embarrass myself further*, she silently added as she shoved her papers in her bag.

Meline took off for the door feeling like an utter fool.

"Wait," Roc called after her.

She spun around to find him still holding half her research.

Oh, holy hell. She rushed back and grabbed her papers, but he refused to release his grip on them.

"I'm holding a benefit at Chateau Frontenac tonight. Come, be my guest. It's the least I can do for knocking you over."

"That's not really necessary."

"I'll add your name to the list." Roc released her papers.

"Um, thanks. I'll think about it." Meline cast him an awkward smile before turning and heading for the door as fast as her feet could carry her.

"I'll see you at eight then," he chuckled from behind her.

Her heart skipped a beat and her cheeks heated further, hearing the rumbling sound. This had to be the most pathetic encounter she ever had with a perfect stranger, must less a man. The fact that he knew it by the way he snickered made it all the more embarrassing.

She couldn't get out of the building fast enough, only to realize once she made it through the doors that she hadn't bothered to consider the stalker. Meline heaved a giant sigh of relief when she didn't see him.

"Because you're imagining shit, you nut case," she moaned.

Meline hung her head, replaying everything as she hustled to her hotel. It wasn't like she was incredibly smooth on a good day, but that performance was just shameful. She couldn't believe he'd taken pity on her for being a klutzy head case and asked her to some party he was throwing at the chic old hotel.

Like I'm going to risk a repeat of this fiasco. At least in the bookshop there was no one to witness her misery. If she took him up on his overly kind offer there'd be tons of people with front row seats to her nightmare. *Uh, uh. That is so not happening.*

She reached her room and flopped on the bed, throwing one arm over her face.

What is your problem? she lamented.

Her cell rang and Meline jumped. She scrambled for the phone and answered it.

"Hello!"

"Hey," Jen said on the other end.

"Hey," Meline sighed, relieved to hear her girlfriend.

"Are you all right? You sounded surprised."

"No, I'm not all right," she groaned in abject misery.

"Well that answers the question about how your vacation's going," her friend replied, sounding sympathetic.

"I've been a total nut from the moment I got here."

"Why? What happened?"

"I told you how my ten-times great-grandfather wrote about meeting something that looked like the devil, right?"

"Uh, yeah," Jen said hesitantly.

"Well, obviously his story has gone to my head. Since I

arrived I keep thinking I'm being followed, spooking at damn shadows." And it didn't help she'd wandered at night when she had no business being out alone.

"I'm sorry, but it's no wonder, you have been spending a lot of time dwelling on dead people lately."

"I know. I know." Meline nodded.

"I know connecting to your roots was important to your parents, but don't you think they'd also want you to enjoy yourself?"

"Yes. I get that, and believe me, I brushed the nonsense off." At least she'd tried.

"I'm hearing a but there."

"But before I could pull my head together, I totally embarrassed myself with a man who was just trying to help me. I babbled, stared like an idiot, spilled my papers everywhere, butted heads with him, fell on my ass exposing my panties then ran like a chicken shit. Oh god, Jen, it was awful."

"You met a guy!" Jen squealed in glee.

"Did you not hear a word I just said? I made a total fool of myself! No, that doesn't even begin to describe it. It was like the nightmare where you wake up naked in public."

"Was he hot?"

"Roc was enormous, but yeah, he was good looking in a rugged masculine way." Meline smiled as she thought of him, then shook her head remembering the catastrophe.

"Ooh, his name was Roc."

"Jen, I ran off like my hair was on fire."

"Oh. Well that's a shame. And you said he was trying to help you?"

"He found me gawking in a book shop and offered to help

me find a book, since like a moron I admitted I couldn't read French."

"So, he came to your rescue," Jennifer gushed.

"I was a babbling loon and he felt pity for me, Jen. You should've seen him. He was dressed in an obscenely expensive suit, talking about how he traveled the world buying and selling art. I know I don't lead a glorious life, but I don't need some rich playboy rubbing my nose in it, inviting me to fancy benefits out of pity."

"Wait just a minute. Are you telling me some rich man named Roc invited you to a party and you said no? Meline Lauber!"

Meline closed her eyes and smacked her forehead. Jennifer was impossible. She was missing the whole point.

"I know the face you're making, Meline. I don't care what kind of fool you made of yourself, you are going to that party."

"And what, trip over my own feet and fall face first into the buffet this time?!"

"Donkey balls! First off, you're the funniest biatch I know. Remember that time you tripped in the club?"

"Ugh, yeah. I'm a total klutz."

"Well you jumped up and threw your hands in the air like you just completed the best gymnastic routine ever. After I finished snorting my mojito through my nose, I totally gave you a ten."

"I appreciate the assist, but my floor routine was probably a seven at best," Meline chuckled.

"Shut up. The point is you are funny and so quick with the snarky comebacks it's like an art. And you're smart. Look how fast you got your associate's degree. And don't get me started on how awesome you are. So, beautiful biatch, you're going to put on that fancy dress we bought just for this trip, and you're going to show that man what you're made of," Jen insisted.

"Yeah, okay," Meline laughed at her friend's pep talk. "I'm hanging up now. Thanks for lightening my mood. You know I love you, girl." She didn't know what she'd do without Jen. The girl had been a life saver over the last year.

"All right, fine, but don't disappoint me. I expect stories. Love ya." Jennifer hung up.

Meline stared at the suitcase holding her dress, debating what if, then shook her head. Yes, she was being ridiculous, but there was no way in hell she could go to that party. Just thinking about Roc twisted her in knots. God only knows what she'd do being around him, in public. She tugged her messenger bag onto the bed. Her time would be better spent planning what she'd do tomorrow. The phone pinged and she glanced down at the message.

'Go to that party!!!'

Meline snorted at her friend's text.

ROC

He'd watched Meline's movements throughout the day, plotting his approach like he did with all his marks. When he saw her go into the old bookstore he knew it was the opportunity he'd been waiting for. Roc put on his game face before going in, his goal in sight. That's where everything went to shit and his attempt to keep things strictly business flew out the window.

The idea was to gain her trust and get a look at her research. Except the instant he saw Meline he got distracted, like the night before. She looked so small and lost standing amidst the rows of books. The driving need to ease her derailed every other rational thought. And rather than making things better, he royally fucked it up. He didn't think he'd come on too strong, but apparently he had, from the way Meline screeched in surprise, babbled, then grew shy and quiet, scrunching up her button nose. She was damn cute when she got flustered. He might've gotten somewhere with her if he hadn't practically knocked her out, almost exposing his horns in the process. In the end it wasn't a total shock when she turned tail and ran.

"Sacrament!" Roc cursed, scrubbing a hand over his face as if that could wipe away the memory of the disastrous afternoon.

He opened his eyes and glanced around the hotel dressing room. He was supposed to be changing into his costume for the masquerade already under way in the ballroom. That was a joke. The costume was what he wore the other three hundred and sixty-four days of the year. This event was his rare chance to be himself and mix with people. He should be happy, like the other times he held these soirées, instead he was worried whether or not one guest in particular would show.

Fuck it. This is my party after all. There was no point torturing himself anymore. He'd replayed his earlier failure all evening and it changed nothing.

Roc hastily peeled off the specially tailored suit jacket and dress shirt that allowed his wings to extend. As he tugged on the black leather pants, his tail uncoiled from around his waist and flicked in agitation, a reflection of his mood. Roc glanced in the mirror. He'd let his horns grow in for this occasion, rather than sheer them short like he usually did. He grimaced at his reflection, exposing his sharp canines. For some reason they were bothering him.

"Now for the last touch." Roc shifted his skin tone till it was as dark as his pants.

He unfurled his wings, flexed them a few times to get the blood flowing then threw open the door, uncaring if the performers in the adjoining room were dressed to play their part or not. He was done waiting and wondering.

"Oh wow. That's an amazing rig," a woman with red hair wearing a striped bodysuit exclaimed as she ran her hand over his wing.

"Thanks." Roc tried to move past her, but she shifted into his path.

"I'm Aimee." She extended her hand, while her eyes roved his bare chest.

"Nice to meet you." Roc nodded but didn't offer his name. Any other time he would've talked with all the performers and soak in Aimee's admiring glances. But he was on a mission tonight.

"George said we'd have a guest performer joining the crew for this gig, but he didn't tell us your costume would be so remarkable. Who did this work, Barrett?" Aimee continued, undaunted by his dismissal.

"Yeah. Pardon me. I need to get out there." Roc brushed past her and headed out the door.

"It's time to mingle," he heard the eager redhead announce to the rest of the troop.

Roc ignored the oohs and ahhs, and the sound of the performers hustling behind him to begin their routine, as he wove through the crowd. His head swiveled every which way searching for Meline. He wasn't quite sure what he'd do if she didn't show. Not only would he be back at square one, trying to invent a way to cross paths with her, but he'd also be disappointed. His steps faltered, surprised by the realization and the totally unexpected way the delicate female had burrowed under his skin.

MELINE

Meline fretted with the long skirt of her pink dress as she gingerly made her way through the ornate revolving door of the palatial hotel. The moment she entered the reception hall, she was struck by all the dark wood paneling and shiny reflective brass. She wanted to take a tour of Chateau Frontenac, but never imagined this was how she'd see the place. She panned from the reservation desks to the opposite end of the vestibule, wondering where this party was. Her eyes widened when she spotted a bunch of poshly dressed people filing past a reception table.

"That can't be where I'm supposed to go." But she had a sinking feeling it was. "There's still time to turn back," she muttered.

She had an inkling this was going to be a swanky event, but she'd drastically underestimated what that meant. She was totally out of her element among the elegant women in colorful designer dresses and men in tuxedos. She was better suited to the casually dressed hotel guests being relegated to one end of the lavishly decorated foyer.

Meline scrubbed a finger over her teeth one last time, hoping she didn't have lipstick on them. She rarely wore make-up. It made her feel more like a circus clown than beautiful. Then again, she'd never really learned how to do it properly. The lipstick and eyeshadow she picked out in the store always seemed garish once she got them out of the package at home.

What was I thinking? She fidgeted as she joined the back of the line. *Jen will kill me if I don't text her photo evidence that I showed up, that's what I was thinking. I blame her for any carnage that ensues.*

"Your name?" the man at the reception table asked, capturing her attention.

She focused on the man in the black and silver half mask. Not only was she clueless just how nice this event would be, she wasn't aware it was a costume party either.

Well, it is that time of year.

The way he looked her up and down, wearing a flat gratuitous smile, made her want to groan. It was obvious she didn't belong here. That's what he was thinking.

"Meline."

"Meline Lauber?"

"Yes," Meline replied, slightly surprised he actually had her on the list. Somehow, she expected Roc to have forgotten.

"Wonderful. Right this way, madame."

Unlike the other guests, who were checked off the list and sent on their way, the masked man escorted her past the arched entry everyone else was milling through. She nervously followed, wondering why she was being singled out.

He's taking me to the servant's entrance or the exit, she snickered wryly to herself.

"The host asked that you be given your pick of our complimentary costumes." The man pointed to the selection hanging up in a coatroom.

"Oh." Meline smiled in embarrassment as she admired the glitzy accessories.

After toiling all afternoon, she'd decided that Roc might not have been taking pity on her after all. She was being overly self-conscious. No doubt he felt just as bad as she did when they knocked noggins. It was probably that foreign hospitality she'd heard about that made him extend the invite. That was why she finally made up her mind to take a chance and come. Although her curiosity about Roc, and Jen's constant haranguing might've helped. But this was too kind. Roc knew she wasn't from here and likely wouldn't have been able to get a costume in time. And if he had told her this was a costume party she would've worn the wrong thing. She was used to the kind of parties where the guys showed up dressed like greasy-haired vampires and the girls were slutty kittens.

I've never been to a masquerade.

Meline grinned as she perused the various accessories covered in sequins, feathers and gossamer fabric. A warm feeling filled the pit of her stomach that Roc was considerate enough to think about her. Her dress couldn't compare to half of what she'd seen the other women wearing, but at least now she'd fit in a tad bit more. Her eyes were drawn to a pair of white angel wings and she gravitated toward them. She ran her hand over the downy feathers. There were little sparkly jewels dotting the wings looking like dew drops.

"Wonderful choice. They're fabulous." The way the man said fabulous, she got the impression he preferred guys over gals. "Here let me." He kindly helped her slip them on.

The wings were positively amazing, reminding her of the ones the Victoria's Secret models wore, but better. She stood up straighter, her shoulders back, chin up. It was funny how such a trivial thing made her suddenly feel elegant.

"You can select a mask, but I don't think you need it." The man admired her as if seeing her in a new light.

"So, you think I'll pass in this crowd, looking less like some bum who wandered off the street?"

The guy grimaced hearing her comment.

Yeah, I noticed your judgmental look earlier.

"Madame, you are a personal guest of our anonymous host. You could wear rags and most of these patrons would fall over themselves to make your acquaintance."

"Anonymous?" Meline tilted her head in confusion.

"Yes. This is the event of the year, yet no one knows who's throwing this fundraiser for the museum. But I bet you do." The man lifted his mask and gave her a conspiratorial look, obviously hoping she'd clue him in on the secret.

"Oh no," Meline giggled. "I'm not spilling the beans." She hardly knew Roc, but if he wanted anonymity, she wasn't about to spoil it.

A thrill of wicked excitement filled her that she knew something all these fancy people were gossiping about.

"Well you should be sure to check out the Bosch painting your friend donated. It's the theme for this whole party," he commented as they left the coatroom.

"I will, thank you."

Meline wandered out of the vestibule and found her way to the back of a crowd milling in a clump. When they thinned, she saw the oil painting. It was like a macabre nightmare with garish creatures, angels, black-winged demons, and people being tormented. The medieval piece was colorful but still came off very, very dark.

"Judgment," she read the label. "Well that looks about right." And it did make the perfect theme for a masquerade.

Movement caught her attention and Meline turned to see a performer on stilts, decked out in feathers and a beaked mask. He was a perfect version of the vulture in the painting. She didn't feel odd gawking at him as he hopped, gyrated and cocked his head like a real-life creepy buzzard, because all the rich attendees were just as taken with his performance. The man was so steady on his feathered stilts that she wondered if Roc hired Cirque du Soleil to entertain his guests. That seemed like something a man who rented out half this hotel would do.

I can't even imagine how much all this costs.

She turned in circles, taking in the yards of black and burgundy fabric, potted trees and everything else that had been brought in to turn the hotel into the embodiment of the medieval torment. And she hadn't even entered the grand ballroom yet. She found Roc daunting before, knowing he was behind all this didn't help. Meline stopped as she came to a magnificent split staircase. She froze, her gaze riveted to the character at the top.

Oh God.

A demon larger than life and black as night stood surveying everyone below, judging them like they were the damned in the painting. His massive leathery wings arched over his back, nearly touching the ceiling with their clawed tips, gruesome and glorious.

A cry rose up from the crowd when the demon leapt from the height. Everyone scattered as he landed amidst them. Their fright swiftly turned to awed gasps and clapping, but she was too shocked to be amused quite yet. There was something familiar about the beastly man.

Meline panned up the leather pants that clung to his thick muscular thighs then paused seeing the tail that flicked behind him. It seemed so real, moving the way a tiger's would. And he swaggered with the grace of a predator, too. Her eyes widened when she realized the demon was coming straight for her. These performers were taking their roles just a little too seriously.

She backed up but her angel wings kept her from melting into the crowd. Her gaze shifted from his stacked abs, corded thick arms, to his impossibly broad chest. He had to be a demon, no man was built like this. When she reached his face the first thing she noticed were the pair of horns jutting through his wavy black hair. They weren't curled over on themselves, just sharp points, a few inches long, the same raven color as the rest of his harsh features.

"I'm glad you decided to come," the deep voice spoke from a broad mouth sporting wicked canines.

Her gaze darted to a pair of silver-gray eyes and recognition dawned on her.

"Roc?" she gasped. If he hadn't approached her she never would've found him in that wild costume.

"Yes," he chuckled. "I didn't frighten you, did I?"

When she made up her mind to come, she promised she wouldn't act like a freak around Roc. She assured herself the incident in the bookstore was just a fluke. But seeing him standing there in that intense costume, surrounded by the glamorous party he was throwing, made holding to her promise twice as hard. Plus, he was bigger than she remembered. And holy hell his muscles had muscles. He even had that vee of muscles below his six pack, disappearing into his leather pants.

You have to be kidding me. She bit her lip to hold in another shocked sound. The bulge in his crotch was daunting but also made her weak in the knees at the same time. She darted her gaze back to Roc's face before he caught her gaping at his dick.

Jesus, I'm so out of my league. He's rich, captivating, built like a god and hung like a horse. Her nerves frayed and the confidence she built up just to get here wilted.

No, no, no! Get it together! You may not be rich or worldly but that doesn't make you any less. You're just as awesome as all these people, she channeled her friend.

"Meline?" Roc cocked his head.

She needed to say something before he started to think she was some mute idiot.

You're playing a role, that's what this is. She lifted her chin, looking more confident than she felt.

"What does an angel have to fear from the devil?" Meline coyly asked as she toyed with one of her wings.

"You do look utterly divine," Roc replied with a panty-dropping smile, making her blush.

The butterflies that had been vibrating in her stomach took flight as he stepped incredibly close. She was forced to stare straight up to maintain eye contact. With his skin dark as night, those horns, and wings blocking out the light, Roc looked wicked, and yet she was drawn to him.

"But are you honestly telling me, little angel, you aren't tempted to sin?"

Her heart stuttered in her chest at the suggestive comment. It was like he truly was the devil, reading her thoughts.

He's flirting with me. Her mouth gaped in shock, not so much from what Roc said but that he said it to her—her!

A woman nearby choked into her hand, and Meline remembered they had an audience. The woman was giggling even though she tried to hide it as she watched the Meline and Roc floor show. Meline glanced back up at Roc to find him grinning like a Cheshire cat. She narrowed her eyes at him.

He might have been flirting, but he was also laying it on thick just to get a rise out of her. And he was goading her in front of all these people. The man was truly rotten.

Everyone's expecting to be entertained, I best not disappoint.

Meline took two steps back and slowly, confidently looked Roc up and down. She didn't shy away from staring at the part of him that filled out his pants, even though she had to shove down the giddy feeling coursing through her, so she didn't blush or trip over her words.

"And you think you've got what it takes to make me fall from grace?" She cocked one brow at him as she rolled her shoulders, shimmying her wings.

One of the onlookers snorted and Meline couldn't help turn and wink at them. She glanced back at Roc in time to see his eyes flash as he swiftly closed the distance between them. Meline drew in a sharp breath when his massive dark wings enveloped her.

"You have no idea all the ways I could sully you. I'd drag you into the pit, and with every glorious scream from those luscious pink lips you'd declare it was heaven."

Roc's husky voice was so deep, his breath tickling the shell of her ear, making her shiver. Meline knew this was good-natured rowdy banter, but someone needed to tell that to her body. She was so close to his chest she could feel the heat radiating off the wicked man. His washboard stomach made her fingers itch to reach out and follow the peaks and valleys. And the spicy masculine scent he exuded mixed with leather had her salivating. He'd called her bluff, then one-upped her, throwing her off balance again.

Touché, she nearly squeaked out loud.

ROC

Roc couldn't help showing off his true nature. This was his excuse to stretch his wings for once. It was the reason he donated this particular painting to begin with. When he saw Meline, something inside him stood at attention, and it wasn't just his cock. He had to reach her before she got away. Leaping from the mezzanine was probably a bit over the top, except he was unable to resist the urge. She was a vision, standing out in the crowd of masked guests. The white wings she wore combined with her unadulterated beauty and he was certain she'd dropped from heaven. As angelic as she was, her body was temptation pure and simple. Her breasts weren't ridiculously large, but they were perky, hidden beneath that pink dress that hugged her squeezable full ass. Roc wasn't kidding when he said he wanted to corrupt her. He thought it was her shy nature that riled something primal in him, till she straightened her shoulders and gave him a taste of his own medicine.

Holy Macero!

A fire blazed to life inside when she laid down the challenge while brazenly admiring him, wings and all. He'd underestimated her. Meline wasn't as shy as he made her out to be. His little angel had a fiery side and he wanted to possess it. Before he knew it, he had her wrapped in his wings, ready to act out the salacious visions burning in his mind.

"You're incorrigible," Meline deflected his scathing comment, again looking like she might bolt.

Wrapped in his wings she couldn't go far, and he wasn't about to let her. But it did remind him that he needed to crank it down a notch.

"Yeah, but I have a lot of fun in the process," he chuckled.

"I bet you do. You've got everyone talking, between this unbelievable costume and the mysterious benefactor for this party," Meline whispered.

"Costume?! This is the real me," he admitted, knowing full well she'd think he was joking.

"Oh, I completely believe you're evil with that rowdy display," she laughed.

He loved the bubbly sound. And as much as he liked seeing her blush and the erotic tension zinging between them, feeling her relax while still enfolded in his wings was satisfying on a deep level.

Meline caught him off guard when she reached up and tugged one of his horns. It shocked him how sensitive they were. No one touched his horns, certainly not a female with delicate little fingers. But more than that was the strange sensation that radiated through him. It started where her fingers grazed him, then moved down his spine and radiated through his limbs. He nearly groaned but repressed it.

"Roc! Did you superglue these horns on? You're never going to get them off," she admonished.

At any other time, he would've been amused by such a tiny female taking him to task. But the way Meline smirked at him, concern lacing her expression, while her fingers still traced the base of one horn, amused was not the emotion that was riding him. Dammit, she made behaving impossible.

"Don't worry." Roc swiftly unfolded his wings and took a step back from Meline before he did something foolish. He just needed a breath of air, not filled with her gentle perfume and whatever that maddening scent was that only she seemed to exude.

"Please tell me you aren't going to have to take a bath in Goof-Off to remove all this." Meline closed the distance, thwarting his effort to get a little space so he could pull his head together.

"I'll be fine." He scrubbed a spot on his forearm, letting his skin change back to its usual bronze tone. "See." He showed her, then pretended to smooth the black make-up back over the spot.

"If you say so. I guess a craftsman talented enough to do all this has a trick to getting it all off." Meline shrugged.

Besides Meline, several of the party-goers were also curiously watching his demonstration. The one thing he'd learned over the centuries was that if you gave humans a reasonable excuse, they willingly believed it.

"Have you eaten?" he changed the subject.

"No, I just got here. By the way, thank you for inviting me and for these." She pointed to her wings.

"Of course. You wear them well."

Meline smiled at him.

"Shall we?" He held out his hand, gesturing to the staircase.

Unexpectedly, she placed her small hand in his upturned palm, so he went with it, ignoring the sensation it elicited. They headed up the staircase, but she stopped abruptly as they reached the ballroom, her eyes widening.

He was about to ask what was wrong when Meline drew in a sharp breath, then blurted, "Roc, this is amazing."

He watched her with a broad grin as her eyes swiveled

from the angelic performers nimbly spinning on silk ropes hanging from the ceiling, to their demonic counterparts' acrobatic floor routine.

"You like it?" he asked even though he knew the answer.

"I've never seen anything like this, like any of this. The fabulous creature costumes are insane. They remind me of the characters from that old movie *Labyrinth*. They're just that good. How do those acrobats not break their necks doing those moves? And then there's this ballroom with all the warm wood and sparkling chandeliers. I'm so glad I came. This is why I want to travel and see the world. It's like an amazing, strange sort of dream," she rambled in a breathy whisper.

"Surely with your job..." he started to say, slightly surprised by her wonderment.

"I wish, but I mostly answer phones." Meline shook her head emphatically while still staring at everything in awe.

He'd seen great spectacles like this in one way, shape, or form over the centuries. But seeing it through her eyes somehow made it all feel new. Suddenly he wanted to visit all the wonders of the world again and bring Meline along, just to see her reaction.

"Wine?" Roc asked, as a server passed.

"Yes."

He grabbed her a glass and she sipped it while watching people pass. She was so caught up studying everything, he had to gently steer her with one hand at her back to keep her from running into things as they moved toward the buffet.

"What do you like to eat?" he asked when they made it through the crowd.

"Anything. I'm not picky," she replied, taking a plate.

She grabbed some crackers and dished out the accompanying pâté.

"You do like liver pâté," he commented, seeing her sizeable pile.

"Liver?" Her eyes widened as she gaped at her plate.

"You better try it."

Meline dipped a cracker into the pâté and popped it in her mouth. She blanched, then scrunched up her nose as chewed. He saw her throat work as she attempted to swallow.

"Good?" he asked with a quirk of his brow.

"It's…um…fine." Meline covered her mouth as she finished choking it down.

"You're a horrible liar," he laughed, and traded her plate for his clean one. "You might want to be careful when you visit France if you don't like pâté. Oh, and watch out for anything called cretons while you're here."

"Okay." She nodded and washed the pâté down with the last of her wine, so he grabbed her another glass off a nearby tray.

"Better?"

"Yes. Thank you." Meline grinned. "So, I don't like everything. But this is good. I like trying new things even if I discover I don't like them. I've never been a fan of liver, whole or otherwise," she laughed as they continued down the buffet.

"You have an adventurous side begging to be free, don't you?"

"Yes!" She lifted her glass almost like a salute. "I know this trip to hunt my ancestors probably doesn't seem adventurous to someone as well traveled as you, but to me it's like a scavenger hunt."

He was smiling at how animated Meline was as she explained the inspiration behind her trip to Quebec, till it reminded him of the reason he met her in the first place.

You can learn what she knows about Nicolas and still enjoy her company.

That was true. But why did it feel like he'd crossed a line?

5

MELINE

"Look at how high that lady's heels are. I like girly shoes but can't wear them. I'd break my ankle for sure."

Meline paused after making the comment, a disturbing notion shoving through the warm fuzzy high she'd been drifting in all evening. She'd been monopolizing the conversation with her trivial stories for some time now.

I blame the wine. It was a dry red, but it went down so smooth that she had one glass too many. *Crap, I hate it when guys I meet do nothing but talk about themselves, then what do I do… Ugh.*

Roc was super kind as he listened to her babble. She couldn't tell from his cryptic half smile if he was tired of her drivel and just humoring her, or couldn't get a word in edgewise. Either way she'd probably overstayed her welcome.

"I guess I should head back to my hotel. I've occupied enough of your time. Thank you again for inviting me." She squeezed Roc's bicep.

She had a really good time, much better than she feared. Hopefully Roc hadn't felt obligated to hang out with her because she knew nobody else.

"Let me walk you back to your hotel," he offered.

"Oh, that's okay. It's only a few blocks."

"I won't hear of it. It's late and dark." Roc shook his head.

"You're right," she conceded, recalling her harrowing walk the night before. "Thank you."

They headed downstairs, out the door and into the cool night air. A man on a cell phone glanced up at them and paused his conversation, his eyes going wide as saucers. He dropped his phone, and she heard it break.

"Serves him right. So rude," she whispered to Roc.

"You are wearing angel wings and I look like a demon," he whispered back, a slight chuckle rumbling in his chest.

"Oh my gawd, I completely forgot. We should go back in and change. Don't you need a jacket? You've got to be chilly." She tried to not overtly stare at his muscular chest now that she was reminded again that he was half naked.

How could I forget?

"Change? Don't you like me how I am?" he teased.

"I do like how you're a wicked smart-ass," she snorted, playing along with his terrible pun. "And even the wings and such have grown on me, but you're going to give everyone between here and the hotel a heart attack.

"No I won't, 'cause you look just as weird, little angel, but together we look normal. Besides, you'll be waiting 'til the end of time before I get these off." He quickly gestured to his, horns, wings and tail.

"I knew it, you used a truckload of some fancy special

effects superglue." She shook her head. "Are you sure I can keep these wings?"

"Call it a souvenir."

"Alrighty then, let's go."

Meline led the way. As they passed the bald guy by the car, he was still staring at them.

"What? Haven't you heard, opposites attract?" she asked the man, then giggled when his mouth dropped open.

"Don't be fooled, she's a devil in the sack," Roc called over his shoulder.

She burst into all out laughter and stumbled off the sidewalk.

"Careful there," he chuckled as he caught her and kept her from falling on her butt.

She liked the sound of his laugh and the way his broad smile made his eyes crinkle, lessening the harshness of his features.

"What?" Roc asked, sobering slightly.

"I was just noticing how white and shiny your teeth are against your dark skin. You should smile all the way back to my hotel, you're better than a flashlight."

"Who's the smart-ass now?" He cocked his brow and snorted at her pathetic excuse to cover up for staring.

Maybe I was wrong. Meline smiled to herself as they walked. *Maybe I didn't come off too gabby and frivolous.*

They reached her hotel before she knew it and she paused outside the big red door. She didn't want to say goodnight just yet.

"You want to come in?" she boldly asked, staring up into Roc's luminous gray eyes.

"Meline, I think we both know that's not a good idea." His easy smile shifted to a smirk, a crease forming in his brow.

He was probably right, but still it was hard to hear.

"Thank you again. I had a great time," she swiftly replied, then turned to go inside so he wouldn't see the disappointment in her eyes.

She barely made it a step before frustration got the best of her. Meline spun back around and scowled at him.

"You know what, no, I don't know that it's not a good idea. You flirted with me half the evening, and well, I just thought, hey, why not. It's not like I have delusions we'll spend one night together, and suddenly you'd profess your undying love for me, I'd move here, and we'd live in a little house with a white picket fence and have a litter of children," she huffed.

Roc stared wide-eyed at her. He had nothing to say for himself, so she turned to go inside.

Well, it was *a nice evening.* Till she went and ruined it. But she meant every word that she said and refused to apologize. They got along like a house on fire, however she wasn't so daft to think a rich, tall, dark and ruggedly handsome man was interested in her for more than a fling. Obviously, she was reading things wrong, he wasn't even interested in that. *So stupid,* she berated herself as she grabbed the doorknob.

"Meline." Roc pressed a palm on the door, halting her retreat. "Please hear me out."

"What?" She turned back to face him, her foot tapping the pavement.

"I'm an asshole. I've had more one-night stands than one man should, and you're too sweet to do that to."

"That's such bullshit, but fine, if that's the excuse you

want to go with." Meline tried to tug on the door but he wouldn't remove his hand.

"It's the truth," he countered with a slight growl.

"Oh, so you're saying that I'm just so damn sweet…" She made bunny ears with her fingers. "…that suddenly you grew a conscience, and have decided to reform your man-whore ways rather than break the silly innocent tourist's heart and send her back to her mundane life pining for the rich and worldly Roc? Don't flatter yourself."

"Dammit, I do want to go to your room. And the things I'd do to you would make it hard for you to look me in the eye in the morning. And that's real, the truth. But you don't know who I am. I'm a deceitful bastard, because I'm still trying to figure out a way to see you again, knowing full well that I'm using you. I can't go up to your room on top of everything else," he rumbled, making absolutely no sense at all. It sounded like he wanted to see her again, but somehow that was worse than a one-night stand.

Real fucking nice!

"All right. Whatever. Goodnight." She shook her head.

Meline tugged on the door again. Roc relented and stepped out of her way. She rolled her eyes, seeing the conflicted look on his face, as she headed inside. It was inconsiderate to the other guests, but she stomped up the stairs, trying not to cry till she got to her room. She was so worked up, it took a few attempts to jam her key into the lock. When she finally got it unlocked, she attempted to storm inside, but her wings got caught on the door jamb.

"Stupid wings," Meline growled in frustration as she shrugged out of the feathery ensemble. They tangled with her purse strap, making her angrier. She yanked the mess off and hurled both onto the floor.

She slammed the door, but at the last second changed her mind and shoved her hand into the door jamb before it banged shut. That would certainly wake everyone in the small hotel if her tirade up the stairs hadn't already.

"Ow, dammit," she barked when the door hit her knuckles, the smarting pain bringing the tears she'd been holding back rushing to the forefront.

Moisture slid down her cheeks as she eased the door closed then held her sore hand. It was the icing on the cake. She glanced at the wings lying on floor and her tears came faster. They were lovely, straight out of a fairy tale. Too bad, like every fairy tale, it disappeared at the stroke of midnight. And yet they were too nice to throw away. She would just have to edit out the end of the story in her mind whenever she looked at them.

As Meline bent to grab them, an arm wrapped around her waist. She shrieked but it was muffled by a dirty calloused hand.

"Arret," the man growled.

That meant stop, but she struggled harder, frantically clawing at the bastard behind her. Her gaze darted around the room as she fought. She'd been so worked up when she got to her room, she failed to notice her suitcase had been dumped out at the foot of the bed. In the mirror she saw the man attacking her wore a ski mask. He growled when she aimed for his menacing dark eyes, but she refused to go down without a fight. The man grabbed her arm and violently swung her away from him. She cried in pain as her hip hit the corner of the nightstand, knocking over the lamp which shattered on the floor. Meline spun to face her attacker then screamed in terror as he rushed her.

Please, God. What does he want? She screamed again as she scrambled back, bumped into the bed and fell atop it.

ROC

"For the love of *Lar*," Roc growled as he stared at the hotel door Meline disappeared through.

He couldn't believe Meline propositioned him or that he turned her down. He grew hard just thinking how sexy she looked as the words fell from her pink lips.

You had to grow a conscience. He adjusted his cock as it strained painfully against his fly.

But he couldn't take advantage of her, not like that. Not when he'd already deceived her. And it was downright pathetic the way he lied to himself, claiming he was merely getting to know her. To sleep with Meline on top of all that he'd already done was unforgivable. The thought of hurting her made the bile in the pit of his stomach churn.

"And why the fuck do my teeth hurt?" The throbbing pain added to his misery.

A couple heading to a nearby pub gaped at him. Before they laid eyes on him they looked disgustingly happy, something he knew nothing about.

"Haven't you ever seen a gargoyle?" Roc snapped, uncaring if they gossiped.

If Meline had been by his side, looking the way she did, they wouldn't have stared. They joked earlier about being quite a pair, an angel and demon. It wasn't quite a joke. The more time he spent with her, the deeper she worked beneath his skin. She was funny and so damn cute. The way she took him to task would've been unbelievably sexy if he didn't feel like such an ass.

But I am a bastard. And the illicit thoughts he was having about her couldn't happen, because he wasn't wearing a costume and she was an angel.

The hair on the back of his neck stood on end as a pained scream split the night.

"Meline!"

Roc turned and ran the dozen paces back to her hotel, his feet barely hitting the pavement. He nearly tore the door off its hinges and stormed up the stairs, pushing past the people coming out of their rooms. Meline screamed in terror and the sound stabbed at him.

"Meline!" he roared.

Roc reached the top floor and shoved past a man in the hall who couldn't get out of his way fast enough, then nearly knocked over a woman, he was so desperate to reach Meline's room. He threw open the door and froze seeing her huddled on the bed. Her face was swollen, tears streaming down her cheeks. The sleeve of her pink dress was torn, and he could see an angry red welt on her arm. Someone hurt her. Rage unlike anything he'd ever known overwhelmed him. Roc felt his skin shift as his body reacted to his turbulent emotions. His gaze darted around the room looking for the vile filth that needed to die, but no one was there. Her assailant must've been one of the people milling around in the hall, blending in with the guests who fled their rooms to see what was wrong. He growled in frustration.

"Roc?" Meline keened with a wavering voice, as her glossy hazel eyes peered up at him through her disheveled brown hair.

The way she looked at him, confusion and relief lighting her gaze, instantly took the wind out of his sails. His anger at whoever did this would have to wait. He was by her side in an instant, but he wasn't sure what to do. Meline melted against him as he wrapped his arms around her. The way she trembled made keeping his temper in check damn near impossible, but he would. Going beast mode would only traumatize her further.

"I've got you," he rasped, her waning terror making him physically hurt.

Repressing the need to enfold her in his wings, since there were humans gawking from the hallway, was nearly impossible. She was so small, and someone had savaged her. He desperately wanted to shelter her from it all.

"Is she okay?" a concerned woman asked from the doorway.

"I'm fine, now." Meline's words were punctuated with a ragged hiccup.

"It's a costume. We were at a masquerade," Roc reassured the woman when she continued to stare.

"Oh, I see. I think someone called the police already. They should arrive soon," the woman said then kindly shooed the other nosy hotel guests away.

"What happened, angel?" Roc tried to keep the snarl out of his voice as he looked at the busted lamp and her clothes strewn on the floor.

"I didn't see him. He had a mask. But I scratched him."

Meline showed him her nails. The notion that she had to defend herself with those benign things made him see red.

If I get my hands on the bastard, I'll show him claws. His fingers flexed, itching to release the claws he usually kept retracted.

Roc sniffed, attempting to pick apart the scents in the room. Lavender hung heavy in the air, along with the salty scent of her tears.

I got you, Roc nearly grinned in triumph when he picked up the odor of dirty sweat and motor oil clinging to Meline. He was glad to have something to track the bastard who did this, but at the same time, he wanted to wash it off her, as if that would wipe away what happened here. *How dare the fucker touch her.* He made a point to memorize the scent.

"My purse! He stole my purse and my bag with all my family info," Meline exclaimed as she frantically looked around. She scrambled off the bed and stood on wobbly legs as she searched the room. "What am I going to do?"

"Don't worry about that right now," he insisted and meant it. Yes, Nicolas' diary was gone and possibly his lead on finding the sigil, but that was the furthest thing from his mind.

"Don't worry?! All my money is gone. What am I going to do for the next two weeks?" she cried as she stared at her clothes strewn everywhere.

Roc was about to comment when his gaze landed on a flicker of gold near the baseboard.

"Is this yours?" he asked and picked it up.

"No. Maybe I knocked it off the guy who attacked me."

A bad feeling struck as he studied the lapel pin. The bald man who'd been talking on his phone outside Chateau Frontenac had been wearing the same symbol, a compass rose with an actual flower in the center. Even if Meline hadn't commented on the nosy man, he would've noticed the guy. The man reeked of Old Spice, like he'd bathed in it. But the stinky spy couldn't be her assailant. His scent wasn't in the room. No, the asshole that did this had to be someone else wearing the same unique pin.

Dammit. This wasn't a run of the mill robbery. He wasn't the only one who'd been following Meline.

Or maybe it wasn't Meline they were after. Over the centuries, groups of humans had become aware of Khargals, each with their own crazy reason for hunting them.

"Meline, you'll stay with me. This place isn't safe," he insisted. Until he figured out what was going on, he wasn't going to let her out of his sight.

"Okay." Her shoulders slumped in defeat.

6

MELINE

"John, I managed to lose my keys," Roc called out as he knocked on the door of his penthouse."

"That happens a lot, sir," a skinny, gray-haired man said as he answered the door. "Oh, my apologies, you've brought a guest. Welcome, madame." He bowed.

"Meline will be staying with us. She was attacked at her hotel." Roc set her suitcase down in the large foyer.

"Oh dear, come in. I'll go make some chamomile tea to calm your nerves. Or perhaps you'd prefer a stiff drink?"

Meline nodded.

"That was a yes to the stiff drink. Little John can't see you nodding," he explained.

"Oh, sorry. Yes, please." She pulled out of her haze and studied John's unfocused stare.

"Don't apologize. You relax, and I'll see to everything, well, in a manner of speaking." John smiled.

"Jokes, right now? Seriously, John," Roc admonished.

She snorted in amusement. "No, it's fine. I could use a little levity. I wasn't hurt, so I should be thankful for that."

It really was a blessing.

"Thank heavens for that." John toddled off.

"But you were hurt," Roc growled as he scowled at her torn sleeve.

She looked up at him, grateful he showed up when he did. After the way they parted, she never expected to see him again.

"I'm fine. Just a little bruised. Why did you come back?"

"I heard you scream." Roc's brow furrowed in concern.

"Oh."

"Are you sure you're fine?" He gingerly touched her arm.

"Yes, I'm fine. It probably angered the guy when I tried to gouge out his eyes. He tossed me into the bedside table." She shivered, reliving the moment.

"Were you supposed to just let him accost you?" Roc snarled, menace flashing in his steely eyes. "Now that you're safely here with John, I'm going back to that hotel."

Anger contorted his features, making his brow appear sharper. He was truly pissed she'd been attacked.

"Please stay. I don't know what else you'll find that the police can't." She put a hand on his arm to stop him as he headed for the door.

"I have my ways. I told you, Meline, you don't really know who I am," he rumbled, seeming hell bent on finding her assailant.

"No, you're right, I don't. And you don't really know me. You've already kindly given me a place to stay, so I don't have any right to impose, but I don't want to be alone right now."

He looked conflicted, a deep crease furrowing his brow. "Meline, we need to talk—"

"Here we are. Would you like this in the parlor?" John interrupted as he entered the foyer holding a tray with two glasses of ice and a decanter.

Meline took a look around the penthouse as she followed Roc and John to the living room. It was spectacularly decorated with modern décor and paintings on nearly every wall. John set the tray on the glass coffee table and she took a seat on the long black sofa.

"If you need anything else, just call," John said after expertly pouring two glasses.

"Thank you," she said as he left.

The need to apologize hung heavy on her mind, but she didn't know how to even begin. With the way he came to her rescue it was obvious Roc wasn't a total asshole. He didn't deserve the reaming she gave him for not wanting to sleep with her. She grabbed one of the glasses and took a big swig to calm her nerves. The whiskey burned going down, making her choke and sputter.

"Easy." He frowned at her as he sat in the leather chair nearby. His dark wings conveniently arched over the low back.

"Thank you for keeping me company, and for all this. You didn't have to give me a place to stay after my behavior. I'm sorry, by the way. I feel like such a fool. Don't worry, I won't impose on you long. I'll be heading home as soon as I can get replacement keys for my car."

"Don't apologize. You should've yelled at me. I was coming on to you, because I like you, but I've got no right, not after what I've done and who I am." After draining his glass, he poured himself another.

"I don't understand."

He wasn't making any sense again. Meline frowned and took another gulp of whiskey. It went down much smoother this time.

"I don't think you were robbed for your money. That bald man outside Chateau Frontenac was wearing the same pin as the one we found in your room."

Her heart sped up and she started to hyperventilate at Roc's observation. She finished her whiskey and he was ready with the decanter to pour her more.

"I thought someone was watching me. I felt it since the night I arrived. I thought I was crazy. Who would follow me? I'm nobody. Less than nobody." She took another large drink.

Who wears matching lapel pins? Some sort of freaky mafioso wannabes or a secret society of nut jobs, that's who.

"I was watching you," Roc mumbled behind his glass.

Her gaze flew to his.

"Excuse me?" Her voice rose an octave.

"You weren't crazy. I was following you." Roc refused to make eye contact for the first time since they met.

"That was you!" She abruptly stood, everything that happened today spiraling through her mind. "You're behind what happened at the hotel?" Meline screeched.

That's why he invited me to that fancy party—to get me out of my room. Oh God, the guy at the reception table knew my full name! I never told Roc my last name. Meline clenched her fist, angry that she let Roc's larger than life persona blind her. *But why?* It didn't make sense. *It doesn't matter.* She shook her head. *I should've known this was too good to be true. How could I be so stupid?*

"No!" Roc growled and shot to his feet.

Her eyes widened when his fake wings shot wide, the clawed tips bristling, making him look even more imposing. Her fear spiked, and she backed up. She'd known Roc less than a day. She had no clue what he was truly capable of.

"No. I would never." He softened his voice and dropped back into his seat. "Please hear me out." He held up his hands.

"I'm listening." Meline halted her retreat, but kept a wary eye on him.

"The other night when you visited the archaeological site, I overheard you mention your ancestor, Nicolas Peltier, and recognized the name. Your ancestor and one of mine were good friends. So, I followed you to your hotel and then again when you went sightseeing. But I didn't send that goon to your room."

"Okay," she drew out the word and started pacing, trying to get a grip on the emotions assailing her. Roc had been very upset about the assault, he hadn't seemed to manufacture the reaction. So maybe he was telling the truth. "Why didn't you just introduce yourself?"

"You're saying me creeping up on you at night as you walked alone wouldn't have freaked you out?"

"Well, when you put it that way, you have a point." Meline paused as she thought of how they did meet, and her eyes narrowed on him. "Wait, then why didn't you say something at the bookstore? Or at the party?"

"I could say our meeting at the shop was so brief I didn't have a chance to bring it up, but that would be a lie. Or at the party, you looked so damn hot I didn't want to ruin it having this conversation, which is the truth, but hardly a decent excuse." Roc's lips twisted into a shit-eating grin.

She blushed, the heat moving over her cheeks and down her chest. Meline shook her head, disgusted that she let the flirty comment derail her. Clearly the booze was messing with her.

Focus!

"Dammit, Roc, you're flirting again," she growled.

"Fuck, I know." He drained his glass a second time.

"So, our ancestors were friends. As much as I'd love learning more about that, I'd never stalk someone. Do you know how freaking crazy that is?" she snapped at him, her fist balled up to keep from slapping his handsome stupid face.

"I don't think the truth's going to make this any better." He cringed.

"Try me."

"So, my ancestor gave yours a valuable family heirloom, that looks like an elongated ruby set in precious metal. I thought that if I got a look at the journal you mentioned and could pick your brain, I'd find it."

Meline crossed her arms as she considered what Roc revealed. This explained what he was babbling about when he turned her down. If she learned all this after sleeping with him it really would've been a kick in the teeth. So, kudos to him for not being a total prick. It also reasoned that a treasure hunt for a family heirloom would peak his interest, he was an art collector. Hell, it had her intrigued. But as she looked at Roc, he appeared nervous and she got the feeling there was more.

"What aren't you telling me? If you didn't pay that man to break into my room, why do you look so guilty?"

"I would never pay someone to break in anywhere, or

have a woman attacked. And when I find who's behind this, I'll make them wish they never laid a hand on you."

The way his voice rumbled with malice, she believed him. She almost felt sorry for the mugger if Roc ever got his hands on him.

"Fine, you didn't hire those guys. I'm sorry, but can you blame me for asking?"

Roc's shoulders slumped. "No, I can't. And you're right, I haven't come clean about everything. A man like me has a lot of skeletons in his closet. But please, trust me, I don't want to hurt you in any way."

Meline sat back down as she let all this sink in. So, he allowed his excitement over finding a long-lost family treasure overrule his common sense, but he'd come clean. However, that meant there was still someone out there who was after her.

ROC

Confessing was a relief, but now Meline had him twisting on the end of a line as she sat quietly considering him. She seemed to relax, yet suspicion still danced in her eyes. For some inane reason he wanted to blurt every minute detail of his life, just to wipe that look off her face. He couldn't bear the thought of her hating, fearing or distrusting him in any way. He worried if she pressed further he'd even tell her about Khargals and the real purpose behind the sigil; then she really would fear him. He couldn't have that.

"Tell me what you think is going on," she finally spoke.

"I'm not sure. Because of who I am, I've always had to be cautious. I generally stay very private." Even if he didn't have an ounce of Khargal blood, his acquired wealth and the means by which he obtained it would be enough reason to keep a low profile.

"Except for tonight."

"Yes. I wanted a chance to mix with people."

"That's why it was a masquerade and you donated the painting anonymously, wasn't it?"

"Yes. Sometimes the life I lead grows weary."

"I'm sorry." Meline frowned and the sharp glint in her hazel eyes softened. Even the acrid biting scent screaming of anger and fear which had put him on edge shifted, replaced by something that reminded him of rain.

His eyes widened realizing she genuinely meant what she said. *If she only knew the half of it.* And yet, strangely, her sympathy brought him comfort. He rarely got the chance to admit the way he felt, and it was even rarer someone truly heard him.

"I shouldn't complain," he quickly added, and waved a hand toward his penthouse. It was unwise to dwell too long on the feelings she incited. "Anyway, I don't know if those people went after you because they saw you with me and were trying to get to me. Or if they somehow learned about my family's relic and want it, or a bit of both. But what I do know is anyone willing to hurt you over any of this is dangerous." The bastards already proved that.

"I don't think they're after you," Meline replied as she considered what he said. "Before we met, some guy dressed like a tourist was following me. I ducked into the bookshop to get away from him, then dismissed it, certain I was just being paranoid. I'm nobody, who would stalk me, right? I hardly have a penny to my name, so it doesn't make sense. But they must want something they think I have, so maybe it is your family heirloom."

That's why she looked so startled in the bookshop. He'd been so focused on her he hadn't noticed any of the other people on the street.

Unbelievable guilt and anger assailed him as he thought about those bastards stalking her. Roc clenched the armrest to keep himself under control. The last thing he needed to do was shift. He already scared Meline enough with his last outburst.

Those bastards might've found her first, but he had a strong suspicion ultimately this was about him. Like she said, what other reason did they have to stalk her? The question was, did the assholes have an inkling of his true identity or were they just glorified treasure hunters and thugs looking for the big score?

"Perhaps it was a coincidence these people found you the same time I did. My family heirloom is very valuable. If they think you inherited it that would be enough to go through all this effort. What I want to know is how they learned about it when I've had no luck? Where did you get Nicolas' journal?"

"It was passed down to my dad. He used to belong to a genealogy website, so maybe he posted our family info on there. But, Roc, I don't recall reading about any jewel or medallion in the journal." Meline paused, her face going white. "Shit! When they don't find mention of it either, do you think they'll come back?" There was a tremor in her hand when she downed her glass of whiskey and the sharp fearful scent returned.

He was disappointed when Meline mentioned not remembering any references to the sigil, but not surprised. This had been a long shot. What frustrated him more was she now worried the bastards behind this would come back for her.

Moron, he cursed. *She was just attacked. You could've let her have the night to recover before revealing the world is filled with wolves.*

Roc got up and moved to sit next to her.

"I'm sorry. We shouldn't discuss this now. You've been through enough for one evening." He put his hand on hers. "I promise, nothing will happen to you. I won't let it."

"I believe you. Thank you for everything and for telling me. I know it couldn't have been easy." Meline intertwined her fingers with his and squeezed his hand.

Roc sighed in relief. He meant to console her, instead her forgiveness and the simple gesture brought him comfort. How she didn't hate him after everything he admitted he'd never understand.

She is an angel.

"Let's discuss something else, or maybe you want to take a shower and go to bed," he suggested.

"I don't think I can sleep, but I would like to get out of this dress. I can't believe that fucker tore it. This cost me sixty dollars and that was off the sale rack." Meline pouted.

"Forget about it. I will buy you ten more to replace it," he reassured her.

"Roc, you're letting me stay here, you're not going to buy me a new dress, too." Meline stumbled as she stood.

"Careful." Roc jumped to his feet and wrapped an arm around her waist.

"Shit, I'm so clumsy, and the booze probably hasn't helped much. Can you imagine if I wore heels?" she snorted.

"If you want to wear heels, I could buy them too and then carry you around."

"Hush, Daddy Warbucks." Meline slapped his bare chest, making him grin.

"I don't know if John got one of the spare rooms set up, so you can sleep in my room tonight." He led Meline through his bedroom to the bathroom.

"Jesus, Roc, your bedroom is almost as big as my whole condo. I love this bathroom. The marble is gorgeous. Ooh, look, a swimming pool!"

"I guess it is big enough you could take a swim, but it's not a pool, it's just a jacuzzi tub." He chuckled at her.

"I know, I was teasing," she added with a wink.

"Maybe you'd like to take a lap anyway."

She grinned. "That would feel good on my muscles." Longing filled her gaze as she stared at the tub and rolled her delicate shoulders.

"You relax and I'll go get your bag."

"Thank you," Meline called out as he left the bathroom and headed for the foyer.

"Looking for this, sir?" John greeted him in the hall holding her suitcase.

"Yes, thank you."

"Will the lady be all right?"

"Yes. But I can't let her out of my sight. Do you recall why we left Madrid?" Roc growled.

He'd told John a ring of art thieves were plotting to break

in, but had suspicions that wasn't the case. It was the only other time, at least since John had been with him, that he had to pick up and leave in the night. This modern era was a blessing, but with the internet it was making it harder for his kind to hide.

"Not those people again," John scoffed in disgust.

"I don't think it's the same people, but the motives are just as vile. I really don't have more than a symbol to hunt them down."

"Describe it for me."

"I found a gold pin with the open bloom of a rose set in the middle of a compass."

"I'm on it straight away, sir, you leave it to me." John nodded and headed for his study.

If anyone could find information about this group, it was John. He might not be able to see but he had the latest technology, and even some that wasn't on the market yet.

Roc carried the suitcase back to the bathroom and knocked on the door.

"Roc," her voice echoed through the door, but he could also make out the violent rustling of fabric.

"I'm just going to set your bag inside." He cracked the door and slid the suitcase in.

"Um, Roc, wait. God, this is so embarrassing. I need your help," she said, her words muffled.

"I'm coming in."

He swung open the door and froze. His gaze panned up Meline's bare calves, to her creamy full thighs and round hips. She wore a tiny lacey pair of panties that did little to hide the tuft of hair on her mound. His gaze shifted higher, and he burst out laughing as he realized what was wrong.

"Don't laugh. I'm stuck." Meline struggled as she tried to tug her dress the rest of the way over her head.

"Stop squirming, you're going to fall," he said, mostly because it was making her ass shake. Any more and he wouldn't be able to repress the hard-on straining in his pants.

He grabbed the dress, ignoring the way his knuckles grazed her ribs as he worked it up over her breasts. It was a test in patience keeping on task as he revealed her bra. It was a lacy bit of nothing. Her ruddy areolas were just peeking over the top of the cups.

Sainthood, that's what I deserve, he groaned.

"I know, it's tight," she commented at the sound he made.

Roc closed his eyes. The woman just had to say that word, tight, conjuring a host of thoughts in his head, none of them good. He got the dress over Meline's shoulders and swiftly released her, backing away.

"I think that did it."

With the way his gums and canines ached, he could barely speak. He desperately wanted to sample her flesh. Just one kiss, as if his life depended on it. And yet somehow he knew one kiss wouldn't be enough. He headed for the door before he pounced on her like a beast in heat.

"Thank you." Meline's voice was no longer muffled but she sounded funny.

He glanced back to find her bent over the tub, checking the water temperature. Seeing her heart-shaped ass stuck up in the air had the hard-on he'd been fighting instantly throbbing.

The woman's going to kill me. Roc shoved at his cock as he quickly shut the door.

7

MELINE

Oh, that's nice. Meline groaned as she slipped into the churning hot water. *So embarrassing. Too much whiskey.*

The way she was acting, stumbling and getting caught up in her dress, you'd think she was totally shitfaced.

You should've seen that coming when you had to pour yourself into the dress to begin with.

It had been one thing after another this evening. She rolled her head from one side to the other, working the kinks out of her sore muscles. That awful man had done a number on her.

"It could've been so much worse," she repeated like a mantra, not sure if it was calming her nerves or making things worse.

Maybe she shouldn't have been so quick to forgive Roc for his part in all this, and there was still something about him she couldn't put her finger on, but she kept coming back around to that moment in the hotel. She was beside herself, totally freaked out and without a clue of what she was going to do, then she looked up and there he was. An inexplicable sense of relief cut through her fear. Which was ironic considering he was dressed like the king of demons.

And he has the hots for me. Meline grinned, recalling his shameless flirting, while she reached for the bottle of shampoo.

"Oh shit," she cursed as the bottle slipped out of her hands and fell into the water.

Okay, so maybe I'm a bit more than tipsy. She fumbled around in the water till she captured the bottle, flipped the lid closed and placed it back on the ledge. *Well, I guess I don't need any more soap*, she snorted.

She ducked beneath the water and scrubbed her head. She came up for air and mopped the suds from her eyes.

"Oh fuck. No, no, no!" she yelped at all the suds bubbling up in the tub. The jets mixed with the spilled shampoo, turning the tub into an out of control bubble bath. "Shit, where's the switch?" She scrambled, looking for the button as the suds spilled over the rim.

"What's wrong?" Roc asked in concern as he threw open the door. "Are you okay?" He peered around the door when she didn't instantly answer.

Roc froze, his jaw dropping open. He shook off his surprise, rushed over and hit the button, halting the jets.

Jesus, why am I a total mess around this man?

"I thought since I was staying for free the least I could do was clean up a bit to earn my keep," Meline joked to cover her embarrassment, then sank into the mountain of suds hoping to hide.

"Is that so?" He laughed as he knelt and began scooping suds back into the tub.

"Here, let me. I'm the one that made this mess." She leaned out next to him to help. "Never drop the shampoo if the jets are on. I can't believe this," she prattled on.

"Meline!"

"What?"

"Your bubble bikini is slipping."

She glanced back to see the suds covering her were sliding into the tub, revealing her bare ass. Her cheeks heated, and her gaze swiveled back to find him a breath away. His gray eyes met hers and she was instantly ensnared. They looked like swirling quicksilver the longer she stared. Meline always believed what they said about the eyes being windows to the soul. Roc was the ultimate enigma, yet in his eyes she saw a tempest of emotion. But it was the fierce longing and desire that struck her the hardest.

She pressed her mouth against his. Roc's lips were full, broad, and warm, like the man, so strong and hot-blooded. But they were also smooth, unlike his stubbled jaw or his hands, that were rough from work. The man was a host of contradictions.

Suddenly she realized he wasn't kissing her back and pulled away in horror. Maybe she'd read him wrong.

"I'm sorry," she started to say.

Roc growled when she tried to retreat, and his hand shot out, tangling in her hair. He gripped the back of her head and smashed his lips against hers again. Meline sucked in a deep breath, surprise and desire coursing through her. He took advantage of the opportunity, his tongue spearing into her mouth. There was something about the way he tasted that struck her as deeply satisfying. A strange tingling sensation spread through her mouth and down her spine. Her tongue delved into his mouth, seeking more. She couldn't believe how turned on she was, and he was only kissing her. She was ravenous, and bolder than she remembered ever being. Her tongue dueled with his, tasting, exploring.

"Meline," he rumbled. The erotic sound made her shiver with need. "Meline," he repeated.

She pulled back and saw the barely restrained passion twisting his rugged features.

"You are so damn sweet, Meline. You don't even have a clue how sexy you are, do you? The way you blush, laugh, and the funny things you do and say. From the moment I saw you, you had me turned inside out. I wasn't feeding you a line when I said I wanted to do unspeakable things to you. So, angel, this is your chance to turn tail and run."

No one had ever said such things to her. The way he flattered her made her feel just as sexy as he claimed, but also nervous. Roc was such an imposing man, and if the desire burning in his eyes was any indication, she wasn't sure she'd be able to withstand the kind of passion he was threatening. Meline found herself nodding anyway.

"I gave you fair warning." His lips twisted into a cocky grin as he leaned in close to her ear. "If you had run, I would've chased you. And I always catch my prey."

She gasped, her mouth dropping open in surprise when he scooped her out of the bath like she weighed nothing at all. He didn't bother with drying her off, just headed straight for the bedroom. She stared up at his dark rugged face. The horns and enormous black wings arching over his head captured her attention. She was about to say something about removing the costume, then thought better of it. It would take too long, and —well—she found it sexy.

The ultimate bad boy.

She grinned wickedly as she leaned in and nibbled his neck. He made a delicious sounding groan, so she nipped him harder.

"I'm not that sweet," she whispered when she reached his ear.

"I think you are," Roc husked and released her.

A shocked squeal burst out then turned into a laugh as she hit the springy bed. Her laugh died when Roc came down on top of her, his weight pressing her into the mattress. God, the man was positively massive, hunched over her. He gripped her wrists, stretching her arms above her head as he kissed her neck.

"In fact, I'm going to see just how sweet you are."

His voice rough with passion, the salacious suggestion and the way he dominated her were overwhelming enough, then he began sampling the skin at the base of her throat. His kisses were hot against her cool wet skin, and goosebumps pebbled her flesh. Her heart beat hard and fast as Roc kissed an agonizingly slow path between her breasts. Her nipples were so stiff they ached, begging for attention. She was going to die from the anticipation.

With his free hand, Roc grabbed something draped over the headboard and she felt silky fabric graze her wrist.

"Roc?" she exclaimed when she saw the blue and yellow necktie, and what he was debating dawned on her.

He cast her a rogue smile, showing a hint of fang, and her breath sped up. She didn't have a lot of experience with a man like Roc or a situation like this, and she'd certainly never been tied up. A frisson of excitement and trepidation shot through her. Her fingers itched to stroke his muscular shoulders and corded arms, but Roc had her pinned. This was sheer torture, she couldn't imagine withstanding it all night.

"I—you—I," she sputtered, not knowing what to say.

He stared at her for what seemed like forever. The expressions crossing his face reflected a fierce debate waging within.

"All right, angel." Roc relented and tossed aside the necktie. "Like I said…" he kissed the tip of one turgid nipple, making her draw in a sharp breath. "So sweet." Roc kissed the other breast, then pinned her with those mercurial eyes. "But if you prove naughty, I'll be forced to restrain you. Maybe I will anyway," he husked the illicit promise.

Meline was stunned speechless, her mouth agape. The breath she was holding burst out when his raspy tongue circled one areola then swiped at her nipple before sucking it into his hot mouth. Her back bowed as he took a long, deep pull before switching to torment the other needy bud. The sensation coiled around her, making every cell in her body scream. She rubbed her thighs together as her pussy cramped in response. That caught Roc's attention and he glanced up again.

"Am I neglecting something?"

Before she could reply, he reared back, snagged her ankles and splayed her legs. There was hardly enough time for her to be embarrassed about being totally exposed. Her eyes widened when Roc growled and dove for her pussy. His large palms shoved at her thighs, forcing them wider to make room for his broad shoulders. But it would've taken the splits to accomplish that.

"You're so little," he huffed impatiently.

Roc wrapped his arms beneath her knees and hoisted her

legs over his shoulders. It was convenient the way his folded wings cradled her calves, holding them put. Meline was stunned by the ravenous way he struggled to reach the most intimate part of her.

"Oh yeah," he took a deep breath and groaned as his face burrowed between her thighs.

Such a personal act usually gave her pause, but his reaction made her forget her reticence. She reveled in the way his large fingers kneaded her fleshy hips, not minding that his grip was nearly bruising. Staccato breaths heaved past her lips at feeling his hot breath caress her slick folds. A surprised sound burst out when Roc's tongue met her heated flesh. She was so incredibly sensitive and aroused she nearly orgasmed right then and there. Her panting turned labored when he found her eager clit and laved it like he had her nipples. It throbbed harder with each slow concentric circle, till he reached the swollen peak. Her pussy spasmed, sending a flood of moisture leaking down her cleft.

The demi-god wedged between her thighs rumbled in pleasure, vibrating her clit. Meline bit her lip to repress the needy sounds fighting to get free. He hummed, and the vibration got stronger. Unbelievably she felt it not only in her clit, but deeper.

"Roc!" she cried, when two thick fingers pressed into her wet vagina.

Her hands shot out for him, clamoring for something to hold onto, as he curled his fingers, aiming for her g-spot. Meline found the two horns and gripped them tight as she bucked her hips. It was a shock she didn't pull them clean off his head.

A savage sound erupted from Roc and it was like he

snapped. He latched onto her clit and sucked ravenously as his fingers began thrusting into her, stroking mercilessly at her g-spot. The pleasure assailing her was pure insanity, making her writhe.

ROC

Roc knew it was selfish, but he rarely let women touch him, for obvious reasons. But Meline wasn't just any female. Although maybe he should've tied her up. Her mere touch did things to him, made his blood boil. Not only were his canines throbbing but so were the talons that tipped his wings. It was a completely foreign sensation. If he were human, he'd say he was sick, but that wasn't possible. All he knew was that he needed to touch Meline, needed to feel her, taste her and everything in between. He'd let her do anything, just as long as she didn't flee his bed. And since she'd been reticent, he didn't bind her wrists. What harm could it do? She already saw everything, though she did think it was a costume.

The first taste of Meline was like heaven. Her sweet nectar was better than anything he'd ever known. The gasping squeaks coming from her pink lips turned him on even more. He was positively evil for using the subsonic hum to make her come undone, but couldn't help himself. Then she grabbed his overly sensitive horns and he was the one who lost all control. He really should've tied her up.

The heady scent of her desire was overwhelming, actually made him dizzy. With every pump of his fingers, her silky pussy spilled more desire. It was shocking how wet she was, spurring him on. He ravenously lapped up the offering in between sucking the pearl of flesh straining from her folds. The way he feasted on her, you'd think he'd never gone down on a female.

"Roc. Roc. Roc," she chanted his name, her pitch getting higher and needier with each word.

His cock jerked, and Roc snarled against her swollen clit, realizing, frustratingly, that he still wore pants. Meline's legs tightened around his head and her fluttering pussy locked onto his fingers, his growl driving her over the edge.

"Fuck," Roc cursed. He wanted to be buried balls deep in her sweet body when she finally came.

He couldn't complain, though, Meline's warbled cry was music to his ears. And she was beyond gorgeous, her breasts thrust out as she arched off the bed.

"No more," Meline gasped as she wedged her fingers between his face and her pussy, attempting to halt his still stroking fingers.

"Hardly, angel, I'm just beginning." He was so turned on, he hardly recognized his own voice.

Roc pulled his fingers free of her body. She shuddered and collapsed against the mattress, her legs sliding off his shoulders. He impatiently gripped his fly and tugged it open, releasing his cock. The languid spent look on Meline's face shifted, her brow furrowing as she stared at his arousal. Roc realized Meline was having second thoughts as she opened her mouth then speechlessly closed it again. Maybe he should ease back, but something in him wouldn't allow it. He needed to make her his.

Get control of yourself!

MELINE

The room was dim, yet when Roc pulled off his pants, Meline couldn't help but gape at what he revealed. Nothing about the man was small, right down to the turgid cock jutting from his pelvis. His crown was so broad, her thighs clenched on reflex. The way he hovered over her, he looked ready to pounce with his intense silver gaze riveted to her naked body.

"Roc?" she said nervously when she found her voice.

"Roll over, angel," he husked.

Meline swallowed hard, recalling his promise to do unspeakable things to her as she rolled onto her stomach. She'd bitten off more than she could chew and yet if she turned back now, she knew she'd regret it.

"No, no," Roc chuckled in that deep rumbling voice of his.

She rolled back to her side, confused, as he stretched out next to her.

"Just relax," he whispered.

That was easier said than done.

Roc wrapped one large arm around her waist and tugged her back against his firm chest. He gently stroked her belly while placing chaste kisses on her shoulder.

He wants to spoon. She was a bit surprised but also touched.

With nothing between them, Roc's stiff cock pressed hot and heavy against the back of her thighs. He wasn't prodding or insistent, yet there was no ignoring it. As daunting as he was, she wasn't about to leave him hanging. Meline turned her head.

"Kiss me." She smiled back at him.

"With pleasure."

His lips met hers and she poured herself into the kiss. She took his hand on her stomach and guided it to her mound. Meline lifted her thigh and draped it over his. Roc groaned into her mouth when she shifted her hips, pressing her ass against his crotch. She kept her hand over his, but he didn't need to be shown what to do. Roc found her still pulsing clit as he insinuated his cock between her cheeks. He slowly rolled his fingers over her swollen nub with gentle pressure, while curling his hips, sliding his cock through the soaked folds guarding her pussy.

Her kisses became more insistent as the heat between them rekindled. Roc sped up his tempo, adding more pressure as he worried her clit. Each time he pumped his hips, his rock-hard cock sheathed in silky smooth flesh grazed her labia. She clenched her thighs, desperate for more of the delicious sensations that kept spiking through her with each stimulating lunge. His cock jerked in response.

"Fuck, angel, you're going to make me come before I get a chance to sink into your sweet little pussy," he groaned.

She smiled at the way his muscular body trembled against hers. It was a heady thing knowing she was able to affect him this way. Roc buried his face into her hair and nosed around 'til he found her neck.

"Oh." Meline drew in a sharp breath when his teeth latched on, holding her firm like a lion would his lioness.

Primal instinct made her freeze, her body stiffening as a tremor moved up her spine. She had no clue being bitten on such a sensitive spot would be so pleasurable. Roc shifted his hips and notched his cock at the mouth of her pussy. Meline's mouth opened wider, feeling the pressure of his broad crown as he demanded entrance to her body. He growled an inarticulate sound into her neck and his mouth tightened its hold, when her quivering channel spilled another flood of desire. He worked his pulsing arousal, stretching her open incrementally.

"Roc," she gasped, and gripped his arm.

Roc vigorously stroked her clit while he continued to slowly impale her on his shaft. He just kept going and going. The sensation was unbelievable. His engorged crown pressed and rubbed against the bundle of nerves on the roof of her channel as he delved deeper. A needy sound she didn't recognize escaped her throat, and her pussy spasmed hard. Roc's hips bucked in response. Her cry echoed off the walls when his cock punched deep. He instantly froze.

"Fuck, relax, angel. You're clasping me so tight." Roc's voice was so deep it was a snarl.

She couldn't speak, it felt like he was in her throat. And the way his shaft pulsed, the twitching head bumping into the over-sensitized recesses of her pussy didn't help. Even his warm fingers resting against her swollen clit were too much. Tortured pleasure coursed through her in waves. Meline panted as she tried to rectify being possessed by such a large man. After a moment Roc started pulling out and she clamored to grab his hips, uncertain she was ready for him to move as his cock grazed her slick walls.

"Oh God," she gasped.

Her back arched when Roc resumed teasing her clit as he retreated. The spikes of pleasure had her stomach doing mini crunches. She writhed, conflicted between trying to escape while chasing the mounting ecstasy. Roc's arm tightened around her waist and he stroked back in. His straining cock rubbed against every inch of her channel, kicking off another hailstorm of convulsions.

"That's it," he groaned.

"Oh," she moaned deep, when he hit the spot deep inside that was quickly driving her wild.

Each stroke was faster and deeper than the one before and the ache morphed into the agony of impending orgasm. She was riding the knife's edge, ratcheting higher and higher. Roc sank his teeth into the back of her neck while pinching her clit and she burst at the delicious bite of pain. Something in his bite set her on fire, like she'd been injected with pure unadulterated nirvana. Meline screamed as the pleasure stole through her, shoving her over the cliff she'd been teetering on. Her muscles seized, her fingers and toes flexing.

Roc snarled a deep feral sound and rolled them, pinning her on her stomach. He restrained her hands above her head, twining his fingers with hers as his muscular body pressed her into the mattress. Savagely, he thrust into her at an inhuman pace, forcing his thick cock past her jerking inner muscles. The powerful lunges drove her up the bed. The sound of his hips slapping into her ass and the headboard slamming into the wall weren't enough to drown out her cries or his primal grunts. His heady delicious scent surrounded her, adding to the delirium.

The ecstasy he was wringing out of her body was unbelievable. Her pussy should've given out by now but it continued to seize around his hammering cock. There was no escaping the fierce passion threatening to consume her entirely. Her orgasm raged on and on, burning through her like a wildfire. Roc slammed in, going deeper than before, his balls grinding against her ass. Meline screamed into the pillow as his cock jerked, spraying her insides with a jet of heat that forced her to climax again.

"No more," she whimpered deliriously as she went limp. This time she meant it. He was going to kill her.

Roc grunted an incoherent sound, his body shuddering atop hers. Meline sighed when he rolled them back onto their sides. He kissed her shoulder, and she smiled sleepily then gave into exhaustion.

❧ 8 ❧

ROC

Roc awoke with a yawn as light streamed in through the windows. He smiled, feeling Meline's warm soft body pressed against his, recalling the glorious evening they'd spent together. Making love to her was unlike anything he'd ever experienced. He felt better than ever. The jittery sensation he'd been experiencing and the ache in his jaw was gone. Roc stilled and his smile faded as his gaze landed on her creamy skin pressed against his chest.

Shit! Sometime in the night he'd relaxed, and his skin shifted back to its usual bronze tone.

Attempting not to rustle the sheets, Roc retracted his wings and eased his arm out from beneath Meline.

"Sacrament," he softly cursed, realizing his tail was wrapped around her leg. Gingerly he uncoiled it.

"No more pâté," Meline mumbled, and he froze.

He needed to get out of here before she awoke, but couldn't help pausing to watch the way her face scrunched up in displeasure, her tongue darting out to dispel the imaginary taste in her mouth.

"Don't worry, angel, I've got it," he whispered.

"Roc." She smiled, her eyelids fluttering before her expression went lax again.

Something inside jumped hearing her say his name in her sleep, looking so happy and relaxed. Then his chest clenched. He had no business going soft for a woman he couldn't have. He knew in the back of his mind this was a bad idea and yet he'd pursued Meline anyway.

Just get out of bed, you fucking moron!

Roc eased the rest of the way out, taking a last look at Meline peacefully sleeping before he retreated to the bathroom. He softly closed the door, sighed and got into the shower.

⚜

MELINE

Meline awoke the instant the door clicked open.

"Hello!" She scrambled to cover herself when John walked in, then remembered he couldn't see her.

Meline glanced at the other side of the bed, her brow furrowing when she didn't see Roc, then she heard the shower running.

"Oh, my apologies, madame, I should've knocked," John commented as he carried a tray to the small table near the terrace.

No, no, it's all right, just come right in. This wasn't how she imagined being awoken after the night she had. *Don't go making mountains out of mole hills. This isn't your home, and what do you know about having a butler?* She shook her head at herself.

Her clothes were still in the bathroom, and as intimate as they'd been she didn't feel quite right just barging in on Roc. Meline noticed a dress shirt and a pair of boxers tossed on the nearby chair. Hopefully Roc wouldn't mind if she borrowed them.

Oh.

She paused as she got out of bed, taking stock of the lingering ache between her thighs. Meline blushed as snippets of the evening darted through her mind. Roc was a wild man. It was a wonder she could walk at all. Her hand stilled at the sight of the necktie as she reached for his shirt. The heat tingeing her cheeks spread down her chest. Their encounter was torrid enough, what would it have been like if Roc tied her up with it, like he'd threatened?

As Meline threw on the oversized white shirt, she almost poked her head through the odd slit down the back. His boxers were large enough she had to roll down the waistband to get them to stay up, but eventually she got it.

I guess that'll do. She snorted, looking down at herself and headed to the table.

"Coffee or tea, madame?"

She smirked, seeing he brought two sets of everything. He'd known full well she was in here when he entered the room but still acted surprised.

"Coffee, please. You're just as wily as Roc, aren't you?"

"I'm sure I don't know what you mean, madame. Cream

and sugar?" John asked, his mouth quirking up ever so slightly.

"Uh huh," she replied to his feigned ignorance. "Both, thank you. So, is this the usual routine?"

"Pardon?"

"Do you usually shoo away Roc's conquests after a quick breakfast while he hides in the bathroom?"

"Madame, I…" John nearly spilled the cream.

"Oh, careful." She steadied his hand.

"Thank you. I must apologize for rudely entering uninvited. You are correct, I did know you were here, clearly." He gestured to the spread of coffee, tea and scones. "But it wasn't my intent to frighten you away. I know you will be staying with us for a while."

"Oh yeah, sorry." Meline suddenly felt stupid for her bout of insecurity.

Why did the morning after seem to always bring doubt? Does he like me? Doesn't he? Should we have done this? Are things going to be weird? Will we do it again? *God, I hope so.*

"I know it's not my place to say this, but I have been working for Roc for many years now and this is the first time I've brought breakfast for two."

Meline gaped at the bombshell John dropped. *Really?*

"Well, I must see to some things at the museum and Roc has some errands he needs me to run." He quickly excused himself, leaving her alone with her thoughts.

Don't go making a big deal of things.

She forced the swirling thoughts from her mind, grabbed her coffee and wandered out onto the terrace. It was a brisk morning, way too cold to be out half dressed, and from the looks of it, it might rain. Meline took a big gulp of her hot coffee as she quickly took in the skyline before deciding to head back inside.

"Fuck." She heard Roc's barked curse from the bathroom. It sounded like he hurt himself.

She rushed over, opened the door and peeked inside to make sure he was okay.

"Dammit, that always fucking hurts like a bitch," Roc muttered as he blotted up the blood on his scalp.

Along his hairline, there were two raw welts where the horns had been. She panned down and noticed the two stumps laying on the counter, then saw the biggest pair of bolt cutters she'd ever seen.

"What are you doing?" She stared in confusion at his reflection in the mirror. From the looks of it he'd cut them off, but that didn't make sense. Why would he have to cut fake horns off?

Roc's gaze darted toward her and the large wings on his bare back swiftly retreated into two long slits, disappearing beneath his shoulder blades. No costume was that amazing. Her breath sped up and she dropped her coffee, the mug shattering on the tile, as she took in the unbelievable scene.

"Meline," Roc said, his rugged face contorting.

He tucked his tail into his loose jogging pants and tugged on a baseball cap. It was sufficient to fool anyone who wasn't studying him too closely, but she'd already seen more than enough. Not that she had a clue what the hell was going on.

"I don't understand," she stammered while backing up.

"Please, Meline."

"You...you…" She shook her head, unable to fathom any of this.

"Just let me explain," he insisted as he came toward her.

Oh, God. That's why his costume looked so real, felt so real, moved the way it did. Even the shirt she was wearing with the slit in the back now made sense. Yet none of this made any sense. Meline felt like her mind was fracturing. *I'm not insane.* But that was the only logical solution.

Meline froze as the description of the creature in her great-great-grandfather's journal churned to the surface of her turbulent thoughts.

"You're the thing in Nicolas' journal!"

ROC

Meline stared at him in horror. She called him the thing in Nicolas' journal and a part of him died. He had to hide who he was his whole life because people thought he was a monster. As much as society had progressed, some things hadn't changed.

"Yes, but that wasn't me. It was my father. And we're not things or demons. My sire saved Nicolas from falling off the old church. Believe it or not they were friends, not that you'd know it from the description Nicolas wrote."

The moment the words fell from his lips he knew he'd made a grave error. Meline sucked in a sharp breath, her face turning red as she retreated farther into his bedroom.

"You *have* read his journal! You—you *broke* into my room, kept opening my window," she screeched, making him cringe.

Fuck me!

"That was before I knew you. I only read a few pages and I didn't take the journal. I don't steal from innocents."

"Meaning what, you do steal from people you deem guilty?" She gestured to the painting on the wall in disgust.

"I don't just steal treasure and horde it. I find things and return them to their rightful owner, like Nazi loot," he defensively replied, feeling like utter trash in her eyes. "But clearly that doesn't make amends for anything," Roc snapped, years of anger surfacing.

"Yes, I lied to you. My whole damn life has been a lie. I knew your ancestor Nicolas. For hundreds of years I've lived in the shadows, surviving off the spoils I take from people too rich to know what to do with themselves, but what else do you expect me to do to survive since I'm a monster?

"And yes, I broke into your hotel to take your journal, but I didn't. You want to know why? This is the really sad part," he barked a morose laugh. "I saw you and something called to me. But that's just me lying to myself about shit I'll never have, because I'm not human. I'm not privileged to walk among you, to have a normal life. But I'm not fully Khargal either," he snorted at how delusional he was.

"I must be a fucking moron, looking for that damn family heirloom so my sire can go home, a father who fucking abandoned me once and refuses to wake up. Another fucking lie. Like he's going to wake up and be grateful. He'll just get on that damn ship and abandon me again. Sure, I could go, but there's no way in hell I'm going someplace I've never known, just to wind up another damn outcast."

Meline stared at him in stunned horror, her whole body shaking, her mouth hanging open. Roc felt how tight the skin on his face was and the way his wings vibrated and realized he'd exposed the darkest part of himself in his fit of anger. He sighed and retracted his wings, letting his features relax, though it didn't matter now, he'd already put the final nail in the coffin.

"I have to get out of here," Meline stammered when she found her voice and sprinted for the door.

"No!" He couldn't let Meline leave, not while she was worked up. Not after seeing him like this. And certainly not with the people who posed a threat on the hunt.

"You can't keep me here." Fear made her voice tremble.

As Meline reached for the doorknob, he scented pungent cologne and another recognizable smell.

"No! Meline!" he bellowed as she turned the knob, but couldn't get to her fast enough.

❧

MELINE

No matter how she tried, Meline couldn't catch her breath. She felt dizzy. Her heart was racing, the sound thundering in her ears. Nothing was what she thought it was, not Roc, not even her perception of the world. She no longer knew what was real or who to trust. She just knew she had to get out.

Meline tugged open the bedroom door then stopped dead in her tracks, her eyes widening in fear, seeing the two men waiting on the other side.

"I must insist you stay." The nosy bald guy from the masquerade grabbed her.

Roc growled and lunged.

"I wouldn't do that. Stay over there," the second man, the one who'd been stalking her in town, insisted while waving a gun.

Roc instantly halted, his gaze darting from her to the barrel pointed straight at him.

"Oh God," she screamed. Meline was in turmoil over what she just learned, but she didn't want Roc dead.

"Where is it?" The bald guy tightened his arm around her ribcage, making it hard to breath.

She gripped his arm, trying to get him to loosen up as he herded her into the room.

"We know your family had the gem and you're here to sell it to this smuggler. So where is it?" the stalker demanded, eyeing her maliciously.

Meline gasped and started shaking uncontrollably. She recognized those dark eyes. The stalker was the same man who'd attacked her in her hotel room.

"It's going to be okay, angel." Roc's snarl was anything but comforting.

"Okay? *Okay?!*" she choked. How could he say that when things were just getting worse by the moment?

"You are mistaken about the gem. And it was a mistake breaking into my house, threatening my female," Roc rumbled, his voice filled with rage, the terrible sound echoing off the walls.

His silver eyes seemed to glow, his anger making them burn. As he took measured steps, closing the distance, Meline was sure his face changed, his brow and cheek bones growing sharper.

Sweet Jesus, these fools have no idea who they've pissed off.

"Don't be stupid." Her stalker aimed for Roc, but he just kept coming.

Oh God, Roc, what are you doing?

He was suddenly a blur. The gun fired, and she screamed. Abruptly everything went dark, like when he wrapped her in his wings at the party. Roc's bare chest was pressed against her, his arms snaked around both her and the bald bastard, pulling them off their feet. She clasped his biceps but couldn't get a good grip, his skin had taken on a rough texture and was hard as rock.

"What the..." the asshole at her back yelped as the world started spinning.

"Let her go," Roc snarled over the sound of breaking glass, gunfire, and the muffled shouts of the other assailant.

"Fuck! I knew it. You're one of those creatures," the bald guy declared, rather than letting her go.

"Suit yourself," Roc warned.

Meline felt something coil around her waist and then they were falling. She screamed in terror as the dark cocoon lifted to reveal they were spiraling through the sky. Why wasn't Roc flapping his wings?

"Fuck!" the bastard clinging to her shouted in her ear.

Meline scrambled to lock her arms around Roc's neck. Her terror doubled when he released the bear-hug he had on them.

I don't want to die. The biting wind rushing past them whipped the tears from her eyes before they could hit her cheeks.

"Please, Roc, I'm slipping," she shrieked as the intruder's strangle-hold threatened to rip her away.

But she didn't know if Roc heard or even cared. His

expression was deadly serious, his lips lifted in a snarl as he looked past her at the vile man trying to climb her back. Meline thought Roc was going to grip her arms but she wasn't the one he was reaching for. There was a dreadful pop and the intruder's death grip on her disappeared. He screamed a blood-curdling sound that grew further away by the second. Meline shrieked as she glanced down and saw the man falling. Roc's arms wrapped around her and her stomach was suddenly in her throat as they instantly reversed direction, shooting toward the cloud cover.

"I've got you, angel," he rumbled as he cradled her against his chest.

She was shaking so badly, she was certain he was going to lose his grip on her as she stared at the retreating ground far below. Each time his large warm hands shifted as he rubbed her back, she startled.

"Please, Roc, don't drop me," Meline sobbed hysterically.

"I wouldn't let you fall. I've had you the whole time. My tail's been wrapped around you and now both my arms."

Roc's words were meant to be soothing and the growl in his voice had disappeared, but it was hard finding any comfort in it. Her world had turned upside down. She'd been deceived, learned humans weren't alone, held at gunpoint, watched a man fall to his death and was now flying through the sky. Solace and comfort were a distant memory.

❦ *9* ❦

ROC

Roc hated that he wasn't able to take out the other intruder, but at the moment he was more concerned about Meline. She was still shaking violently when he landed on the veranda of the hotel he often frequented across the Saint Lawrence.

"Dammit," Roc cursed as he vigorously rubbed her ice-cold skin.

He had leapt off the high-rise, fearing if he didn't get Meline out of there she was going to be severely hurt, or worse, killed by a stray bullet. As it was, it took every acrobatic move he could muster to avoid the wildly firing bastard. But in his haste to get her to safety, he forgot she couldn't withstand the elements and nearly froze her to death.

Humans are delicate, idiot. He shook his head as he recalled his sire insisting his mother bundle every inch of herself before they went flying all those years ago.

"I'm so damn sorry. I forgot how cold it gets up there. We're going to get you warm."

112

Meline didn't respond, just kept trembling. Roc used his subsonic tone to unlock the balcony door and swiftly entered the hotel suite. He glanced around the empty room. The place was tidy, bed made, and bar stocked, but of course he paid to keep it ready for whenever he needed it. Roc headed straight for the bathroom, set Meline on the counter and turned on the shower. He glanced back to find her staring at his wings and tail with the same shocked expression that hadn't left her face since she discovered his secret.

Losing your temper and those bastards breaking in didn't make things any better.

If he hadn't been preoccupied, he might have sensed them sooner. He repressed a snarl, recalling the way they threatened her. Meline's terrified screams still echoed in his ears. The way she begged him not to drop her twisted his gut. As if he could do such a thing.

Of course that's what she thinks, she watched you throw a temper tantrum then drop that bald fucker to his death. She thinks you're a monster.

"*Ostie d'câlisse de sacrament,*" he cursed under his breath.

Roc's shoulders dropped, and he sighed as he stared at his freakish reflection in the mirror behind Meline's small trembling form. This was hopeless.

"I wish things were different, but this is who I am. I'm a demon of a man. I live my life in the shadows, lying to everyone and constantly hunting for something that eludes me."

MELINE

With all the unreal things going on and thinking she was going to die, Meline found herself caught up in a similarly surreal moment in time.

She was sitting on her couch, staring at the picture of her parents hanging on the wall. She'd just returned from the morgue where she identified their remains. It was the worst thing she ever had to do. The wreck was so horrific, she wasn't even sure she'd be able to have open caskets at their funeral. So, she stared at their pictures, committing to memory the way they looked, perfect and whole. Then she burst into hysterical laughter, because they weren't perfect, not at all. The last time she'd seen her mom and dad, they were arguing in their kitchen.

"I can't believe you, Alan. We've been married close to thirty years, and in all that time you couldn't bring yourself to mention you didn't like my cherry pies."

"I wasn't about to complain when you were making all those pies just for me," her father replied.

"So you just let me go on thinking you liked them. That's as bad a lying to my face. Am I such a shrew you can't voice your opinions?" her mother snapped.

"Come on now, Celeste. It wasn't a big deal and Meline likes cherry." Her dad nodded toward her.

"Oh no, don't get me involved in this," Meline snorted as she kept her distance.

"And I love your apple, your peach and meringue." Her father snagged her mother around the waist despite Mom's protest. "I love all your pies." He tickled her suggestively.

"Oh God, Dad, gross." Meline fled the kitchen as her mother's angry huff turned into a giggle.

The thing was, her dad found more joy in the love Mom showed when she cooked him sweets. The pies could've been filled with paste and he would've eaten them with a smile on his face. At the end of the day it was the intent that was important, no matter how badly the follow through was botched.

Her attention returned to Roc as he started speaking. His powerful wings were still exposed but they just sort of hung at his back, and the long tail that kept her from falling to her death dragged the floor. Sometime during the struggle Roc had lost his hat and she could easily see the raw welts where he'd cut off his horns.

He mutilated himself to fit in, to be accepted by everyone —by me. The thought brought tears to her eyes.

The mystery behind Roc's life came into focus and the picture was a lonely one. All because of something that in the end was as trivial as cherry pie, when so much more made up the man than his appearance.

"Please don't be frightened of me, angel. I know after what I did it's hard to believe, but I'm not a danger, not to you. I'm so sorry—so sorry for everything." Roc reached out to touch her then stopped and let his hand drop, his expression looking lost and bereft.

She couldn't take any more, he was breaking her heart. Meline lunged forward and kissed his frowning lips. Yes, this new revelation was hard to process but he needed to know she saw him, the man inside, the one who'd come to her rescue more than once.

Roc was still for a moment then started kissing her back.

His arms wrapped around her, his large palms cupping her bottom. She gripped his thick biceps and locked her legs around his waist. Meline gasped when he carried her into the shower, clothes and all.

"Meline…" Roc rasped in between kisses, sounding pained and confused.

"I understand everything now." She traced the spot where one of his horns had been, then caressed his stubbled cheek.

He closed his eyes and leaned into her hand. "I'm not a demon, though the things I've done, I sometimes wonder."

"I'm sorry. I can't imagine the life you've led to keep this secret." Meline brushed her lips against his as she whispered.

"I need you, angel." The emotion in his voice stabbed deep.

Roc was so different from her and they'd known each other for such a short time, but their fate had been intertwined for centuries. It was like she'd been waiting her long dreary life for him to swoop in. Despite being frightened and attacked these last few days, she never felt so alive.

"Then I'm yours." She gripped his broad shoulders tight.

Roc caressed her cheek, his eyes overflowing with adoration. His lips descended and gently met hers in a kiss that was shockingly tender for a man so rough and powerful. Adept fingers traced her ear, as his mouth worshiped hers then kissed the tip of her nose and each eye. He was the one doing all the exploring, like he had last night. She'd been so overwhelmed she missed the opportunity to reciprocate, but here was her chance.

"I think we're wearing too many layers." She wiggled, encouraging him to put her down.

Reluctantly he loosened his grip, letting her slide down

the length of his body. Meline shivered, a frisson of desire coursing up her spine as his erect cock rubbed against her, all the way down. A deep, sonorous groan rumbled in Roc's chest, making her nipples stiffen, poking through her soaked shirt. His heated gaze fixated on her chest and he released the growl, reaching for her shirt. She shook her head and danced out of his reach. Roc frowned, doubt entering his gaze.

"I want to touch *you*," she insisted.

He hesitantly nodded, his expression serious. She now understood why he was reluctant to let anyone touch him and wanted to tie her up the night before.

The way the water sluiced over Roc's bronze wings then down the valleys of his tan chest and washboard abs had her salivating with desire. Her gaze traced the path the water traveled. The solid vee of muscles bracketing his waist were pure temptation, and the trail of hair from his belly button disappearing beneath his jogging pants was just plain cruel. That sight alone had her breath coming out in little pants, then she glanced lower. The wet fabric clinging to his cock revealed the pronounced ridge on his crown, and her pussy cramped with need. Meline nearly stopped right there but she wanted to know Roc, all of him. Her hand grazed his stomach as she circled around his back.

"No, please let me see them," she encouraged when Roc swiftly retracted his wings.

His shoulders rolled forward, exposing barely noticeable slits beneath his shoulder blades. Speechless, she watched while his wings slowly re-emerged, like a bud unfurling. She skimmed one pinion as it unfolded, noting the leathery texture. Blood pumped through his veins, filling the membranes between the bones till his wings extended to their full breadth. It was wholly unbelievable and yet there they were in all their glory, their clawed tips scraping the ceiling. Meline caressed Roc's back, feeling the powerful muscles that worked the appendages. She glanced up to find him staring back at her, uncertainty still filled his intense liquid silver gaze. She had to show Roc she accepted him in every way.

"They're amazing," Meline whispered, and meant it, as she leaned in and kissed one powerful limb.

Roc released a deep sighing breath, his shoulders easing. His wings extended back, flanking her in their immenseness, like a backwards hug.

"You're amazing." She rubbed her cheek against one leathery wing while stroking the other.

The muscles in his back trembled beneath her wandering palm. It broke her heart seeing what such a simple gesture did to the man. He deserved so much more than mere acceptance. He deserved love and affection.

Her hand skimmed along his spine, to where his tail hung over the waistband of his pants. She ran her finger down the length of it and watched his tail flick in response. Meline smiled when the long appendage coiled around her calf.

Hooking her thumb in his waistband, she lowered his pants, revealing the muscular cheeks of his ass. She'd never seen one as nice as his. Meline knelt to worship the sight. The pair of dimples at the top of each cheek was irresistible. She traced them before moving to caress his firm globes. Her hands cupped both magnificent swells, reveling as they flexed. Meline leaned in. For some reason she felt the burning desire to sink her teeth into his tempting flesh. Roc jumped as her teeth closed, even though she barely nipped him. His flesh hardened with her teeth marks still embedded in his flesh. Roc spun around and looked down at her, surprise etched on his face.

"Maybe I was wrong about how sweet you are, angel."

She couldn't help but grin up at him. Her smile faltered as her focus shifted to the thing staring her in the face. It had been too dark last night for her to note more than his daunting size. Meline swallowed hard. That certainly hadn't changed. Roc was so engorged, the veins stood out on his thick shaft. There were several unusual ridges along the frenulum beneath his flared crown that complimented the more familiar crest on top. She must've been too incensed to notice it before. Roc drew in a sharp breath, his cock jerking when she reached out to explore his foreign anatomy. A shocking realization occurred to her.

He's never had his cock sucked!

ROC

He couldn't move a muscle with Meline's delicate fingers wrapped around his arousal, her breath ghosting over his heated flesh. He thought he was going to come out of his skin and inadvertently shelled when the vixen dared to bite his ass, but this, he was ashamed to admit, this had him ready to bolt. It didn't help that she looked up at him with that half-lidded gaze, her pupils dilated with desire. She saw everything he was and still wanted him. He dreamt his whole life of being known like this, touched like this.

Roc choked on his next breath when she engulfed the head

of his cock. The sight of her pink lips stretched around him was the most erotic thing he'd ever seen. His hand shot out to steady himself against the shower wall when her tongue rolled around his sensitive tip. He threw his head back as the pleasure assailed him. In his wildest fantasies he never imagined this would feel this good.

His breath came out in chuffing growls as he tried to hold onto his sanity. Meline started sucking with long strong pulls, then her hand joined in. She stroked him as she pulled back, her tongue teasing his slit, only to swallow him again.

"Fuck," he groaned as his cock bumped into the back of her throat and she swallowed around him.

Roc punched the wall, cracking the tile. He was losing it. He could feel his features shifting. Meline might accept him but the last thing she wanted to see was him all beastly. He needed to hold on to his composure. She wasn't making it easy, though. Her sweet, musky perfume laced with her unique, addictive scent that drove him wild filled his nostrils with each breath.

"Mmm," she moaned around his length.

Roc glanced down to find Meline had one hand shoved down the borrowed pair of boxers, furiously working her clit. That was the last straw. He reached out to pull her off the floor but had to pause to retract his claws before tangling his hand in her hair. He got distracted as she again sucked him in deep, her tongue flicking the ridges on his cock. Instead, he found himself cupping the back of her head, guiding her movements as she blessed and tormented him. His legs quaked as his balls drew up tight.

No. Roc adamantly shook his head. He refused to find his pleasure before she had hers.

MELINE

The way Roc growled and jerked each time she sucked him in deep turned her on. He was unbelievably sexy as she stared up the length of his body. The sight of his flexing washboard abs, impressive pecs, broad shoulders and powerful wings splayed wide fueled her passion, ratcheting it higher. But it was the heat in his silver gaze that gripped her the most. She couldn't resist playing with herself as she pleasured him.

Oh yes, she moaned around his girth as he thrust deeper into her mouth. He was too large for her to swallow, but she tried anyway, gagging in the process.

Shockingly, Roc tasted like salted caramel. With each pull he spurt in her mouth. She laved his cock and sucked harder, seeking more of the unexpected treat, but he refused to come, much to her frustration.

"Sacrament," Roc cursed and pulled her off him.

"I was just getting to the good part." Meline pouted in disappointment, then saw the determined expression on his face.

Oh. His features were sharper, more intense. His canines pronounced, wings vibrating. She was learning his features shifted in response to his mood. And from the look of it, he was feeling some very strong emotions. The feeling was mutual.

"My turn," Roc growled, his voice inhumanly deep, then tossed her over his shoulder and stormed out of the bathroom.

Hanging upside down over his shoulder, she had a perfect

view of his sexy flexing ass and thrashing tail. Impatiently, Roc tore off her borrowed boxers as he stalked toward the bed. His tail rose, hooked her shirt and tugged at it. Clearly, she'd riled him. It just came as a shock that he'd never received a blowjob and she couldn't resist. Now she had a feeling she was going to pay for her boldness.

Suddenly nervous, Meline squirmed. She startled, her eyes widening when he growled in warning as his palm fell against her behind. Roc was not a normal man and she'd awoken something primal inside him. She stilled, unwilling to tempt him further. Her beastly lover huffed, sounding satisfied, and roughly kneaded her stinging cheek.

The room spun when Roc flipped her over and she landed face down on the bed. Meline started panting as he tugged her hips backward, so she knelt at the edge of the mattress. He meant business.

"My kind are gifted with the ability to move things with subsonic sound. It has many uses," Roc rumbled as he knelt behind her and kissed her upturned ass.

He shoved her knees wide, splayed her fleshy cheeks with both hands and crammed his face into her pussy. Roc's tongue speared into her and began vibrating like a sex toy on crack. It felt inhumanly long and thick as it undulated inside of her. She never knew anyone who loved eating pussy like Roc. Meline gasped and instantly spasmed around his tongue, releasing a flood of desire.

"Mmm, yes," Roc growled, adding to her pleasure.

He wedged his hand beneath her hips, found her swollen clit and started rubbing it mercilessly. The slick bead throbbed like it had a heartbeat of its own. She pressed her face into the blankets to muffle her cry of ecstasy.

Meline jumped when his thick finger teased her ass. "Roc?" Nervous, she glanced over her shoulder and discovered him intently focused on her rear.

Anxious breaths burst past her lips and she trembled as his fingertip circled then eased past the ring of muscles. Her mouth gaped in surprise, not realizing how sensitive she was there. The unexpected sensation of him breaching the dark opening had her reeling. Roc speared his vibrating tongue deeper into her pussy as he worked his knuckle past her constricted rosette. He twisted his finger as he pressed further, all while mercilessly stroking her clit. The shocking pleasure made her shake uncontrollably. On the next roll of his tongue and twitch of his fingers, the orgasm rocked through her.

"Oh yeah, my wicked angel likes having her tight ass played with, don't you?" Roc husked as she spasmed, bathing his mouth with her release. "Don't you?" he asked again, punctuating the question by sliding his thick finger the rest of the way into her ass.

"Yes," Meline groaned into the blankets as her orgasm spiked in response to his wicked prodding.

Roc grunted, pleased with himself and her admission, then reared back. But instead of giving her a reprieve his cock replaced his mouth. She was barely able to handle him last night. With his finger burrowed in her ass, she didn't know how he'd possibly fit inside her. Bent over the bed, and him at her back, she was entirely prone, no place to go. She clenched the blankets as nervous desire threatened to overwhelm her.

His unbelievably broad crown stretched her slick lips, forcing her quaking muscles to let him in. Every one of the prominent ridges on his cock sent a frisson of tormented pleasure coursing up her spine as he worked past the strained opening of her vagina. The all-consuming full sensation was pure madness. She didn't know how much she could take of this and yet she didn't want him to stop.

She writhed as he slowly stroked his finger in and out of her ass, lighting up the nerves she never knew existed. And his cock impaled her equally painfully slow.

"Roc," she cried as the insidious climax roiled like a building storm on the horizon.

"Yes, angel," Roc groaned, his free hand gripping her fleshy hip to keep her where he wanted her.

"More," she demanded with a breathy growl.

Meline was desperate to again find release even though her body still vibrated from her first orgasm. She was teetering on the brink of something dark and delicious, but he was teasing her with this slow possession. Meline bucked, shoving against him, clenching her inner muscles around his arousal.

Roc snarled an animalistic sound, pulled his finger from her trembling ass and gripped her hips with both hands. His cock stabbed into her, forcing a cry of pleasure and pain from her throat. His hips rolled, grinding against her ass. Meline tossed her head back and forth, her pussy spasming around the pulsing invader. No sooner had she gotten used to his girth than he pulled free and rammed back home, going balls deep. The powerful thrust was enough to wrench a passionate scream out of her, while the ridges on his cock grazed her sensitive walls and g-spot, adding to the exquisite torture.

The beast of a man was unhinged. He yanked her back on his engorged cock as he pistoned forward. His crown rammed against the far recesses of her convulsing channel with each lunge. She clawed at the blankets, gripped in a pleasure that was sure to break her. Roc dropped forward, his muscular chest pressing against her back, shoving her into the mattress as he continued his erotic assault. His skin felt rough, like he'd shifted further. Meline keened in pleasure and pain when he gripped the back of her neck with his teeth. Liquid nirvana invaded her, radiating from his bite. The exquisite sensation flung her over the edge. Stars burst in her vision and every muscle in her body seized, caught up in the cataclysmic orgasm. Roc snarled and bucked, flooding her with his release.

Once he'd calmed and she stopped panting, Roc eased out of her vagina. He wrapped her in his arms and shifted them onto the bed. Meline bit her lip when he came down on top of her and slid his still erect cock back into her trembling pussy. He caressed her cheeks, his thumb tracing her lips as he slowly stroked into her body.

"You really are mine," he rasped, his voice thick with emotion.

The primal beast had receded. The storm that raged in his silver eyes had calmed. Now there was just the man. A man who desperately needed to be loved.

"Yes." She nodded then wrapped her arm around him and held on tight.

Roc kissed her deep as he slowly made love to her again. No man had ever possessed her as wildly as he did or in this unhurried, poignantly sweet pace. And she'd never loved a man the way she was falling for him.

10

MELINE

As she hung their wet clothes in the shower to dry, Meline noticed the rough patch of skin on her elbow and forearm. She hadn't seen it when she bathed last.

"Well that's attractive." It looked like she'd never seen lotion a day in her life.

She found a complimentary bottle of lotion on the counter and rubbed it into her skin. Meline glanced in the mirror and giggled. Why was it her hair looked its best after a good roll in the hay? She turned, admiring herself with a grin, loving the rosy glow of her cheeks. Meline bit her lip seeing Roc's teeth marks on her neck. He was a biter and surprisingly she liked it.

Meline wandered out of the bathroom to find Roc on the phone. He mentioned he needed to warn John to stay away from the penthouse and check in with the hotel manager. It sounded like he was talking to the latter.

"I'm in my usual room. What's on special today in the

kitchen?" Roc nodded as he listened to the person on the other end. "Yes, that's fine. Send up two of those and whatever wine pairs well. I have a few more requests that I'd like you to put on my account. I need clothes for my girlfriend, size twelve jeans, medium shirt and size eight shoes."

Roc glanced up at her and she nodded to confirm he got that right. Meline pointed to her head.

"Oh, right, and a man's hat, any larger size will do." Roc nodded, appreciating the reminder, as she joined him on the bed. "I also need the envelope I keep in the safe, and a rental car." He paused. "It's a long story, Henry. Thank you, I appreciate everything as always." Roc hung up the hotel phone and leaned back against the headboard.

Meline was impressed he could get whatever they needed at the drop of a hat, but apparently he stopped at the posh riverside resort regularly and they were more than happy to cater to their high end clientele.

"What are you going to wear?" she asked.

"The pants I had on and the shirt you were wearing. I don't really need shoes. Besides, finding clothes in my size is nearly impossible. I have to have everything tailored."

"But they're still wet," she pointed out.

"I have ways of drying them." He shrugged.

"Of course you do." She shook her head. There was no end to the tricks the man had up his sleeve. "So, I'm your girlfriend, huh?" She snuggled against his bare chest.

"Is that a problem?" Roc trailed a finger slowly up her spine.

"No." She grinned as a thrill coursed through her. "But no more lies, Roc. Not about anything. And I better not one day find out you don't like my cherry pie," Meline warned as she played with the bit of hair on his chest.

"Huh?" Roc's head popped off the pillow to stare at her in confusion.

She snorted seeing the way his head cocked like a perplexed puppy.

"My father ate my mother's cherry pies for decades before admitting he didn't like them. But you, sir, have already used up all your chances in that department."

"Oh, I can imagine how well that went over," Roc chuckled with that rumbling laugh that made her insides melt. She loved the way his eyes crinkled, softening his rugged features. But then his expression turned serious and he tipped her chin up to look into her eyes. "I don't want to hide anything anymore."

Meline nodded. She believed that wholeheartedly. "You unloaded a hell of a lot in a short time and I only caught half of it. I think it's best you start at the beginning."

"I know. I'm sorry I lost my shit. I still can't believe you kissed me instead of kicking me in the balls." As he made the comment his tail protectively cupped his crotch, making her wonder if it was intentional or a subconscious response.

"Your nuts are safe for now. Down boy." She patted his tail and package. "How about you start with—shit this sounds crass, but I don't know how else to put it—what are you?"

"Don't apologize. It's a fair question. I'm half Khargal, half human. You'd call us gargoyles."

"You're kidding me, right?" she snorted.

"No." He smirked.

"You're a gargoyle named Roc."

"Yeah. I get the irony. You can blame my mum for that one." He mussed her hair.

"I guess that explains why your skin felt so hard and rough when those thugs were attacking us."

"Yes, that's my *duramna*. It doesn't make me invincible, but bullets don't do as much damage."

"Amazing. Okay, go on."

"Well, my people crashed here on Earth about a thousand years ago and have been waiting for rescue ever since."

"You're aliens!"

"Yes. We're not some magical creature or something shunned from heaven, like myths suggest. We're just stranded."

"Oh," she giggled.

"What's so funny?" Roc's sharp brow furrowed.

"Well, I knew there had to be some logical explanation, but I guess I needed to hear you say it."

"So, you did think I was a demon?" Roc cocked his brow at her.

"I guess there's always this corner of your mind where all the impossible things live, like the boogey man from your childhood. And when you're scared or presented with something you don't understand, the improbable suddenly seem more possible. But I kept telling myself there had to be a reasonable explanation."

"And you think aliens are a reasonable explanation?" His eyes widened in surprise.

"Yes. Granted, coming to terms with aliens here on Earth isn't easy. But that's mainly because I never expected to meet one, not because I don't believe they're possible. I mean the universe is beyond huge. The thought of other life not existing out there would be kind of sad, lonely on a cosmic level. Aliens are far easier to rectify than the idea that there's this whole realm of myth like you said. That leap is just too big for me to handle."

"Good." Roc squeezed her tight, looking relieved. "I was really worried I sent you off the deep end earlier."

"You kinda did. This is a lot, Roc, but I believe there's more to us than the fleshy bits on the outside."

"I thought you liked some of my fleshy bits?" Roc grinned evilly as he thrust his hips, grinding his semi-hard cock against her.

"Oh, I do. In fact, I find the whole package wickedly sexy." She grinned back.

Roc rumbled seductively. His hand strayed to her ass and suggestively squeezed her cheek.

"Behave. Talk," she giggled and slapped his chest.

"Fine," Roc huffed. "So, my sire, Petronus, was on the ship that crashed about a millennia ago. After several centuries passed with no rescue, they lost hope and went their separate ways. My sire was still in France, when one day a group of drunken randy noblemen strayed into the remote woods where he lived. It was the 1600s, and in those days you had to be a member of the privileged class to hunt. Well, those overentitled fools decided to hunt some very special prey, a lowly peasant girl, my mother. They didn't care that she was barely of age or had never known a man. And there was nothing she nor any of the other farmers could do about it," Roc sneered.

She was starting to see why Roc had such a low opinion of the rich, even though technically he was wealthy.

"Please tell me your dad stopped them before anything awful happened to her." Meline held her breath.

"I wish I could." Roc turned his face away, so she couldn't see the sadness and anger that transformed his features. "They made sure she was only too happy to be rescued, even by a demon. Theresa couldn't go back home, not after what my sire did to those men, so he had to flee the area with his new companion and, well, in 1632 I came along."

"I bet your dad was lonely before he met your mom. Having a family must have made him happy." She smiled at Roc but her smile faltered when Roc didn't look happy.

"We're not supposed to get involved in your society, but that's a little hard when we have to live among you," he continued grimly. "My sire broke the rules getting involved and pairing with my mom. And for some reason Khargals have this thing about honor, so, no matter how good the reason was, Petronus always carried this guilt over what he'd done. And it probably didn't help that he had a mate on his home world that he was being unfaithful to."

Hearing the frustration and anger lacing his voice, Meline had a feeling Roc's father took his guilt out on his family. She couldn't imagine growing up living under a shadow like that.

"You don't have to talk about this if you don't want to."

"No, it's okay. We lived in Provence, France in the woods, and when I was about ten, I foolishly decided to practice flying on my own." Roc paused, his brows furrowing. "The villagers saw me, and a band of men followed me home. They trapped me and my mother in our cabin and set it on fire. Petronus arrived just in time but he was forced to…"

Roc's skin hardened beneath her and the way his silver

eyes darkened, she could tell he was reliving a very bad moment.

"I think I understand." Meline rubbed his chest, feeling absolutely horrible. It wasn't her intent to open old wounds.

"We were forced to leave our home. Petronus decided to come to the New World since there were less people here and I had to learn to stretch my wings."

The way Roc growled, she had a feeling he was made to feel guilty about that, too. She kissed him, letting him know she was there and sympathized.

"The first night in Quebec, my sire saved your ancestor from falling off the old church. Although Nicolas probably wouldn't have fallen if Petronus hadn't surprised him."

"Did your dad just pop out and go boo?"

"No." Roc smiled, and she was glad to lighten the mood. "Anyway, it was a big risk. I'm actually surprised my sire bothered. Thankfully Nicolas didn't betray our trust and we considered him a friend. But from what little I read in his journal, now I'm not so sure."

She'd read what Nicolas wrote and at no point did her ancestor mention being saved or claim to be friends with Roc's dad. Instead he described being at the mercy of the devil. Now it was her turn to feel guilty because obviously that wasn't true.

"I'm sorry my family did that. You must feel betrayed."

"It's disappointing. Nicolas used to take me hunting." Roc frowned. The sad far-off look in his eyes was heartbreaking. The way he spoke it sounded like Roc had considered Nicolas a part of his family.

"Wow. It's just sinking in how old you are. You know, you look pretty good for being a geezer," she teased, hating how morose the conversation was. He'd had too much pain in his life.

"Thanks. And I've still got the moves, too." Roc gave her a cocky grin as he rolled, pinning her beneath him. He rocked his hips, grinding his cock against her stomach.

"Well, old man, this explains you calling me doll when we first met. You're the ginchiest daddy-o," she giggled as she shoved at his chest.

"Very funny. I do have a little trouble keeping up with slang." He relented and rolled off her.

"I'm just teasing you. You're not doing that bad," she commented, recalling how sexy he looked in his suit when they first met, and he called her that.

James Bond eat your heart out. She bit her lip.

"What?" Roc asked, seeing the expression on her face.

"Nothing." Meline traced a circle around his nipple. "I've felt your skin harden a bit, but can you actually become stone?"

Roc suddenly froze, the texture of his skin turning course like sand and unforgivingly hard. She reared back, her mouth dropping open as she looked him up and down. He had turned entirely to stone, like the statue David. His usually black hair, bright gray eyes and pink lips were the same beige tone as the rest of him. But the eeriest part was how cold he was.

"Okay, that answers my question. Nice demonstration."

Meline waited but Roc didn't respond.

"Hey. You can stop now." She patted his stiff, rough arm, but he didn't change back.

He was starting to unnerve her. Meline stuck her finger beneath his nose to feel if he was breathing.

"Boo!" Roc sprung alive.

"Dammit, Roc!" she screeched as she grabbed a pillow and swatted him over the head.

"I'm sorry," he snorted, way too pleased with himself.

"Mmm hmm," she smirked. He thought he was so funny spooking her like she'd accused his father doing to her ancestor.

Her frown broadened as she was again reminded of Nicolas.

"Nicolas never mentioned you, your mom or the family heirloom. Maybe that's not even his journal." She hoped. The idea someone in her family wronged Roc was hard to swallow.

"It's possible, but the description of Petronus was spot on. No one else but Nicolas would've been able to give that kind of detail."

"So then the part about imprisoning the demon in stone could be true, too." Meline frowned, recalling Nicolas relating how he vanquished Petronus.

"Yes." He nodded. "Nicolas actually wrote that?"

"He did. Are you seriously telling me my ancestor pretended to befriend your family then imprisoned your dad? Where were you and your mother?"

"My mum died trying to give me a sibling."

"Oh God, I'm sorry. I lost my parents a year ago in a car wreck. I know how much it hurts." She tried not to tear up.

"Both at the same time? I can't imagine how hard that must've been." Roc cupped the back of her head and kissed her forehead, genuine compassion reflecting in his eyes. His fingers aimlessly stroked the bite mark on her neck as his sympathetic frown shifted to a wistful smile. "My mum was the most beautiful person I had ever known, patient and kind.

How she put up with my sire is a wonder. She's the reason I gave humans a chance. Like you, I was already of age when she passed, so I should feel lucky, but still it was hard. And we couldn't even attend her funeral."

Meline bit her lip to keep from apologizing again and interrupting him. She couldn't fathom not going to her parents' funeral. As different as they were, some things were common no matter what your heritage is, like the loss of a loved one.

"After she was laid to rest, I couldn't put up with my sire alone, we just kept butting horns. So, I decided to see the world and try to find others of my kind. Time passed so quickly that when I finally returned, my sire was nowhere to be found. Nicolas' grandson was a senile old man and all I could get from him was the rumor Petronus was entombed in the foundations of the governor's mansion. I didn't expect Petronus to retreat into the *duramna*, but I wasn't really shocked either, since he always acted like living on Earth was a chore. I assumed he passed the medallion onto your family since they had other trivial things he'd left behind."

"Wait, are you saying your dad was willingly buried alive?" Her eyes widened in horror.

"Yes. I know that's odd to wrap your head around but Petronus isn't dead. I guess the best description is that he's hibernating." Roc paused, his brow furrowing. "Shit, I hope the surly bastard isn't dead. Maybe he is. Never once has he stirred in all the visits I've made to that damn mansion. For the longest time I gave up. I just assumed he was being stubborn, but maybe…" He stopped and frowned.

I hope his dad's not dead. She kissed Roc's chest.

From the sound of it, Roc's relationship with his father

wasn't stellar, but it was clear he'd been very hurt to discover his father went into hibernation when he returned home. It was a hard concept for her to fathom, not so much the gargoyle being buried alive part, but because neither of her parents would do that to her. No loving parent would. The fact Petronus hadn't woken up after all this time didn't bode well. But if he wanted to believe his father still lived, she wouldn't dash those hopes. Roc had already suffered enough. If she had any say in it, those days were over.

ROC

Roc shook off his morose thoughts. He was making Meline sad and that was the last thing he wanted, since being here with her was anything but sad. He was still floored by her reaction when she finally had a chance to calm down. He thought he'd lost her for sure, then Meline did the last thing he expected. The way she showered him with affection filled a void he never realized was so vast till she showed up in his life.

He hated they were having this discussion and were faced with this bull shit. All he wanted to do was make love to Meline till they both passed out, then wake up and do it again. Whenever he wasn't kissing her, he salivated, and his canines itched, desperate to taste her some more. She was an addiction he'd never get enough of, and now that she knew *who* he was the need had only deepened.

Roc hugged Meline close and sighed as he forged ahead. "My sire aside, we still must find the sigil."

"Why do I have a feeling you're not just being sentimental about the family heirloom?"

"Because you're as smart as you are gorgeous." He kissed her forehead. "From what little I gleaned from Petronus, our people were exploring for resources to aid them in a war back home. When they passed through the wormhole into this system, there was a bit of trouble and they crashed. To add insult to injury, their distress beacon malfunctioned."

"So, your people didn't know where to rescue you from."

"Exactly. But according to my friend Zaek, this beacon has gone live after all these years, which means the cavalry is coming to pick up its soldiers."

"Well that's good news." Meline smiled, but it didn't quite reach her eyes.

If he had doubts before about going to Duras, Meline's worried expression cemented his resolve to stay. There was no way he'd leave now.

"I see what you're thinking, angel." He grabbed her hand and kissed her knuckles, reveling in her sweet scent. "I have no intention of going to Duras. I was born here. This is my home."

"Oh." She smiled sheepishly at him.

Lar, I love that smile. How did I get so lucky? He smiled back at her.

"But you're right, it's good news for many like my sire. Except there's a catch. The only way the mothership can locate him is if he has that family heirloom. The sigil is a bit like the communicator insignias on *Star Trek*."

"Oh, well shit."

He hesitated to tell her the rest. She'd been so brave, he didn't want to frighten her further.

No, I promised there'd be no more secrets.

"Unfortunately, it gets worse. Apparently bad things happen if we don't find all the sigils."

"What do you mean by bad things?" she asked slowly.

"They self-destruct." He made an explosive gesture with his hands.

"Oh God. Well of course we have to find it then." She suddenly looked frantic, her fingers fluttering over his chest.

"Yes, I know. I don't mean to make excuses for myself, but that's why I followed you to begin with."

"And now those nut jobs are looking for it, too." Meline gripped his arm tight. "Do you think they know it's more than a fancy medallion?"

"Probably, and I just confirmed they were on the right path," he growled in frustration.

The bastards might have arrived at his penthouse thinking he was merely a smuggler or art dealer Meline sought out to sell the sigil to, but his dramatic getaway exposed who he really was. The assholes threatened her, what else was he supposed to do?

"So, where do we look? Like I told you, Nicolas didn't write about a medallion or jewel." She bit her lip, looking worried.

He regretted she was involved in this mess.

"I'm starting to think Nicolas might have taken the secret to his grave," he huffed, his tail slapping the bed in agitation.

Meline bolted upright. "That's it." She excitedly smacked his chest.

"Ow, hey." He reflexively hardened his skin. "For a little thing you're awfully strong."

He wasn't exaggerating, she was surprisingly strong,

although he kinda liked the way she rough-housed with him. Unfortunately, now wasn't the time for play.

"Oh, I'm sorry." Meline gently massaged the spot she slapped, and his skin returned to its fleshy texture. "You gave me an idea. Nicolas and several of his direct decedents are buried in Three Rivers. People often bury sentimental things with the dead, maybe the sigil is there."

"That's as good a place to look as any." He tugged her hand and she toppled onto his chest. "I knew following this sweet little tail was a good idea," he growled seductively, grabbing both her butt cheeks.

"Mmmhhhmmm." Meline kissed him.

He growled as his tongue delved into her mouth. Meline tasted amazing. Kissing had never been so satisfying. She both caused and eased his restless hunger.

Things were just getting good when there was a knock on the door.

"I'm going to tell them to take a hike," Roc groused as he pulled away.

"Mmm, something meaty and creamy," Meline moaned and he heard her stomach growl.

"You smelled that from here?" His eyes widened in surprise. Few humans had that good a sense of smell, although from the sound of it she was very hungry. "I hope you like *tourtière*. It's a meat and potato dish. They make a good one here."

"Well it certainly smells good." She climbed off his chest, taking the sheet with her, leaving him entirely exposed.

Roc wasn't embarrassed by his nudity, then he glanced down at his cock. *But this probably isn't the tip the porter is looking for.*

"I'm starting to think you aren't as angelic as you look." He hustled out of view of the door.

"I tried to tell you," Meline giggled as she wrapped herself in the sheet and headed for the door.

"Don't tempt me to test that theory. If you behave yourself, we might get to Three Rivers by nightfall."

Meline grinned over her shoulder and wagged her brows before opening the door. Roc shook his head incredulously. She'd learned she was sleeping with an alien and there was dangerous technology that had to be found before some crazy secret society used it to do god knows what, and yet she was teasing him, and he was deliriously happy for once in his life.

Life is crazy!

11

MELINE

"There, I think that's the church." Meline pointed as she caught a glimpse of the old church in the dark.

"That's what the phone says." Roc drove to the back of the lot.

The headlights lit up the gravestones, casting long, ominous shadows over the cemetery.

"Roc, exactly how do you expect to find this thing?" she asked, suddenly feeling nervous.

"We're going to have to dig."

"I had a feeling you were going to say that," she groaned.

I just had to have the bright idea Nicolas took the medallion to his grave.

"It'll be okay. I'll do all the digging." He shut off the SUV and everything went dark.

Him doing all the work really didn't make this lunacy any better. She gave him a sideways glance.

"Okay, if it helps, when we get done, we'll go straight to

my place in Montreal. It's only an hour from here." He pulled up the satellite image on his phone.

"Is that a freaking castle?!"

"No, my castle is in Scotland." He snickered, but she had a feeling he wasn't joking about having a castle.

"Of course it is." Meline rolled her eyes at him.

"You can wash all the dirt off in the hot tub and you'll have your pick of any bottle of wine from the cellar. I'll wait on you hand and foot," he coaxed.

The man drove a hard bargain. She begrudgingly got out of the SUV and trudged after Roc. A car passed on the road and she ducked.

"We're going to get arrested! I can already see the mugshot," she hissed.

"No one will see a thing, it's too dark. And if anyone does come nosing around, I'll get us out of here."

"Fine, but I want two bottles of wine," she huffed and continued walking.

"Deal," Roc chuckled.

If this weren't a dire situation, she wouldn't be caught dead in this old ass cemetery at night. Meline nearly jumped out of her skin every time the wind rustled through the trees, or a dog barked in the distance.

Don't be a chicken shit. It's not like the bodies are going to spring to life and claw their way out of the earth. She shook off the image of a horde of zombies coming after them. It was such a foolish notion. Meline paused. This morning she thought gargoyles weren't real, so maybe zombies... *Don't be stupid,* she shook her head.

Meline glanced at Roc's larger than life silhouette. He didn't look the least bit ruffled. Tomb raiding was probably old hat for him. Roc was like a mix of Indiana Jones and Batman, except his wings were real. He just forged ahead, doing what had to be done to keep everyone safe from the power-hungry lunatics hell bent on gaining the fancy communicator. She smiled. Having him near was a big comfort. It was silly to worry with her very own superhero by her side.

"Do you need the mobile's flashlight to see the names?" he asked.

"No, it'll stand out like a beacon." There weren't any street lights surrounding the old church and cemetery, but luckily there was enough moonlight to see the headstones.

"Let's start down there. It looks like the oldest section." Roc pointed.

"I wanted to have an exciting vacation and dig up my family history, but this isn't quite what I had in mind," she mumbled under her breath as they traversed the rows.

Roc chuckled, but wisely didn't comment. They were on their third row in the older section of the graveyard when she recognized a name.

"I found Nicolas' grandson."

"And over here is Nicolas." Roc nodded to the next stone over.

"Which one do we start with?" She looked at the various plots. There were four generations concentrated right here, and more throughout the cemetery if she remembered correctly.

"If my sire were here, he'd know. Supposedly the pure-breds are connected to the sigils somehow. But he's not, so, I guess we start with good old Nic." He shrugged.

Her eyes widened when sharp claws extended from Roc's

fingers. He knelt and started scraping the grass away from Nicolas' grave.

"Neat trick, Wolverine. I'm glad I didn't notice those things when I let you play with my lady bits."

Roc paused as he choked on a laugh.

"As handy as you are, no pun intended, I think I saw a shed at the back of the church. I'm going to see if I can find a shovel."

"I don't mind digging." He scooped up a handful of dirt and tossed it aside.

"Yeah, but I want to get out of here sooner rather than later, I got a hot tub and two bottles of wine calling my name. And believe me, it's going to take every drop to forget this."

"And you shall have my best." Roc gave her a deep bow.

Meline wandered back up to the church. She glanced back down the hill to see Roc digging away like an overgrown groundhog and shook her head.

I'm officially a grave robber. Jen's going to either kick my ass or high five me over this one, she mused, but knew full well she couldn't tell her friend half of what happened on her vacation. *She'll have me locked up in the loony bin if I do.*

Her thoughts were still circling around what she was going to tell Jennifer when she reached the shed. Thankfully it was unlocked, and she walked right in. They probably didn't bother securing the old shed, since anyone who wanted in could just yank the door off its hinges if they were desperate. Meline fished around in the dark till she felt the long handle of a garden implement, unfortunately it was a rake. The rickety door creaked, and she glanced back.

"Roc, if you pop out and scare me, I *will* kick you in the

nuts." It would be just like the man to sneak up and go 'boo' again.

The wind blew, making the door creak again. She laughed at herself and continued the search.

ROC

The cell rang, halting his digging. Roc brushed the dirt off his hands and glanced at the screen before answering.

"Little John, I'm glad you called. Did you get my message?"

"Oh, he got the message all right. And I've got a message for you, you fucking abomination. You killed my brother, so I'm going take everything you've ever loved."

Roc instantly recognized the voice, it was the other bastard from his penthouse, the one who'd stalked then mugged Meline in her hotel room.

If this asshole has his phone then John didn't make it out of the penthouse to run errands after all.

"Enough, Cohosh. You promised you were going to contain your emotions." Another more civilized voice interrupted the bastard's rant. "Roc, I must apologize for my associate."

"Clearly you know my name. So, who are you?" he demanded.

"You may call me Nightshade." Obviously an alias. "And I believe we have aligned interests."

Doubtful.

"Sir, don't…" John hollered in the background.

"Shut up!" the piece of shit stalker, who apparently went by Cohosh, yelled, cutting John off.

Roc heard the distinct sound of the bastard striking something and John's responding groan. He snarled viciously, a red haze invading his vision.

"I said enough!" Nightshade hollered to the thug. "All this distasteful business could've been avoided, Roc, if you would've taken a moment to hear us out in Quebec. We were merely interested in acquiring the relic and were willing to make a very fair offer."

"You call breaking into my home and holding us at gunpoint a discussion?" Roc attempted to ask as calmly as possible.

"Ah yes, well, my associates were a bit eager."

"I gather you want the combination to my safe in exchange for my butler, since I'm guessing you didn't find whatever it is you want in my flat."

"Ah monsieur, your safe posed little obstacle," Nightshade laughed but it wasn't sincere. "No, I believe given your true nature, you know exactly what we are looking for and that we didn't find it in your safe."

He didn't reply. Acknowledging the existence of the sigil wasn't a good idea. Neither would admitting he didn't have it. They'd just kill John and be done with it.

"Regrettably, not finding the relic, the unfortunate demise of Cohosh's brother, and given your formidable capabilities, my associates feel like you've forced their hand. Despite my efforts to reason with them, they have made some hasty decisions." This time the over ingratiating bastard did sound genuine.

Roc didn't like the sound of that, not at all. "If you're threatening me, get to the point."

"I fear it is too late to undo what's in motion, but if you agree to bring the relic to us, I think I can persuade them to spare your friend here," Nightshade replied.

"Sir, it's a…" John called out but was struck again to shut him up.

"You tell your associates that if they touch another hair on John's head, I'll rip out their entrails and shove them down their throats," he snarled, at the end of his patience.

"I'll give you a day to think on it and text you an address." Nightshade hung up without saying more.

Roc repressed the urge to crush the phone. John didn't know all his secrets, but he was his oldest friend, besides Zaek. His gut churned with guilt and rage.

I never should've involved him. I knew the risk. He snarled, repressing the urge to shift and take out his wrath on the ancient headstones. *There's still time. Just calm down and think.*

The sound of tires spinning on gravel caught his attention and Roc glanced toward the main road in time to see a van take off.

I fear it is too late to undo what's in motion, Nightshade's words echoed in his head.

"Meline!" Roc roared as he looked frantically toward the shed. This had all been a distraction.

His wings burst from his back and he launched into the air. The van disappeared. They didn't have their headlights on and trees obscured the road, but he could still hear the engine as they sped off. Roc barreled over the church rooftop, fear and rage fueling him. These fuckers thought they'd seen his dark side, but they were wrong. They were going to pay for threatening Meline. But if there was a single scratch on his female, the assholes would learn the meaning of true agony as he peeled their flesh one shred at a time.

The wind shifted, and he caught scent of something that instantly brought him to a halt midair. He looked back at the church in horror.

"No!" he bellowed as he dove for the entrance. "Meline!" He threw himself against the old double doors, splintering the wood.

☙❧

MELINE

Meline coughed as she came around. She was lying on tree roots and they dug painfully into her back. But her head hurt the worst. It throbbed, nearly bringing tears to her eyes. She didn't remember hitting her head. Meline reached up to feel the sore spot and her hand slammed into something plush above her. She opened her eyes in confusion, but it was too dark to see.

"Where am I?" She certainly wasn't in the shed. "Roc?" When she called out, her voice echoed strangely.

Another cough threatened to choke her. Wherever she was, the scent of smoke was getting stronger by the moment. It was starting to burn her eyes and she was beginning to feel warm, no, hot.

"Oh God. *Oh God.*"

Panic took hold as she frantically explored the confined space, desperate to find a way out. Her hand froze feeling the long knobby object stabbing into her thigh. It wasn't a root at all. Meline screamed in horror, suddenly realizing where she was.

"A coffin. I'm in a coffin." And she wasn't alone.

Her breath burst out in rapid pants as she started to hyperventilate, her heartbeat thundering in her chest. She had to get out of the small box and away from the dead body that shared it. Meline pounded and clawed at the lid, her nails shredding the fabric lining the casket.

"Roc!" she choked on the scream and punched the lid harder. "Roc!"

Tears rushed down her cheeks as more smoke poured through the thin gap around the lid. She held her breath to keep from sucking in the noxious smoke that seared her lungs with each labored breath, but could only hold it for so long.

Please don't let me die like this, she prayed.

Her head swam. She blinked, trying to chase away the stars floating before her eyes. One side of her cramped prison was getting so hot, she didn't know if she'd burn alive or succumb to smoke inhalation first. Her hands dropped from the lid, her knuckles bloody and raw from the futile struggle. It took all her energy to roll onto her side and shove the corpse to the hotter half of the casket.

Roc flashed through her mind and more tears streamed down her cheeks. She hadn't let herself think about what the future held with him, but in the back of her mind she hoped there would be something. This wasn't how things were supposed to go. She certainly wasn't supposed to die over some stupid alien communicator she didn't even have.

Meline's eyelids slid shut. She snapped them open, but they were so heavy they drifted closed again. The loud crackle and a gust of scorching air forced her awake. A bright, flickering ruby and flashes of gold danced before her eyes. Groggily she wondered if she was hallucinating the foreign medallion or the raging fire as something tickled the back of her mind. A dark silhouette of a man swallowed up the image, his wings blocking her view of the mesmerizing sight.

"Meline!" the vision called to her, sounding desperate.

A pair of hands reached for her. Meline startled as they wrapped around her.

"Meline!" Roc roared.

She blinked and focused on him. He was real.

"Roc!" she choked on the sob as he picked her up.

All around him the crypt was ablaze, fire consuming the other caskets and licking up the walls of the old church basement. She screamed as a ceiling beam came crashing down.

"Hang on." His stony wings enveloped her, sheltering her from the nightmare.

She felt Roc battle his way through the fiery tomb, using his body like a battering ram to escape the collapsing structure. It was unbelievably hot inside her cocoon, but his rocky wings kept the inferno from reaching her. She couldn't imagine how Roc could stand it. He just kept moving forward, leaping over obstacles in their path as he held her tight. A gust of fresh air reached her as Roc finally staggered out of the church. His wings lowered, and she pulled in a deep breath. She glanced over his shoulder in time to see the entire sanctuary succumb to the flames. Her mouth dropped open in shock and disbelief.

"Thank you," she wept as she clung to his neck.

Her skin stung in the frigid nighttime air, but amazingly that was the worst of it. She couldn't fathom how it was possible. Her clothes were singed and burnt in places, yet her skin was only pink, no blisters. Roc had found her just in time.

Roc stumbled, nearly dropping her in the gravel lot. His steps slowed, and he faltered again.

"I think I can walk." She attempted to pull her shit together.

Roc's arms were rigid, and she had to work to get out of his grasp. There was something seriously wrong.

"Roc, are you okay?"

He didn't reply, and she started to panic again.

Of course he's not okay. He just fought through a blazing inferno.

The man was inhuman but not invincible. He was hurt. He had to be. His pants and shirt had been reduced to scraps of ash clinging to his naked skin.

"Let's get to the car." Meline gingerly put an arm around his waist.

Roc's steps were sluggish as she helped him toward the SUV. She noticed the cell phone laying on the ground nearby and paused. He nearly toppled over when she tried to grab it.

"Shit!" She quickly grabbed hold of him again.

Meline was grateful they'd left the car unlocked as she yanked open the passenger door. She physically turned Roc around and gently urged him in.

"Watch your head." She cringed as Roc collapsed into the seat.

Lifting his feet into the car was a struggle but she finally got him in, then shut the door and ran back to grab the phone. A dog howled in the distance, and she jumped out of her skin. Meline warily looked around the lot as she rubbed the knot on the back of her head. She hadn't wound up in that coffin on her own. Meline sprinted back to the car, got in, locked the doors, and started it up.

"Hang on, Roc." She patted his arm. "Oh God!" His skin was rough and harder than she'd ever felt it.

Meline flipped on the overhead light. Her hand flew to her mouth as she stared at him in horror. She knew Roc had the ability to turn to stone, but this time it was different—he was different. His tan skin was mottled red and the darker areas were riddled with cracks that appeared to be spreading. That couldn't be normal.

"Roc, I don't know what to do to help you," she cried in panic. It's not like she could take him to a hospital.

Just get the fuck out of here. Whoever was behind this was undoubtedly watching. She would have to figure out what to do on the road.

Meline peeled out of the parking lot and headed toward the highway, going west. She gripped the steering wheel just to keep her hands from trembling. Her gaze kept darting from Roc's motionless body to the rearview mirror. No matter how many times she looked, he hadn't changed, and she wasn't some super spy so she couldn't tell if they were being followed or not.

"You're going to wreck if you don't watch the road." She dashed away the tears streaming down her cheeks. At the very least her erratic driving would get her pulled over and then she'd have a lot of explaining to do.

It wasn't until they passed a road sign that Meline realized she was just aimlessly driving with no clue where she was going. There was no way she could pull over at a rest-stop or get a hotel with Roc sitting in the passenger seat like a statue. A thought occurred to her. They were a hundred kilometers from Montreal. She grabbed the cell phone and pulled up the map. It still showed Roc's house just outside the city. She hit the button, calculating the route.

"We're going to your house," Meline assured him, but wasn't even sure Roc could hear her. A horrid thought occurred to her. She reached over and felt the side of his neck. "Please don't be dead," she sobbed, feeling only cold stone. Her trembling hand frantically explored his chest, but he was just as lifeless there, no hint of a heartbeat.

Holding it together was impossible and the tears kept coming as she drove. She didn't know what happened to a man like Roc when he died. There was so much she didn't know about him or his people. She just knew that something was terribly wrong, and she couldn't do a damn thing about it except drive and cry.

Eventually she reached the end of the little pink line on the GPS. Numbly she pulled up to the driveway gate of Roc's palatial home. Meline rolled down the window and stared at the keypad.

"Please work." She typed in the number Roc had used on the phone, his birthday. "One, six, three, two."

Her breath burst out in relief when the gate opened with a creak. Meline followed the long driveway to the garage and again used the code to get in. She stopped and turned the SUV off.

"We're here."

Her shoulders slumped as she looked at him. His unseeing eyes stared straight ahead, frozen in the same pose he'd been in for the last hour. It didn't matter to him that they'd arrived. But at least here she felt safe from prying eyes.

Her lip quivered as she traced the sandy surface of his

cheek, following one of the many deep spidering cracks that extended down his neck. It looked like a burn that had split open. She sobbed as she examined him all over, similar gruesome wounds covered his entire body. This wouldn't have happened if he hadn't come to her rescue, yet again.

"You shouldn't have." She didn't want to burn to death in that tomb, but seeing Roc like this was killing her. The hole it was ripping in her heart made her want to double over. "Roc," she sobbed as she leaned in and gently rested her head against his hard shoulder.

Her life had been unexciting before Roc. She'd been relegated to a cubicle farm from nine to five and came home to an empty little condo day in and day out. Then he showed up in a dreary bookstore and her world lit up like a fabulous dream.

"You can't be dead. You just can't be. I've fallen in love with you." She closed her eyes and willed the dream to continue.

12

MELINE

Meline roused to find herself uncomfortably draped over the SUV's center console, her head pillowed on Roc's arm. She rubbed the dried salty tears from the corners of her eyes and noticed the light coming through the garage windows. She'd been asleep for quite a while, it was morning already.

The moment she glanced at Roc she knew she shouldn't have as tears welled up in her eyes again. Nothing had changed, he was still rock hard. She'd hoped there'd be some sort of difference when she awoke. In the light of day she couldn't tell if the red patches and painful deep cracks that mottled his stony flesh were any better or worse. His normally lively silver eyes remained fixed straight ahead. She caressed his rough, cold cheek.

"I don't know what to do." Meline shook her head morosely. That hadn't changed either.

There had to be something that could help Roc. She couldn't just sit here feeling sorry for herself while some clandestine group of nutjobs hunted them down. The assholes found them last night at the cemetery, so it was probably just a matter of time before they tracked them down again. Her eyes widened when she noticed Roc's phone. She grabbed it and quickly yanked out the battery, unsure if that was what led the bad guys to them in the first place.

It was obvious the bastards had decided who was really important between the two of them when they tried to kill her.

Of course you're expendable. They think you already handed the medallion over to Roc and you're just a plain old human. But Roc was special. And now that they knew what he was, they also knew he wasn't easy prey.

Meline shivered at the thought of what almost happened. Roc called her angel, but he was her savior. He arrived in the nick of time, but it was still a miracle she'd escaped unscathed.

How is that even possible when Roc is like this? She frowned in confusion.

He'd sheltered her in his wings, taking the brunt of the inferno, but it had still taken a bit for him to find her. The coffin had grown so hot and the smoke was choking, yet as she looked at her hands and arms there wasn't a single burn, although her clothes were a wreck. Her knuckles weren't even bruised where she punched the lid. At the very least she expected a lingering cough. But there was nothing, almost like it never happened.

But it did. Tears welled up in her eyes as she looked at Roc. *No, no, this is counterproductive.* She scrubbed away the tears and straightened her shoulders, determined to do something—anything.

"I got lucky you came when you did. Now it's my turn to

help you. I'm going to look around to see if you've got anything in this house that can give me answers." She kissed him then pulled herself away.

Meline cast Roc a parting glance as she left the garage. She entered a hallway and opened the first doorway she came to, to find a utility room. The next door revealed a bathroom.

"Oh, thank you." She hadn't realized how badly she had to go until she saw the toilet.

Meline did her business then washed her hands.

"Oh Jesus," she blurted as she caught sight of her reflection. Her face was covered in soot, and her hair was a wreck. "Well at least it wasn't all burnt off." She splashed some water on her face then continued on.

The short hall turned a corner and ended in a kitchen that would be the envy of any chef. She smiled wistfully as she looked through the window at the lavishly stocked wine cellar. Roc promised her any bottle she desired. Funny enough, though she liked good wine, she didn't have the first clue how to pick it. He would've had to choose for her.

Her stomach grumbled hungrily but she was on a mission. She wandered through the connected family room into a formal living room that spilled into an immense foyer. She spun in a circle, taking in the statues, paintings and antiques. They were magnificent, but she expected nothing less from Roc.

I don't even know where to begin.

Meline glanced at the matching grand staircases leading to the second story. They reminded her of the ones in Chateau Frontenac. She then considered the other doors branching off the foyer. One led to a large coat closet. Meline paused when she opened the next.

Well, this is a start. She gaped at the study.

Hundreds of leather-bound volumes filled the ceiling-high shelves. She ran her fingers over their spines as she passed from one shelf to the next. Frustratingly they were no help. Half the books had no titles, the others were in various foreign languages. Meline circled the room then dropped into the desk chair with a defeated sigh.

"Did you seriously expect to find something titled 'First-Aid for Khargals'?" she huffed, exasperated with herself. "Like Roc's going to keep a journal about his kind, knowing how risky it is."

After staring blindly for a minute, Meline pulled herself together and trudged out of the study. At least her little tour had been a diversion. She debated finding a shower and something to wear, but wasn't in the mood to fool with it. As she wandered back through the family room, a notepad sitting by the sofa captured her attention. She moved the pencil and took a better look at the doodle. Her mouth dropped open in recognition as the image on the paper merged with the mirage her oxygen-deprived mind conjured while trapped in the burning crypt. The sketch of the oblong medallion lacked color, but she knew the setting engraved with unusual script was shiny like gold. Roc had faithfully drawn the large jewel in the center. Meline closed her eyes, recalling the way the red stone shimmered. She had seen this before and now she remembered where.

Once when she was young, her father had taken her to a very special museum exhibit. She recalled fondly as he got down on one knee and pointed to a beautiful stained-glass butterfly.

"Your great-grandpapa Lauber was an artist. He worked

for a man named Tiffany who made most of this pretty glass. Papa Lauber made this butterfly as a gift for your nana using a brooch that had been passed down in our family," her father explained.

"Why didn't we keep it?" She gaped at the piece lit up so it cast a rainbow of colors on the walls and floor. Its wings were a dozen jewel tones, its body the most amazing ruby—the medallion.

"Our family loaned it to the museum so other people can enjoy it, and so a rambunctious little girl didn't break it playing ponies in the house." He ruffled her hair and she giggled.

That was the only time she'd seen it, since the museum rarely brought it out of the vault.

Excitedly, Meline dropped the drawing and was about to run out to the garage to tell Roc, then remembered he was frozen in stone. Her shoulders dropped. She might have learned where the sigil was but that didn't help Roc.

Maybe he's just hibernating like his dad. But she didn't honestly think his dad was hibernating, no loving parent would abandon their child like that, and she didn't believe Roc was hibernating either, he was too injured.

Meline walked through the kitchen. Her stomach rumbled seeing the bowl of fruit on the island. She was surprised to see how fresh it was.

No doubt he pays someone to keep things stocked for whenever he pops in. Maybe I'll think better on a full stomach.

She pulled a banana off the bunch, then cracked open the fridge. As she expected, it was full. Meline grabbed a block of cheese along with some sliced turkey, then went in search of a plate and knife. One of the drawers she opened held a bottle opener. Her gaze drifted to the wine cellar.

"I think I've earned it." She grabbed the first bottle she came to and opened it. As she reached for a glass, she paused. "Fuck it." Meline flipped the cabinet closed as she took a swig straight from the bottle.

After collecting her snack, she headed back to the garage and joined Roc in the SUV. Not surprising, he was unchanged.

"You hungry?" she asked, knowing full well he wasn't going to respond.

Meline popped a slice of cheese into her mouth then washed it down with a giant gulp of wine as she attempted not to dwell on the painful questions needling her mind. Questions like; how long did she wait before making the hard decision to leave? How did she find someone to help her deactivate the dangerous relic, now that she knew where it was?

"Are you going to make me drink alone? That's not very nice of you, Roc."

She talked out loud because the silence was unbearable.

"What?" She held her hand to her ear, pretending he'd answered. "Oh, you do want some. Good. I was feeling like a drunk, drinking before noon." She tipped the bottle up to Roc's mouth, wetting his lips just a little.

Meline screamed when Roc's hand shot out, grabbing the bottle. She barely got her fingers free as he gripped it in his stony hands. His mouth snapped open and he poured the wine down his throat without pausing for breath. He still stared straight ahead, his eyes blind as he ravenously drank. If anything, what little he did move added to the craggy fissures in his stony skin. Roc swiftly finished off the wine. Her eyes widened in horror when he opened his mouth and bit down on the bottle.

"Roc, no! I have food," she entreated as he chewed the glass, his throat bobbing as he swallowed the shards.

He ignored her, so she tried to take the broken bottle, but a warning growl had her swiftly pulling her hand back. She gripped her knees and stayed still, so he didn't feel threatened. He reminded her of a wounded animal, unpredictable and potentially dangerous. Roc took bite after bite, chewing and swallowing. Miraculously it didn't seem to cut his lips and she saw no blood each time he opened his mouth.

"I hope you know what you're doing."

Roc took the last bite of the bottle and swallowed it down then licked his fingers. Just as she worried he might try eating his own hand, his nostrils flared as he pulled in a deep breath. His head eerily swung toward her with a terrible cracking sound.

"Oh fuck." She frowned, seeing new fissures in his neck spider down his shoulder then seal again.

She froze as he pulled in another chuffing breath, his mouth open, exposing his long canines, like he was trying to taste the air. His eyes were a murky gray instead of the sandy color they had been, but she still wasn't certain he could see since he didn't focus on her. Yet she was hopeful. It seemed eating was helping. If she only knew, she would've tried this earlier.

"Here." Meline was about to offer him the plate in her lap when Roc abruptly lunged toward her.

Her back slammed into the car door as she reared back. This was an improvement from the way he'd been, but Roc wasn't himself. He was injured, hungry, and moving on instinct alone. That was a dangerous combination. She stayed deathly still as his nose burrowed in her hair, sniffing wildly. Meline started to tremble when he reached her neck and she felt his sharp canines graze her. His tongue made a long swipe over her hammering pulse, tasting her.

"Roc." Her voice quaked as he lingered.

He grunted and continued sniffing his way down her chest till he found the plate in her lap. A relieved sigh burst out when he started shoveling the meat and cheese into his mouth, then ate the banana, peel and all. It was supremely foolish, but she snatched the plate away before he started in on that, too. Quickly, she grabbed the door handle and tumbled out of the SUV, eliciting a frustrated growl from her statuesque lover. Roc glared as she scrambled to her feet.

"Come on, there's more food in the kitchen," she coaxed, waving the plate at him like a red flag.

She didn't wait for him to make it out of the car, she took off for the kitchen like the hounds of hell were nipping at her heels. The sound of the garage door crashing into the wall when he threw it open spurred her on. Meline skidded as she rounded the corner, barely making it into the kitchen.

Roc was on her in an instant, his massive body pinning her against the island. Swiftly she grabbed an apple from the fruit bowl and offered it to him over her shoulder. She jumped when he took a bite of it right from her hand. His lips grazed her as he ate, and she was grateful to discover they were again fleshy. The moment he finished the apple, Meline was ready with another banana, but Roc was again rooting around in her hair. Her eyes widened when he ground his hips against her behind and she felt his hard cock.

"Mmm," Roc grunted hungrily against her neck, making her shiver.

This was not a good idea, not with the state he was in. Roc needed to eat and finish recovering. And yet as he rocked his pelvis, she couldn't help the flood of moisture that soaked her panties. Her singed jeans were a poor barrier as his turgid cock sawed back and forth between her thighs. She squirmed as much from the mounting pleasure as from the desire to get away. He growled in displeasure and nipped her neck.

"Roc," she yelped.

Roc's hot breath ghosted over the sensitive flesh below her ear, his tongue teasing and tasting the place he bit, as his hands kneaded her hips while dry humping her against the counter. He was hungry, just not for food.

ROC

He was dizzy and ravenous, but deliriously happy at the same time. The scent of his female surrounded him. Touching her soothed and inflamed him all in the same breath. The sweet flavor of her skin burst on his tongue. Her body called to something deep inside, a hunger only she could satisfy.

Concern laced his female's voice, making him pause. He heard what she said, yet for some reason it didn't process. Everything was fuzzy, but it didn't matter, she was here with him.

There was something so compelling about the smooth flesh where Meline's shoulder met her neck. He salivated with the desire to taste more of her and resumed exploring. His fingers flexed, squeezing her supple hips. The heat from her pussy made his cock jerk as he thrust between her thighs. He needed to sink into her silky heat more than he needed food or even air, but something was in the way—her clothes.

Roc snarled as the annoying material abraded his shaft. He gripped her waistband and was about to tug when she squirmed.

"No, Roc, you need to eat," she snapped at him, and this time he understood the word 'no' but didn't like it. He could scent her desire. It didn't make sense that she resisted.

Somehow his female escaped his grasp as he toiled over her strange reaction. This was the second time she'd run from him. Fear unlike anything he'd ever known surged inside him as she darted away. He couldn't let her out of his sight. It was too dangerous. Something threatened her. He couldn't remember what hunted them, but she had to remain by his side.

Roc leapt over the island, landing in her path. His female squealed in surprise as she bumped into his chest, her eyes growing large before scowling at him. He snagged her around the waist before she could evade him again.

"Roc, you have to eat." She struggled in his arms.

His stomach rumbled in response to something she said, but keeping his female safe was more important. Roc shook his head as the two needs warred inside him.

MELINE

For *being injured he certainly moves fast*, Meline huffed. The refrigerator was almost within reach. She thought for sure if she revealed the bounty inside, he wouldn't be able to resist.

Roc seemed more lucid, but he still wasn't quite right. He was acting like he got his bell rung in a boxing match. He needed to eat more. It appeared the food was helping heal the red patches and fine cracks, so it had to be good for his mental state, too. Except he was entirely distracted by her.

"You can lead a horse to water, but you can't make him drink," she grumbled as he hovered over her, looking frustrated and confused by her demand.

His fingers hooked her waistband and swiftly tugged her jeans down, panties and all. They put up little resistance having been damaged by the fire. Her eyes widened as he lifted her onto the counter and ripped her jeans in two. Meline's heart kicked into high gear when he took one pant leg and tied her ankle to the island leg. His rough hand gripped her knee, shoved her legs wide, then bound her to the other leg. She nervously stared down at the way her legs were splayed, her bare pussy entirely vulnerable.

"Roc!" she exclaimed and fell backwards when he pulled her hips to the edge of the counter, then planted his face in her crotch. With the way he tied her, there was no way she could close her legs.

"No." Meline tried to shove his face away. This wasn't going to help him.

Roc growled in rebuke as he glanced up at her, his silver eyes flashing. He was an imposing hulk of a man.

"Don't you get huffy with me." She reached back, grabbed the banana he ignored earlier and threw it at him.

Deftly, Roc snatched it out of the air, looked at it then glanced back down at her pussy. Her mouth dropped open in shock when he took the banana and slipped it into her vagina.

"Oh my God, what are you doing?" She tried to bat his hands away. She'd never used food in sex. It was entirely too weird.

Roc grabbed her hands and tugged them over her head. He snagged her shirt and pulled it over, too.

"Hey! Wait a minute." She struggled as he used the t-shirt to bind her wrists to the island faucet. "Shit!"

He grunted, looking satisfied she could no longer interfere then returned to his illicit task. Roc gripped the banana sticking out of her pussy and pressed it all the way in. It couldn't begin to compare to his cock, it wasn't nearly as long or thick, and yet she found herself getting wetter as he stroked in and out. Maybe it was the way he intently stared at her labia as he fucked her with the phallic-shaped fruit. Or maybe it was the way he twisted it, the curve in the banana striking her in sensitive places. Just as she started trembling from the building pleasure, having forgotten how weird this was, Roc pulled it out. Her eyes widened when he licked her juices off the banana then again ate it without bothering to peel it first.

She should've been happy when Roc yanked open the fridge and started grabbing things left and right, tossing carrots, frozen raspberries, and anything else that captured his attention onto the island. Instead, she was nervous.

Meline started to hyperventilate when he approached her with a bottle of chocolate sauce. The anticipation was unbearable as he flipped open the lid and drizzled it over her pussy.

Meline gasped at how cold the chocolate was, squirming as it slid down her sensitive cleft, coating her labia. Her breath burst out when his hot tongue took a long swipe from her slit to her swollen clit. The contrast was startling. Roc made satisfied rumbling noises as he lapped at her labia, consuming every bit of chocolate mixed with desire that spilled from her pussy. The man always ate her pussy like his life depended on it, and she loved every minute of it.

"Roc!" Her hips bucked when his tongue delved between her cheeks and circled her anus.

Meline gripped the faucet, threatening to yank it free, and panted as he pushed the wet tip of his tongue into her clenched opening. The sensation was obscenely pleasurable. Her pussy cramped and fluttered as he explored the taboo spot. Her knees quaked and she gushed, making him growl. Again, he eagerly lapped up her offering.

Nervous didn't begin to describe what she felt when Roc lifted his face and grinned evilly as he grabbed a carrot and bit off the small end. She had a sudden suspicion he was feeling more like himself. He thrust the thick end into her vagina, swirled it around then pulled it free.

"What are you doing?" she asked anxiously as he ran it over her slick, trembling labia.

"Eating," he rumbled then latched onto her clit.

The wicked man pressed the carrot against her ass as he thrust two thick fingers into her pussy and mercilessly sucked her clit. His tongue swirled while he worked the carrot into her puckered rosette while stroking his fingers into her overheated body. Meline tossed her head back and forth. The pleasure overtaking her was unbelievable. Her channel spasmed as he added a third finger. Her ass quivered with each press and retreat of the makeshift sex toy. She tried to clench her thighs but couldn't with her ankles bound.

"Roc," she cried as the orgasm rolled over her.

Her back bowed off the counter as he impaled her ass and pussy faster. She screamed in ecstasy when he flicked her clit with his tongue. She came so hard her whole body shook with agonizing pleasure, and yet she wanted more.

"I need you," she keened.

❧

ROC

He couldn't recall how Meline wound up tied naked to his kitchen counter like a sexy little sacrifice, but he wasn't about to let the opportunity go to waste. Her passionate cries and the way her pink quivering slit clenched his fingers was the most beautiful sight he'd ever seen. Her tight ass stretched around the carrot gave him perverse pleasure. Her virgin rear wouldn't take his cock, but it was clear his female enjoyed the prurient act.

Roc pulled his fingers out and tossed the carrot aside. His cock hurt watching the desire spill from her quaking vagina.

"Please, Roc," she begged.

Sweat beaded her forehead and also trickled between her breasts. He loved how the creamy mounds heaved as she panted. Her stiff nipples were as pink as ripe berries. Roc noticed the frozen raspberries on the counter and grinned.

"You're too hot," he husked as he grabbed several of the sweet treats.

"Roc," Meline gasped when he placed the icy berries so

the hollows cupped her turgid nipples, making the areolas pucker from the cold. "Oh, you're evil," she squirmed.

"Yes," he grunted and grabbed an ice cube from the tray sitting on the counter.

"What are you doing?" Meline squealed as he trailed one frigid cube down her stomach.

"Very hot." He slid the ice over her mound.

"Roc, no! Oh God!"

She bucked when he touched the ice to the engorged clit jutting from her slick folds. Her pussy spasmed frantically, spilling more nectar that leaked down her pink cleft to her puckered rear.

"Is this better?" He warmed her rosy little clit with his fingers, circling round and round.

"No!" Meline wailed, her back bowing off the island. "Fuck me!" she growled.

His cock strained and throbbed with a life of its own. Hearing his sweet angel's cursed demand nearly had him coming. He'd have to do something about that, or he wouldn't last a minute.

A salacious thought entered his mind and he grabbed several more chips of ice. Meline's eyes widened in shock and she started tugging, nearly breaking her bonds, as he neared her pussy.

"Roc!" she snapped in warning, but he ignored it.

Her ecstatic cry echoed off the walls when he slipped two cubes into her tight little ass and another in her pussy. Roc quickly crammed his aching cock into the mouth of her trembling vagina before she pushed the ice out. He reveled in the way her delicious shriek deepened, and how her hot, wet slit grasped him. It was as painful as it was glorious. If it weren't for the ice teasing his crown as he pressed in, he would've burst instantly.

"It's too much, Roc, I can't take it," she cried.

A twisted part of him loved hearing her ardent cries as he tested the bounds of ecstasy. But she wasn't the only one being pushed to the limit. Through the thin trembling membrane, he felt the ice in her ass. Each time her pussy spasmed, the cold cubes slid along his overheated shaft. Hot and cold, it was a wonderful maddening mix of sensations.

"Yes, you can. I'll warm you up," he husked, although what he had planned wouldn't be a reprieve for either one of them.

His tail snaked between her legs and worked its way into her ass, forcing the puckered ring of muscles to let him in. His demanding cock had her pussy straining, while his tail and the ice cubes stretched her virgin hole. Meline orgasmed, her stomach flexing spasmodically as he attempted to press deeper.

"Fuck, angel," he snarled, and his hips jerked, unable to control himself.

Her mouth opened on a broken silent scream when he punched deep, burying himself to the hilt.

He was a glutton for punishment. As he started fucking her, he couldn't resist rubbing her pulsing clit with his thumb. The spasms in her vagina clenched his cock and tail painfully tight, making it nearly impossible for him to pull out or thrust back into her hot body, though the swiftly melting ice helped.

"Roc. Fuck. Oh. God. Roc." Meline sucked in gasping breaths.

She was beyond sexy thrashing and calling his name. He quickly lost control, giving in to the dark need that drove him to possess and dominate her, so Meline knew once and for all she was his. Roc fucked her with abandon, pounding out his feral lust. He dropped forward and sucked the cold berry off one of her nipples as he repeatedly slammed home. The moment his hot tongue met her chilled nipple, Meline cried out again, all but her glorious wet pussy and tight rear going rigid. Her eyes rolled back in her head as she erupted, her channel flooding with more liquid desire. He gripped her splayed quaking thighs and swung his hips faster. The way she rhythmically clenched his cock, and her ass convulsed, impaled by his tail, made it impossible to stave off the fire churning out of control. His wings shot out as the orgasm surged up his spine. The force of it was blinding.

"Mine!" He bucked and jerked as he roared from the ecstasy.

MELINE

"Angel, I'm so sorry. Did I hurt you?" Roc caressed her cheek as the world came back into focus, and Meline realized she was crying.

"You didn't. That was…" she panted.

There weren't words to describe what she felt. The intense ecstasy merged with the relief that Roc was going to be okay, making her feel delirious. She wanted to laugh and cry all at the same time.

"Thank *Lar*." Roc kissed her repeatedly, looking relieved as he untied her wrists.

"And I'm much better now that I know you're not dying," she sobbed.

"Shhh. It's okay. I'm okay." He pulled her into his arms and Meline realized he'd already freed her legs. "I'm really hard to kill." Roc cradled her against his chest as he strode to the living room and sat on the couch.

"I can see that now." But it didn't make last night any less frightening.

She trembled as she clung to Roc, stroking his bare chest as she examined him. The thought of losing him was devastating. It was hard to believe he was completely healed after the way he looked earlier. But his skin was warm and smooth again. His eyes were bright and filled with life as they flashed with concern for her.

"It's you I'm worried about. I thought the fire…" His voice wavered as he held her tight. "And I could've hurt you coming out of the *duramna*."

"But you didn't, and we're okay," she laughed. It was crazy they'd survived. She shook her head in disbelief. "Although you were kind of freaky. You ate a glass bottle and got growly when I tried to take it from you."

"My kind does that. We need the minerals, especially when we have to heal fast. I really could've hurt you. Did you try to take it away? Is that why I tied you up?" he asked, looking very worried.

"Not exactly. You did that when I tried to get you to eat something besides my lady bits." She blushed, remembering how insistent Roc was at having his way with her.

"Oh." Roc cast her a cheeky grin. He then sighed, looking guilty.

"What?" She caressed his stubbled cheek.

"I should've had better sense when I came to and found you tied to the island. I should've checked you over, instead of giving in to the instinct demanding I claim you. I don't know what's come over me." His hands roamed her naked body, checking for injuries.

"Don't be hard on yourself, you were out of it. I promise I'm fine. You found me just in time." She kissed his collar bone, relieved that he was back to his old self.

"You are fine." His brow furrowed, looking just as confounded as she was about how she survived the fire without a scratch. "What happened?"

"I don't know. I was in the shed looking for a shovel and the next thing I know I'm waking up in a burning coffin with a body." Meline shivered at the memory.

Her hand drifted to the back of her head, but it no longer hurt, and the bump had gone away.

"The bastards called, distracting me. They have John!" Roc snarled, his wings snapping to their full height as he suddenly recalled what else happened.

"Oh God, no! I thought he was out doing errands when those creeps raided your penthouse." Tears welled up in her eyes.

Please be okay. She really liked John.

"Where's my phone?" He looked around.

"It's in the SUV."

Roc cradled her tight against his chest as he stormed out of the living room.

"Dammit, we didn't have a chance to find the sigil. I have to get back to the cemetery. Sigil or not, the second those bastards text me an address, I'm going to rip their..."

"Roc!" she shouted, interrupting his spiraling rant.

His gaze darted to her in surprise. "They almost killed you. I won't let that stand," he growled, the skin on his face tightening, his brow sharpening.

"The sigil's in the Queens Museum," she blurted before he started snarling murderous threats again. Although the people behind this more than deserved it.

They kidnapped her new friend, hurt Roc and tried to kill her. She wasn't nearly as invincible as Roc, but she was pissed. *And they're going to regret it.*

🏵 13 🏵

MELINE

Roc was quiet as they drove. In fact, he'd been that way since their conversation about the sigil. He barely said two words when they showered, just kissing and touching her. Like he was reassuring himself she was okay. She understood, feeling somber herself. His touch brought her comfort and yet she was sad at the same time because they were hardly out of danger. They couldn't even be contented by their small victory, discovering where the relic was and surviving the fire, not knowing if John still lived.

It'll be okay. We just need to be more alert. We'll rescue John, retrieve the sigil before it goes supernova and Bob's your uncle, all is well again. Meline attempted to get her nerves under control as the weight of the task ahead threatened to overwhelm her. *No, no, we're going to kick ass*, she rallied. They'd made it this far.

"It's a good idea to ditch this car, they probably bugged it at the cemetery. But I think we could drive back to Quebec as fast as we can fly," Meline commented as they pulled up to the airport outside Montreal.

"We're not going back to Quebec." Roc drove onto the tarmac and headed for a small plane.

"You want to go to New York first? I know the sigil's dangerous and we need to get it back, but John's more important! I don't trust those people to keep their word, they tried to kill me. And I don't have my passport, remember?" She frowned at Roc's dispassionate expression. He knew how dangerous this crazy group was. They couldn't leave John with them for a minute longer.

God only knows what they've done to him. She couldn't even think about it.

Roc stopped the SUV and faced her. She didn't like the stern expression on his face.

"Meline, you're going back to Connecticut."

"Wait, what?!" She gaped at him in confusion.

"These people are serious. You nearly died once. I won't risk it happening a second time. And I can't be worrying about you while I take care of these bastards and get John back."

"So, you're going in alone? I know you're a badass but you're not invincible." She started to panic thinking of him getting hurt. "And don't you think that if they found us once, they sure as hell can find me again?"

"They think you're dead and won't have time to learn any differently. But just to be sure, I want you to stay with a friend for the next few days. The plane I chartered caters to clientele who like their privacy, so you won't have any trouble crossing the border."

He got out of the SUV, effectively putting a stop to their

argument. She hopped out before he could come around and open her door.

"I'm not going home. We're a team." She understood he was worried about her. She was worried about him, too.

Roc held up one hand, silencing her. He placed both palms on her cheeks and tipped her chin up. Before he kissed her, a heartbreakingly sad expression crossed his face. Instead of passion, his kiss was filled with longing, and she got the terrible feeling this wasn't just goodbye for now.

"Roc," she whispered, her voice breaking as they parted. "I'm not going to see you again, am I?"

He closed his eyes. His hand lingered on her cheek for a moment before stepping back. When he opened his eyes again, the usually bright gray had grown cold.

"Meline, I am who I am. I lie and steal for a living. I hide from everyone and have to run from people like the ones who tried to kill you."

"I know who you are and you're going to take care of those assholes," she argued, shaking her head in disbelief.

"And more will come, like they always do."

"I don't care about any of that." She stepped toward him. Her chest physically hurt.

"But I do," he snapped, making her freeze where she was. "This isn't going to work, Meline. We both knew it from the start."

"Bullshit," she countered, her chin quivering as tears filled her eyes.

"Goodbye, Meline."

Her mouth hung open in shock as Roc strode back to the SUV, tears streaming down her cheeks. He didn't even look back at her, just walked away from what they found together.

Meline sucked in several ragged breaths and had to swallow down the bile rising in her throat as her heart shattered. There were so many things she wanted to say but was too stunned. She couldn't even blurt out the three most important words.

I love you.

ROC

Roc watched the plane takeoff before launching into the air, abandoning the rental car. He couldn't get the image of Meline out of his head, or the devastated tears filling her eyes, while he winged it toward Quebec. He was barely outside Montreal when he lost it. The anguished roar that burst from his throat sent birds fleeing from the trees.

Walking away from Meline was the hardest thing he'd ever done; he'd sooner volunteer to be drawn and quartered. He was a selfish man and Meline was the ultimate prize. But for once in his life he couldn't be greedy, not when keeping her would ultimately get her killed. Sending her away was enough to break him but watching her die would destroy him. He deluded himself thinking if he kept her near, he could protect her. Yet it took barely a moment for her to be ripped away in the cemetery. The memory of her trapped in that burning church crippled him with fear and filled him with rage, making it nearly impossible to fly. He couldn't let that happen again, not now, not ever.

She's safer without me.

Even if he could keep her out of danger every waking

hour of every day, she'd be forced to hide like he did, living a lie, complicit in his life of crime. That was the last thing he wanted for her. Meline deserved better.

The sun was setting over the skyline by the time he reached Quebec City. He expected a text message anytime now, it had been nearly twenty-four hours since the bastards first contacted him. Roc found himself gravitating toward the governor's mansion excavation at the foot of Chateau Frontenac. He descended the steps below the boardwalk, bent and hummed into the lock securing the archaeological site. The padlock dropped open, he swung the gate wide and went inside. His eyes swiftly adjusted to the lack of light and Roc found the stone wall that always drew him.

"I know where the sigil is. You're going home, sire." He listened closely for any sound to indicate his sire stirred somewhere inside the stone wall. "Did you hear me? You're going home," he repeated when there was no response.

"Of course, you refuse to answer me. Why would you? I'm just your fucking son," he snarled.

This was the last straw. He felt raw. Saying goodbye to Meline ripped old wounds wide open and all the years of frustration, anger and hurt came pouring out.

"You know what, I'm done trying. I've come here I don't know how many times to talk to you. I know I was a disappointment. I know that everyday you looked at me you were reminded of the perfect progeny you left back home and the vow you broke with mum while you were stuck on this miserable planet," he shouted at the silent stone wall as he paced.

"Is this place so fucking awful that you couldn't bear to wait for my return? 'Cause I can think of at least one thing that makes this world a place worth living in."

And I lost it.

Roc froze in his tracks as a terrible realization dawned on him. His sire was always such a miserable bastard, regretting every day on Earth, taking his mother for granted. It never occurred to him that losing Theresa devastated Petronus.

"No, that's wrong." Roc shook his head, he did know her loss hurt his sire. "I just never understood the weight of your loss, not until now. And you didn't just lose her, did you?" Petronus had lost not just one mate but two. Roc had lost Meline, but she still lived. He couldn't imagine the grief and pain his sire suffered. "And then I left you."

Roc collapsed on the ground and frowned as he stared at the wall.

"I'm sorry," he sighed, this new understanding adding to his pain. "I'd really like to ask you how you dealt with what I'm feeling, except I think I know. But there's still a chance for you to go home. Or maybe you can move over, so I can climb in there with you."

Still nothing stirred deep within the stony walls. He hung his head, feeling dejected.

His cell pinged, and Roc glanced down at the message.

'Are you ready to make a deal?' The message was accompanied by a picture of John sporting a black eye.

'Name the place.' He snarled as he sent the reply.

'Bring the relic to the abandoned pumping station at the old port, come alone.'

"I have to go, sire, and try to save my friend."

Roc shouldered his bag, left the excavation and took off for the industrial sector down by the shore. He slowed midair and focused on the two-story building amid a field riddled with pipes. He didn't see anyone lurking on the roof of the pumping station or the surrounding area, but that didn't mean the kidnapping bastards were alone, like they demanded of him. It didn't matter either way, they had John.

He landed outside, retracted his wings and cautiously approached the abandoned building, every sense on high alert. No one greeted him at the entrance. The instant he opened the doors, the strong scent of chlorine nearly bowled him over. His nose burned as he found his way to a massive central room filled with rusty machines. There, alone in the middle of the room was John, chained to one of the old turbines and nearby sat an empty cage. Roc took two steps toward John but froze as the turbine sprang to life, spinning, yanking the chains attached to John's outstretched arms.

"Stop right there, freak, unless you want to watch grandpa get ripped in two," a voice bellowed from the catwalk up above.

Roc turned to see the fucker who'd hurt Meline and broke into his penthouse standing on the metal balcony. Somehow, he wasn't surprised to see the psychopath, Cohosh. Nightshade was the type that didn't like to get his hands dirty, so he sent his henchman. Roc's wings bristled, ready to launch at the man behind Meline's near-death experience, but John's shout of pain as the chains pulled tighter halted him.

"I brought the damn medallion. You can stop your demonstration," Roc roared, shaking his backpack.

His shoulders eased when the spinning machine halted, and John sighed in relief.

"Sir, you shouldn't have come. It's a trap," John coughed.

He suspected nothing less from the vile assholes.

"Like I was going to leave you," he reassured his old friend.

"Touching. Now drop the bag and get in the cage," Cohosh barked.

"I don't think so. I don't trust you. I'll toss the bag up to you, then me and my friend will be going," Roc countered.

He was about to rush John and break the chains when men with semi-automatic weapons stepped out from behind the large machines and corroded pipes. He expected a handful of men at best, not a small army equipped to start the next world war.

Fuck me. With the strong chemical smell, he hadn't scented all the mercenaries, and hadn't thought much of it since this used to be a pumping station.

"You murdered my brother, so please do something stupid," Cohosh raged and pressed the button starting up the turbine again.

"You fucking kill him and you won't get a damn thing. I'll rip you to shreds," he snarled, but stepped into the cage to appease the bastard.

Roc stared the reprobate in the eyes as he slammed the cage door and the lock snapped into place. The piece of shit was angry but there was a hint of fear lurking in his eyes.

You should be afraid. These bars aren't nearly enough to contain me.

"Now toss the bag out."

Roc shoved the backpack through the bars and John released a groaning sigh when the whirling machine again stopped.

As much as he hated it, he had to comply as long as those mercenaries pointed their weapons at them. A few bullets weren't a problem, but a hailstorm would cut through his *duramna.* With the mood he was in, he would've risked it, but John was entirely vulnerable.

One of the armed men stepped forward, grabbed the bag and threw it up to Cohosh. Roc watched as the fucker pulled out the decoy medallion. The antique ruby brooch was worth a small fortune, however, it wasn't the relic the bastards were looking for. But since he himself had only seen the sigil a few times, he doubted the stupid fucker would know better.

"Nightshade, we have the relic," the thug spoke to a laptop screen.

"You tested it, Cohosh?" the absentee prick asked.

Shit! Roc's heart stilled when the jackass placed the decoy brooch into a piece of equipment that looked way too sophisticated for a numb nuts like Cohosh.

"I'm not reading anything. All the lights are still red," Cohosh grumbled.

"I told you acquiring the relic wasn't going to be easy," Nightshade countered.

"Can I kill them now?" the fucker Cohosh demanded.

Son of a bitch, Roc growled, hearing all the guns click as rounds were chambered.

MELINE

The cabby stared at her in the rearview mirror as he drove toward her condo. Meline knew she looked like a hot mess, she'd cried the entire flight home. But the sympathetic looks were getting old. It didn't help that she'd gone straight to the airport bar and gotten drunk. She ignored the cabby, staring out the window instead. When the taxi stopped, she peeled a few bills off the wad of cash Roc had slipped into her pocket, refusing the urge to toss the entire stack at the driver. She didn't want the cash. It made her feel dirty, like he had paid her off.

I'm sorry for trampling your heart. Here, take some money, she silently railed at him.

Meline trudged through the patio gate at the back of her condo. It took a minute of fumbling around in the dark to find the fake rock holding her spare key. She flipped on the kitchen light, staggered over to the fridge and tugged it open. As she grabbed the bottle of cheap chardonnay, wondering if there was enough left to make her pass out, a scent caught her attention. Something was off, and it wasn't the spoiled milk in the fridge.

She spun, ducking as she swung the bottle. It cracked against some giant thug's head, sending him reeling backward. Meline scrambled out of the kitchen before he could recover. The piece of shit grabbed the back of her shirt as she reached the patio. She stomped his foot and elbowed the man in the stomach. He released her, doubling over with a pained grunt. She barely made two steps before he snagged her leg, sending her sprawling into the grass. Meline rolled as he loomed over her. She punched him in the nose, relishing the crack, but not the disgusting spray of blood. She'd never punched someone let alone broken their nose. Surprisingly her hand didn't even hurt. Meline released the anger she was feeling toward Roc, striking the home invader again.

"Fuck," the man barked, before she shut him up with a blow to the jaw.

Two more greasy bastards piled on, grabbing her arms.

She struggled as they dragged her off the ground, noticing the rose pin on one guy's collar in the process. Meline tugged her right arm free but the bloated mafia wannabe grabbed it again, squeezing her wrist till it hurt.

"Dammit, this bitch is strong." The man looked surprised.

"Yeah, thanks for the help." Her attacker scowled as he spat out a tooth.

It was shocking the way she gave the three men a run for their money. She was half their size, but she was pissed, super pissed.

So stupid, she grumbled at herself as they hauled her back into her condo.

Obviously, the insane secret society didn't think she was dead. She shouldn't have come home. She was supposed to go stay with Jen, but the last thing she wanted to do was rehash what happened with Roc. She just wanted to curl up in bed and go to sleep.

"Miss Lauber, so glad to see you hearty and whole."

She turned from the trio of thugs struggling to hold on to her and stared blankly at the new guy wearing a suit, acting like he knew her. He wasn't one of the assholes who'd broken into Roc's penthouse, at least not the one who was still living. That bastard wasn't among the handful of thugs currently tracking mud through her condo. But it appeared this man was the leader of that whole gang.

"You may call me Nightshade. And now that introductions are done, I'd appreciate it if you'd have a seat." He pointed to a chair at the end of the dining room table.

"I don't have what you're looking for. I didn't sell some stupid relic to that man," she snarled as they tied her to the chair. This whole scenario was the icing on a really shitty cake.

"Sure, lady, where'd you get the pile of cash on the kitchen counter then?" The guy she bloodied shook her.

"Enough." Nightshade held up his hand as he sat at the table in front of a laptop. "I'm fully aware you don't have the relic. Your unusual companion is about to hand it over in exchange for his friend. You're just my insurance policy that he follows through."

He shifted the laptop so she could see the screen and her eyes widened. Poor John was bloody and bruised, chained to a large piece of machinery. And Roc was trapped in a cage with a dozen guns pointed at him.

Oh God. Meline blanched. She was heartbroken and pissed at Roc, but seeing him in danger trumped all that.

"Nightshade, we have the relic." The aforementioned asshole popped up on screen, like she'd said Beetlejuice three times.

What relic? She couldn't get a good view of whatever it was Roc handed over, but obviously it wasn't the real thing. Quickly she schooled her features so they didn't see the surprise on her face. Roc obviously had a plan.

"You tested it, Cohosh?" Nightshade asked, eagerly staring at the screen.

"I'm not reading anything. All the lights are still red," Cohosh grumbled.

Crap! These thugs were smarter than she'd given them credit for.

"I told you acquiring the relic wasn't going to be easy," Nightshade barked in frustration.

"Can I kill them now?" Cohosh growled, and she saw the mob step toward Roc with their guns aimed.

The insane man was all too eager to kill Roc, especially after what he'd done to the other guy at the penthouse.

"No!" she screamed.

"Meline!" Roc roared loud enough it nearly blew the laptop speakers.

Suddenly the screen went dark. Her heart surged into her throat, not knowing if gunfire broke out on the other end or what.

"Don't you dare fucking hurt him," she snarled, her voice growing inhumanly deep.

She stood, despite her wrists being tied, and slammed back down, shattering the wooden chair. Angrily she gripped the broken armrest and stabbed at the guy on her left. The fat guy couldn't jump away fast enough. The jagged wood grazed his stomach, opening a nasty gash. Unfortunately, not deep enough to incapacitate him.

"Don't! My rash associate may have botched his ill-advised attempt to kill you at the church, but I can assure you I won't fail," Nightshade snapped, pointing his gun at her head.

No, no, no! This can't be happening.

✻ 14 ✻

ROC

The lights in the old building cut off, casting them in total darkness.

"I think we've got company. Someone get the lights back on and watch the fucking prisoners," Cohosh barked orders as the gun-toting men scattered.

Roc ignored it all.

They have Meline! He thought he was keeping her safe by sending her away, but he might as well have gift-wrapped her for these assholes. *I'm so fucking stupid. I should've known how determined they were.*

A window shattered, capturing his attention. He wasn't sure if the secret society was being upstaged by a rival sect, and didn't really care, this was his opportunity to get out of Dodge. The iron lock put up little protest when he used his Khargal gift. His high-pitched whistle wasn't audible to the humans, even so the hail of gunfire aimed at the windows drowned it out.

188

The gunmen stopped after their first frantic barrage. Roc froze, only managing to open the creaky cell door a fraction of the way before it grew deathly quiet. You could cut the tension with a knife as the gunmen stared at the broken windows, waiting for a glimpse of the intruders. While they were distracted, he shoved through the small opening, dodging one of the mercenaries blindly aiming his gun in the dark.

"Did you see someone come through the window?" a man nearby yelled, squinting in an attempt to see whoever had broken in.

"Don't fucking ask questions, just do your job, you morons," Cohosh shouted.

Roc didn't bother to look for the intruder as he quietly made his way toward John. The edgy gunman spun, sensing he was lurking nearby in the dark. Despite hardening his *duramna*, Roc ducked out of the man's path before coming face to face with the muzzle of the assault rifle. Getting shot in the head at point blank range was going to do a little more than sting.

There was a flurry of movement followed by a sharp groan and a sickening crunch on the catwalk at the far side of the room. The night-blind mercenaries swung toward the sound and started firing again.

"Stay down till I can clear a path," Roc insisted as he ducked down by John and broke the chains holding him.

"Sage advice, sir," John replied in his dry English accent as Roc helped him take cover under one of the large pipes connected to the turbine.

"I missed you, Little John," he snorted at his friend's oh so characteristic retort and the immense relief at finding John had no life-threatening injuries—yet. "I've got to go finish this."

It was chaos all around, shooting, scuffling, and death moans in the dark. Roc glanced across the room in time to see one of the gunmen being yanked behind a giant machine. He didn't see the assailants but whoever they were, he'd have to thank them for the timely distraction, assuming they weren't after him as well.

Roc crouched low as he approached the closest mercenary, staying below the barrel of the man's gun. He waited for the fucker to turn, stood and snapped the man's neck. Senseless violence wasn't his thing, but these people brought it on themselves. They never should've threatened John and Meline. As the limp man dropped to the ground, a shadow passed above his head.

"Well it is about time! I was starting to think you turned out to be a coward with the way you were hiding behind those conduits," the recognizable gruff voice commented as the mysterious assailant swooped past.

Roc's mouth dropped open and he blinked in shock. "Sire?"

"Are you going to make me do all the work, *mon fils*?" His sire launched at a male, taking the mercenary's weapon before the man knew what hit him.

Roc regained his wits and joined in, angrily lashing out at another gunman.

"I'll have you know, I wasn't hiding. I had to get my friend to safety," he snapped at his sire while grabbing his opponent's rifle and punching the human in the face.

It was unbelievable. His sire was asleep for hundreds of years and his first words were to call him a coward.

Real fucking nice!

"Why am I not surprised an Earthian got you into this mess?" Petronus' retort was almost drowned out by the screams of the man he dropped from thirty feet onto the concrete floor.

"Did you wake up just to rub my nose in past mistakes?" Roc grabbed two men and knocked their heads together.

Petronus landed in front of him, his stony wings looking just as daunting as Roc always remembered them. "No. It sounded like you needed me, and from the looks of it I was right."

Roc paused. For a brief moment Petronus sounded like a concerned parent, then ruined it just as fast.

"I had things handled," he growled as they both ducked a spray of bullets.

"If that is what you call being locked inside a cage."

Roc snarled. His wings shot out, the taloned tips slicing into the two men who approached from either side. Their eyes widened as he opened their gut with a swift brutal slash. Petronus snatched their weapons and the pair of mercenaries staggered back in shock as they bled out.

"Earthians have certainly made some advancements. Their munitions sting a lot more than I remember." Petronus finished admiring the rifle, aimed it and took out the last man standing.

A sound on the catwalk caught Roc's attention. He turned to see Cohosh, the leader of this band of assholes, attempting to escape. He needed to reach him before the bastard managed to contact Nightshade. Roc leapt into the air and dove toward the piece of shit, landing in his path. Roc dodged left and knocked the gun out of Cohosh's hand just as the shithead fired. The bastard turned to run the opposite direction but Petronus landed in his way.

"Time to join your comrades," Petronus sneered.

Despite trying to keep a straight face, Cohosh's eyes were slightly wild as his gaze darted between them. Roc couldn't really blame him. With the way the moonlight streamed in, illuminating Petronus' spiked wings, horns, and sharp canines, his sire looked like a demon summoned from Hell.

"If you kill me, Nightshade will end the girl," Cohosh blurted as Petronus closed in.

"Sire, wait!" Roc barked. As much as he hated to admit it, they needed this asshole alive.

"A female? What is he talking about?" Petronus gripped the front of the Cohosh's shirt.

"These people want the sigil and they're holding Nicolas' descendant, Meline, because of it."

"You do not possess the sigil, do you?" Petronus frowned as he tilted his head, like he was listening for something that wasn't there. "Nicolas was supposed to give it to you."

"Well that was a shitty plan because he was long dead when I finally returned home, and his grandson was a senile old man who knew nothing about it."

"And this female has it?" Petronus asked.

"Not exactly."

"Never mind the female then. I can find the sigil." Petronus tapped his forehead and Roc remembered the purebreds were connected to their sigils, like a weird telepathic life vest.

"No! You don't make the calls anymore, not about this. We're getting my female back from these fuckers," Roc snarled as he snatched Cohosh away from his sire. Petronus thought he could just pick up where he left off, being over-bearing the way he always was. "And you're going to help," he informed Cohosh, tightening his grip on the slimy fucker's throat.

"Over my dead body," Cohosh choked out.

"That can be arranged." Roc knocked him out.

It probably would've been smart to hold off and attempt to pull information from the asshole, but if he had to hear any more, he would've killed the bastard on the spot before learning where Meline was being held.

"Excuse me," John called out as he emerged from his hiding place. "I hate to interrupt this family reunion, sir, but wouldn't it be wise to get away from here?"

"Yes, it would," Roc agreed. "Sire, get this piece of filth out of here and I'll help my friend then clean up this mess."

Petronus nodded, gripped Cohosh's limp body and took off through a broken window. Roc leapt off the catwalk. John turned abruptly, hearing him land nearby.

"This may be hard for you to process but I need you to trust me and not freak out." Roc wrapped an arm around John and lifted off the ground.

"Thank you for coming for me, sir."

"We're friends. I would've come back for you sooner, but we thought you were out doing errands."

"Friends?" John cocked one brow. "Is that why it's taken you so long to reveal this side of yourself?"

"Wait, you knew?"

"Sir, I may be blind, but I'm not stupid," John scoffed at him.

"I'm sorry," Roc apologized, suddenly feeling guilty for not trusting his partner in crime for the last two decades.

"I assumed you'd tell me in good time. Then when you didn't, well, I kept myself entertained dancing around the elephant in the room." John's lips twisted in amusement.

Roc's mouth dropped open as he recalled all the occasions the blind man almost tread on his tail or smacked into his wings. They literally had danced a few times in an attempt to avoid one another, or not, according to John's admission.

"You know, I always suspected you had an evil streak, but that's just diabolical." Roc shook his head in amazement.

"Eh." John shrugged. "Sir, would it be too forward if I asked what you are?"

"We're called Khargals, but humans know us as gargoyles. Our people crashed a thousand years ago," he explained as they touched down on the lawn outside.

"Fascinating." John nodded, looking unaffected by the news. His expression shifted to concern. "Sir, I didn't get a chance to look into these people. But I overheard some things. You need to proceed very cautiously when you go after Meline. Not only do these people want the medallion, they want a specimen, you." Anger laced his usually stoic friend's voice.

Roc nodded, he was gathering that.

"Foolish Earthians picked on the wrong clan if they thought that pathetic cage would hold you," Petronus huffed.

"John, meet my long-lost sire, Petronus. He finally decided to wake up."

"A pleasure, sir. The wrong clan?" John tilted his head quizzically.

"My family is from a line of spies. We have the ability to open locks, can shift our skin color, see, smell and hear well," Roc rattled off.

"That explains your choice of trade. However, I must warn you, it sounded like this group has several loosely organized sects all over the world. They call themselves the Rose Syndicate."

"I'm not surprised, not after what I've seen." Roc nodded.

"We are wasting time," Petronus grumbled, impatiently dropping Cohosh's unconscious body.

"Will you be okay with my sire while I go handle this mess?" Roc asked John, slightly concerned, given the way the other human among them was faring.

"Rochelle, your elderly Earthian will be just fine."

"Rochelle?" John asked, the corner of his mouth twitching in amusement.

"Sire, don't call me that." He scowled at Petronus.

"Why? It is your name." Petronus smirked, knowing full well that was a sore point.

"It's a girl's name. Why for the love of *Lar* did you let Mum call me that?" He threw up his hands.

"But you were her little rock," Petronus teased and John chuckled. His name literally translated to little rock in French.

The pair were going to get along just fine.

"Don't encourage him," Roc groaned then headed back into the abandoned pumping station. Cleaning up a building full of his enemies was preferable to being mocked by his long-lost sire.

MELINE

"Keep trying to reach Cohosh, I want to know what's going on," Nightshade said to the thug across from him.

She was desperate to know, too. Meline never imagined being tied up at gunpoint would be the second scariest thing she'd experience. She was ready to come out of her skin wondering what was happening to Roc. Images of him being riddled with bullets after the angry psychopath discovered the medallion was a fake kept playing through her mind.

I have to do something.

"Tell him to let Roc and John go and I'll tell you where the relic is," Meline blurt, panic getting the best of her.

"I fail to believe that," Nightshade commented, unimpressed, and turned back to his laptop.

"Don't ignore me. I know where it is," she snapped. They needed to listen to her.

The sigil was dangerous in the wrong hands, but it was just a thing. If they killed Roc or John it was permanent. They needed to survive this and then worry about how to get the medallion back later.

"Miss Lauber, I'm in no mood to play games with you. The relic's not here, and it wasn't in your parent's home. I thought your family was tenaciously holding onto this secret, since even with the threat of death, your parents refused to give it up. But I have a feeling I've been wrong."

Meline sucked in a stunned breath. "*You* killed them! *You* ran them off the road!" she shouted, pain making her voice raw. She wasn't crazy, someone had been in her parent's home before she sold it.

She was so devastated and angered by the news, she

couldn't think straight. Meline struggled, the chair groaning as she fought to get free.

"Don't." Nightshade waved the gun at her. "Yes, we engineered your parents' accident. Unfortunately, it didn't bring anything to light. But I must thank you, you did lead us to someone who can locate the relic for us. Assuming Cohosh hasn't done something stupid." Nightshade scowled at his phone silently sitting on the table. "Besides, I'm not gullible and you don't strike me as stupid. We both know that if you give me the information I want, then I'd have no further use for you."

Fuck! She clearly was no good at this psycho manipulation.

Nightshade laughed seeing the expression on her face. He was getting off on torturing her. His phone pinged, and the sadistic bastard glanced down at it. Her heart sped up as he read the text then sent a reply.

Please be okay. She bit her lip.

"Well, Miss Lauber, it seems hearing your voice has encouraged our winged friend to talk. He's offered up just enough to buy you some time. It looks like we're meeting Cohosh in New York."

Thank God, he's alive. Meline's shoulders eased and she let out a relieved sigh.

But her relief was short-lived. She'd made things infinitely worse. If she'd just taken Roc's advice and stayed with Jen maybe he would've fought off these pricks without worrying about her, like he explained to begin with. Instead, he was caged like a dog. And God only knew what they'd do to him, or her, to get the rest of the information.

ROC

Nightshade wasn't expecting him in New York City for another eight hours. That was, the prick wasn't expecting Cohosh till late morning. It was how long the drive would take. Except Roc didn't plan on driving or going all the way to New York City, like he'd messaged Nightshade.

"You weigh a fucking ton," Roc growled in frustration as he shifted his burden.

They couldn't fly nearly fast enough taking turns carrying the piece of shit Cohosh. He would've dropped the fucker bundled up like an Eskimo if he didn't need him for insurance. Setting the pumping station on fire then getting John settled someplace safe had taken longer than he'd have liked, but they were still making good time.

He'd worried about giving the bastards the actual location of the sigil, but he needed Nightshade to think Cohosh was getting somewhere with him. Meline's life depended on it.

And he didn't know what they might've gotten out of her. The vile sons of bitches already tried to burn her alive.

Finally, the Connecticut coastline was within sight. They were so close to Meline's house, he could barely contain himself. It only took breaking a few of Cohosh's fingers to learn that was where Nightshade was holding her.

"We are close, I can sense my sigil." Petronus broke off and headed south toward Long Island.

"Yes, but we're going after Meline first," Roc hollered the reminder over the whipping wind as he caught up with his sire.

Petronus landed in a nearby tree and he followed. Roc propped Cohosh against the trunk and put a boot on the unconscious man to keep him balanced on the branch.

"Rochelle, I know what you said, but we need to get my sigil. We cannot let it fall into the wrong hands," Petronus argued in Khargal. It was odd hearing the old language again.

"Call me Roc," he growled in frustration. "And, yes, I remember the few depressing bedtime stories you told me about the sigil, but we're getting Meline first!" he rumbled adamantly.

"I understand, but it is better you forget about your friends. We will be heading back to Duras soon. It is best to cut ties now."

"Did you forget that I'm half human, that even though you hate this place, it's the only home I know?"

"This is not home, mine or yours!" Petronus' brow furrowed. "You should not have to hide in a place you call home. Do not think I missed how you mutilated your horns in attempt to fit in here," Petronus spat in frustration and disgust.

"And I'll fit in better as a hybrid on Duras?" Roc countered.

"Yes! Our people are not closed off."

Roc shook his head. This was a pointless discussion.

"Forget about Duras and the sigil for a damn minute. There's no way in hell I'm leaving Meline with those bastards. We go that way." He pointed.

Petronus' eyes narrowed on him. "You mated this female!"

Disappointment and judgment rumbled in Petronus' voice. Mixing with the primitive humans was the ultimate sin. They weren't supposed to get involved and alter the human's natural course. Not that he cared. He refused to be ashamed of Meline.

"I haven't married her, but I do care what happens to her! I'm not a complete bastard. Sacrament, you're impossible."

"Marry?! That is an Earthian custom. I am talking about mating," Petronus scoffed.

"How would I know? You only ever insisted I stay away from humans and never bothered to explain the Khargal version of the birds and the bees," Roc railed at his sire. "No, it's not possible."

Roc shook his head in denial, not because he didn't want it to be true, but because in all his years and with all the females he'd met, it had never happened. It was almost too much to hope for. He couldn't imagine being mated to a better woman —or anything that frightened him more. It was because of him Meline was in danger.

Before Petronus could reply and explain what he was talking about, Cohosh's mobile pinged. Roc used the pin he'd forced out of Cohosh to access the message from Nightshade.

'Status update.'

I'd like a status update, too! But it's not like he could demand how Meline was doing, without making Nightshade suspicious.

The thought of what might be happening to her twisted him in knots. Even if they didn't rough her up like they did John, she had to be terrified after what they'd already done to her. The mere thought of her in tears made him want to rip something to shreds.

"Rochelle, you are going to break that device if you do not retract your claws," Petronus warned.

Roc grunted and sent the text, hoping his message was received, then hefted Cohosh off the branch.

"Let's go. We've wasted enough time," Roc huffed.

"The life of your Earthian is fleeting when compared to the risk the sigil poses."

"Enough, sire! I can't believe you. Did Mum honestly mean so little to you that you can't understand what Meline means to me? I was really starting to think maybe I had things all wrong about you, but I guess that was just me lying to myself like always," he snarled in anger.

"I can see there is no reasoning with you, so go, but I have to get my sigil. I will meet you at the rendezvous when I have it." Petronus took off toward New York City and Roc let him go.

It was the same old story with Petronus, honor and duty above all else. Maybe what he had with Meline was fleeting and there was no hope for them, but he wasn't about to leave her at the mercy of those fuckers for another second. He'd managed for centuries without Petronus, he could certainly do this alone.

MELINE

"So, what, are you planning on killing us when all this is over?" Meline demanded, interrupting whatever Nightshade was doing on his computer.

"Well, once we get the specific location of the relic out of him, the gargoyle will go to a facility. His kind has miraculous capabilities, but I think you're aware of that."

Her breath sped up and bile rose in her throat. They were going to turn Roc into a science experiment after torturing him. She started shaking and bit her lip to keep from vomiting.

"As for you, assuming we don't have to kill you to make a point, after my people question you, you're free to go," Nightshade added then shrugged as if it was all routine.

"You'll just let me go?! Why don't I believe that?"

Nightshade wore a suit and acted with a bit more restraint than the handful of thugs in black fatigues who kept eyeing her with malice, but she wasn't fooled. His thin veneer of sophistication hid an egomaniacal psychopath.

"My organization has a broad reach and support in high places, so it would be wise to not make trouble. But you go ahead and tell whoever you want about this. No one's going to believe an uneducated travel agent," Nightshade countered.

The barely veiled threat hit its mark. It was just like she feared; there was no end to this. Who would believe that some shadowy organization held her, a nobody, captive? The story was hard enough to take seriously even if she didn't mention alien gargoyles. The way Nightshade talked, these crazy bastards would always be watching, waiting for her to slip up. Then they'd undoubtedly make her life a living hell. And all the while Roc would be truly living a nightmare, being prodded and cut up.

Meline tipped her head back and looked at the ceiling, desperately trying to hold in her tears. She'd rather die than be faced with a future like this.

"Cohosh just replied." One of the gun-toting soldiers slid the cell phone toward Nightshade. "They just crossed the border into the states. He said it was easy as cherry pie."

Her head popped up at the man's choice of words. It couldn't be a coincidence. A thrill of excitement coursed through her. It was a message from Roc. It had to be. She just needed to be ready.

"Good." Nightshade nodded then glanced at her.

She quickly wiped the eager expression off her face, but he already caught it, his eyes narrowing on her.

"Something's not right. Load up. We're moving out," Nightshade snapped.

Fuck! Roc managed to send her a message and she ruined it.

The gunman with the broken nose cut her ropes, barely avoiding her wrists, then tugged her out of the chair.

"Don't do anything stupid." He gripped her arm and practically dragged her to the SUV parked in her garage.

Apparently, that's all I'm capable of.

The man shoved her into the back of the SUV as the others loaded their gear into the trunk. When he turned to shut his door, she wrenched her arm free and grabbed the handle on her side.

"No!" she screamed when it refused to open.

The thug grabbed the back of her neck and squeezed. "Child safety locks," he laughed.

Nightshade got into the front passenger seat and the overweight gunman started up the engine. As they pulled out of her driveway another nondescript vehicle joined them, leading the way down the road.

What am I going to do? This shit has to end here!

Meline neurotically played with her seatbelt as she stared out the window. It was the middle of the night and the only people on the road were the drunks leaving the bars. It didn't really matter, it could be broad daylight and she doubted anyone could help her. She didn't know what Roc had planned, but she'd obviously screwed it up tipping off Nightshade. Now it was up to her to figure a way out of this mess.

Something large that looked like a body suddenly slammed into the roof of the first SUV in their caravan.

"What the fuck?!" the driver bellowed as he swerved to avoid the careening vehicle, but failed to miss the body in the road.

She drew in a horrified gasp as the SUV bounced, driving over the unfortunate soul on the pavement. Meline quickly regained her wits. This was her chance. Before the driver corrected, she lunged forward and covered his eyes, her fingers digging in. She released every bit of rage and anguish for what they'd done to her family.

"Get her off me," the man screamed in agony, as her nails sliced into his vulnerable flesh.

Nightshade and the other gunman desperately tried to pry her hands away, but she held on, fueled by vengeance, tapping into strength she didn't know she had. Her fingers felt sticky as they sunk deeper into the wailing man's eyes. The SUV veered this way and that. Nightshade grabbed the wheel but overcorrected.

Meline was forced to let go when the car flipped. She frantically gripped her knees as everything somersaulted. Breaking glass cut her shoulder and arm when she slammed into the door and something else struck her in the head as it flew through the cabin. The SUV came to a stop and she hung from her seatbelt, the strap biting into her stomach. Nightshade groaned from the front seat. The gunman beside her lay crumpled and bloody on the glass-covered ceiling. The moron hadn't been wearing his seatbelt.

Despite the pain in her shoulder, she didn't waste any time getting out of her own belt. Meline repressed a cry as she dropped to the ceiling of the mangled car. The roof had caved in too much for her to climb out the broken window. She tugged on the door handle and kicked. Even damaged, the door still wouldn't budge.

"Come on!" she screamed at it.

"Meline!"

"Roc!" she yelled in reply to his frantic shout.

He was suddenly peering in through the mangled window. She couldn't have been more ecstatic if God himself descended to answer her prayer. Roc pried the door off its hinges with a determined roar. He reached in and gently pulled her out of the wreckage then cradled her against his chest. Before she could blink, he leapt into the air. The sound of gunfire coming from the ground below lit up the night, but the way Roc swiftly darted through the sky, they had no hope of hitting them. Meline clung tight to Roc's neck as he flew.

ROC

The sun was just peeking over the horizon when he landed in the only place he could think of that was safe in New York, the rooftop of Evensong.

"Are you okay?" His voice wavered as he stroked Meline's back.

He nearly died when the SUV barreled end over end. He'd missed the mark when he dropped the useless piece of shit, Cohosh. The man was supposed to land in the road as a distraction to stop the caravan, instead it hit the roof of the lead car. In his desperation to get Meline back, he nearly killed her. Everything slowed down as he watched the car flip, like he was watching both his life and hers flash before his eyes.

Roc ignored his minor injuries as he frantically looked Meline over. He ran his fingers up her left arm, cringing as he brushed away bits of shattered glass. None of her bones felt broken, but something horrific had happened to her hands. They were covered in blood. He gingerly took hold of her wrists as he examined her delicate fingers.

"It's not mine. I gouged a man's eyes out," she replied, sounding distant.

"Fuck! I'm so sorry. I didn't mean for this to happen." The thought of Meline having to defend herself made a panicked feeling grip his chest.

"They killed my parents," she admitted quietly, her chin quivering as tears welled up in her eyes.

"No!" The way she talked about her parents, they were good, loving people, like his mum. "I'll kill them all," he snarled.

"I just want this madness to stop." She shook her head.

"I'll take care of this and you'll be safe again," he promised. This was all his fault, but he'd make it right.

As he pulled her close and bent to kiss her, the door to the roof opened. Meline spun in his arms to face the intruder.

"It's okay," he reassured her when Giles, Evensong's bartender, came through the door.

"I thought I heard someone up here," the human said as he approached.

Roc didn't bother to retract his wings. This man was familiar with his kind.

"Sorry, Giles, I would've asked first but it was an emergency." Roc nodded toward Meline.

Giles' brow furrowed as he took in her disheveled appearance, then glanced over the rooftop toward the city. "You haven't brought trouble to my doorstep, have you?"

"Your bar's safe. The bastards who did this weren't able to recover fast enough from the crash to follow. They're still across the bay in Connecticut wondering what happened," he assured the man.

He was persona non grata at Evensong and Alkor's club in Canada. For some reason his Khargal brethren didn't appreciate the cavalier way he lived his life. Some nonsense about drawing too much attention.

Perhaps they're right. He frowned as he considered the position he'd put Meline in.

"Good." Giles nodded, looking more at ease.

"I'm Meline. Thanks for letting us stay." She reached out a hand.

"Shit!" Giles exclaimed, seeing how bloody her hands were.

"It's not my blood," Meline repeated as she pulled her hand back, then laughed morosely. "That has to be the most disturbing thing I've ever said."

"I can imagine." Giles cast a concerned glance at him.

"So where is that *Ray* of sunshine?" Roc asked. He'd only met the owner of this bar, a Khargal who went by Ray, a few times. But like all of the purebreds, the male was way too serious for his own good.

"Ray's away on business. I can't say when he'll return."

"Hmm." Roc nodded. Ray was no doubt on the same mission he was.

"I'll get you something to wash up with, some drinks and a jacket," Giles offered.

"Thank you." Meline smiled in appreciation.

"Yes, thank you. We won't impose on you long," he promised as Giles headed back downstairs.

The instant Giles left, he snared Meline around the waist and pulled her against his chest. They'd been interrupted before he had the chance to express just how relieved he was to see she was safe. His mouth ached with the need to kiss her sweet pink lips. Roc answered the imperative that had been gnawing at him, planting his mouth against hers. Meline stiffened in his arms. When he pulled back, he found her frowning.

"Ain't it a bitch when you want something you'll never let yourself have?" She pulled away from him.

"Meline, I'm…"

"No!" Meline held up her hand as she scowled at him. "I'm really glad you're safe and thank you for coming to my rescue but…" She shook her head in frustration as her face twisted into a sad frown. "I can't just forget the way you pushed me away."

"I'm sorry." He hung his head. "I thought I could take care of them and you'd be safe."

"That's just an excuse! You've been making a lifetime of excuses for holding people at arm's length. What's it going to be next time? I really thought we had something, Roc." Tears welled up in Meline's eyes and her shoulders sagged.

His heart broke watching Meline sit against the roof wall. He could literally see her pulling inside herself and away from him as she tugged her knees up against her chest.

Well, you got what you wanted. You drove her away. He clenched his fists, his claws digging into his palms.

MELINE

She couldn't believe Roc wanted to act like nothing happened. Granted she was so relieved to see him safe that she almost melted in his arms. Then she remembered the way he shut her out. A part of her was angry at him, but mostly she was sad. She wanted him to let her in, except it seemed too many years of hurt had hardened the wall around his heart.

Meline startled when a creature that made Roc look human landed on the rooftop.

"It's my sire," Roc reassured her. "I see you found the place just fine," he commented to his father.

So, this was Petronus. His wings were leathery and the talons at their tips were sharper than Roc's. This gargoyle had not two, but four horns jutting from his hairline, a large and small pair. She could see the family resemblance, but the bridge of Petronus' nose was more pronounced. His eyebrows were sharper, perched over stern, deep-set eyes. Petronus' lips were thin, and it looked like the alien man never smiled a day in his life. Her ancestor had been spot on with his frightening description.

She was surprised to see Roc's elusive father. A part of her was happy for Roc that he wasn't dead, but she also worried. This was the man who made Roc feel unwanted and undeserving of love.

"I see you rescued your female. I told you the Earthian would be fine. They are not interested in her." Petronus barely gave her a glance as he talked about her like she was a possession.

Nice. No wonder Roc was the way he was.

"No. She got hurt and wouldn't have been fine. They already tried to kill her once. But you wouldn't listen and took off after that fucking sigil when I needed your help," Roc growled.

"And if I had your help, I might have been successful retrieving the sigil. You know the risk it poses," Petronus snarled back.

"What did you do?"

"Earthians are far more advanced than last I remember." Petronus cast her an accusatory glance, like she was the reason he returned empty-handed.

"Unbelievable! You set off the alarms, didn't you?" Roc ran a frustrated hand through his wavy black hair.

"I did not expect them to use invisible light beams to

trigger their alarms, when the outside doors were secured with primitive tumblers and gears."

"Well if you were already in the museum, why didn't you just get the sigil?"

"Armed Earthians swarmed the vault before I got close," Petronus snapped.

"You couldn't just follow my lead. *Gracking Macero*!"

"Watch your mouth, Rochelle!" Petronus' tail lashed angrily.

Rochelle? Wow, okay. For such a masculine guy, she never expected him to have a name like that. *No wonder he shortened it.*

"No, sire, *you* screwed up. The people after us know the sigil's in New York City. They're going to see the botched robbery and will know it's not just a coincidence. Dammit!" Roc paced the rooftop.

"So, we go back tonight, when it gets dark again. And you can show me what you have learned since I saw you last." Petronus looked almost excited. It was the first time he showed true interest in Roc since landing.

"And those bastards will be expecting that," Roc huffed.

"What if we went now?" she asked, a plan forming in her mind.

"The authorities will be swarming the place. There's no way we'd get past them, much less into the vault." Roc shook his head.

"Not if we're invited in. I…" she reasoned.

"So, we create a chaotic situation to distract the soldiers," Petronus spoke over her.

Rude. She scowled.

"The building has numerous windows. I will rapidly break

them and create a diversion for you to get past the armed Earthians," Petronus continued.

"What happened to those rules of yours about not harming innocents and drawing attention?" Roc countered, his brow furrowed in frustration. "That stunt could hurt a lot of people and as fast as you can dive bomb a window, it could still be caught on camera."

Meline nodded in agreement with Roc. There'd been enough blood shed.

"This is a desperate situation," Petronus growled.

"Then why didn't you just barrel through the guards to begin with?" Roc snapped sarcastically.

She was done listening to them argue. Meline got up, equally pissed at the posturing men, and headed for the door leading down to the bar.

"Where are you going?" Roc asked.

She whirled angrily to face him. "I'm returning to my house, because we're going with my plan!"

"*Your* plan?!" Petronus scoffed.

"Yes," she growled at the difficult gargoyle. "I've been dragged along on this adventure without any say in what happens." Meline pointed an accusing finger at Roc. "You sent me home even though I begged you not to, and we see where that got us." She turned on Petronus. "And you ditched your son then botched your attempt to break into the museum. Maybe if you helped Roc, we wouldn't have to worry about the assholes hunting us. So, we're going with my plan!"

"Okay, okay. I'm listening. What's your plan?" Roc held up his hands.

"One of you is going to my house to get a few things and

find us a vehicle. Then I'm going to walk right through the front door of the museum."

"Angel, I've broken into a ton of places. You're going to need to do a little more than walk through the front door," he cajoled.

Roc was well meaning but she was so frustrated it felt patronizing.

"Don't you worry your pretty little head about that." She smirked at him. Roc might have a massive bank account and superhero strength, but he wasn't the only one who had the means to get into the museum.

❧ 16 ❧

MELINE

Meline glanced nervously at the entrance of the Queens Museum as she crossed the cobblestone courtyard. The sprawling building wasn't quite like she remembered. The edifice had been remodeled with panoramic glass windows that stretched two-stories high all along the front. She felt totally exposed. Anyone watching for her, inside or out, would see her coming from a mile away.

Maybe I should've thought more about this.

She suspected everyone who made eye contact of being the enemy and quickly hustled to join the back of a large group entering the museum. Roc was somewhere nearby, in a van, waiting for her call, and Petronus was lurking on the roof, but a lot could happen before either could reach her.

No. This will work. She pushed through the glass doors and headed to the customer service desk.

"I'm here to speak with your curator."

"We had a break-in last night, so I imagine Kendra is rather busy," the receptionist replied.

"I heard. I have a piece here on permanent loan and would like to see it."

"Oh. Your name?"

She hesitated to give her name, fearing Nightshade had connections in the museum, but her name was her ticket in.

Here goes nothing.

"Meline Lauber."

"All right, just a moment." The woman picked up the phone and made a call.

Meline stuck her nose in one of the pamphlets, resisting the urge to look around. She had a feeling Nightshade's minions were scoping out the museum. It was best if they didn't recognize her or this venture would go swiftly down the tube.

There's not enough deodorant in the universe for this three-ring circus. She surreptitiously sniffed herself and was grateful to find she didn't smell like a two-day old gym sock. *You wanted adventure. What do they say; beware of what you wish for?*

"Miss Lauber. Kendra Hammond." A smartly-dressed woman with glasses stuck out her hand and Meline shook it.

"Nice to meet you. Do you have someplace we can speak?"

"I apologize, it's been a very eventful morning." The curator frowned.

"I gather and have concerns about a piece my family loaned the museum."

"Of course. Right this way." Kendra held out her hand and Meline followed her lead. "So, it begins," the woman mumbled under her breath.

Meline had a feeling she wasn't supposed to hear that last

part but did. She imagined a lot of donors were going to be calling with concerns after seeing the news of the break-in. This was probably the curator's worst nightmare.

She has no clue. I could show you nightmares.

"I had a chance to look up the piece your family placed on loan with us. The stained-glass butterfly your grandfather created is a stunning example of his work while at the Tiffany Studio."

"Thank you." Meline eagerly looked toward the secure entrance they were approaching.

"The piece is currently in our vault. I guarantee it's perfectly safe," Kendra added.

"Still, I'd like to see it."

Kendra stopped just shy of the doors. *Oh, come on.* Meline wanted to groan.

"That may be a difficult request given all that's gone on." The curator hesitated, placing her access badge to the sensor.

Believe me, lady, you don't want that butterfly. It's nothing but trouble. But she couldn't say that.

ROC

The place was crawling with police and rent-a-cops. Nightshade undoubtedly infiltrated that group since they'd be able to get access anywhere. But the guests going in and out of the museum made him just as edgy. They looked benign but looks could be deceiving.

"What's taking so long?" Roc punched the steering wheel of the van. He should have heard from Meline by now.

He couldn't believe he agreed to let her go in alone without first making her explain the whole plan, but she'd insisted. The way her eyes flashed angrily as she squared off against them on the roof had him worried. Meline was a delicate, sweet creature, but in that moment, he was just a little bit afraid of what she might do. He'd actually looked around to make sure no sharp objects were within her reach. He'd already fucked up big time. Not going along with her plan would've added another nail to his coffin.

A flash on the museum roof caught his attention. Roc rolled his eyes as he signaled back. Petronus was getting impatient. The last thing he needed was his sire doing something rash. The burner cell pinged and Roc glanced at it.

"Thank *Lar*," he sighed, started up the van and pulled out of the parking lot.

Roc found his way to the access road behind the museum. He turned the corner and slammed on the brakes narrowly missing the cop car. Roc tugged his baseball cap low as he rolled down the window.

"This is a private drive. No admittance." The officer looked at him suspiciously.

"Sorry about that. I've got a delivery." He gestured to the crate in the back.

He didn't have a clue what was in the box, but Meline insisted he fetch it from her condo, along with a change of clothes. The mood she was in, he wasn't about to argue.

"The loading dock's at the end. Watch out. There's a lot of us around today."

"Yes, sir." He nodded to the officer.

Roc pulled forward and maneuvered down the ramp. He was relieved when the metal garage door lumbered up to reveal Meline standing on the dock. She looked good in the long-sleeve sweater dress. He could barely tell she'd been in an accident only hours ago. She stood up straight, shoulders back, confident and proud. Meline was handling this better than he was, which was utterly pathetic since he'd been in situations like this a million times.

But you've never had a female to worry about. His nerves were worse than they'd been on his first job.

Roc shoved down his anxiety and smiled at her then noticed the guard wearing a gun on his hip. His tail flicked in agitation, hidden in the baggy cargo pants he wore. Roc forced it to behave as he got out of the van and pulled the box from the back.

"Hello. I'm Kendra, chief curator. Do you need assistance?" The woman in glasses standing beside Meline introduced herself.

"I'm good. It's not that heavy. Nice to meet you." He nodded in greeting.

"Right this way." The woman gestured.

He carried the box through the hallways, growing more eager and restless with each secure door they went through, till finally they were in the heart of museum storage. His fingers itched, seeing the countless works of art hanging on dozens of rolling racks.

"Please, place the box here." The curator gestured to the examination table covered with padding. "Let's see what you brought." The woman looked excited.

Roc sympathized. He was curious, too. Meline couldn't unseal the box fast enough. The scent of old canvas instantly struck him as she lifted the lid. His eyes widened seeing the landscape she revealed. It was a gorgeous port scene. He looked at the signature and saw Meline's family name.

Of course. Her grandfather was an artist.

"This is exceptional," the curator beamed.

"I'm glad you like it." Meline smiled at the woman.

"I just have some paperwork for you to sign to make the donation official."

So that's how Meline managed to get us in. Roc shook his head. He couldn't believe she was giving up her grandfather's painting for him.

But getting into the museum was just half the problem. They still needed to retrieve the sigil and get out without raising suspicion.

The curator stepped away to grab the documents and he edged toward one of the aisles. Meline said the sigil had been crafted into a stained-glass butterfly, but he didn't see any stained-glass pieces in these first few rows.

"Roc," Meline hissed, giving him the evil eye when he started to wander off.

"What?" he mouthed. They were so close. They'd made it into the vault. If he could just get a look around.

"Would you like a tour once we're done here?" Kendra asked as she set the file in front of Meline.

"No. We sadly don't have time," Meline replied.

What? His eyes widened as he glared at her. This was the perfect excuse. Yes, they had time. The private plane ready to whisk them out of Dodge would wait for as long as this took.

She shook her head tersely and signed the documents.

"All right." Meline nodded and headed for the vault exit.

"Well, thank you, Miss Lauber. I was worried when you

first arrived, but I think this will please my director." Kendra shook Meline's hand.

Roc couldn't believe they were leaving. His steps slowed as they reached the door.

"Come on, slow poke." Meline grabbed his hand and tugged.

He gave her a look that spoke volumes and she pursed her lips as she goaded him out the door.

Dammit, his shoulders dropped as the vault sealed behind him.

"I knew I should've put up more of a fight when she said she had a plan," he mumbled as they headed back to the loading dock. Meline wasn't a seasoned thief.

"I heard that." She scowled, squeezing his hand till it smarted.

Shit, he winced.

"I'm sorry, but you're not cut out for this," he whispered back.

"Is everything okay?" Kendra looked back at them.

"He's just grumpy we didn't get a tour," Meline quickly covered.

"Maybe another day." The curator smiled as they reached the van. "All right, here you go." Kendra patted a crate sitting on the dock.

His eyes widened when the curator pulled back the padding to reveal the stained-glass butterfly. There in the center of its body was the sigil.

"Great. Thank you for being so understanding. My family has missed this." Meline nodded to the woman as the crate was resealed.

"We appreciate the exchange, and that you've entrusted us

with another of your grandfather's works, given recent circumstances."

Roc couldn't get the crate into the van fast enough. Meline hopped into the front seat and they pulled out of the dock. He expected a band of thugs or guards to pop up at any moment as they drove around the museum and exited onto the open road, but they never did. Roc flashed his lights, signaling his sire as they headed toward the highway.

"So…" Meline cast a smug glance his way.

"You did good," he admitted sheepishly.

"Yeah I did, and don't you forget it." She jabbed a finger at him.

"I'm sorry." He cringed at her acerbic tone. He felt like a total bastard for doubting her. "You refused to tell me the whole plan and I got worried when it took so long."

"Well I tried, but you guys decided you wanted to argue over top of me, 'cause what could the little helpless human possibly do compared to a big fancy art thief?" Meline huffed. She was angry, but he could hear the deep hurt lacing her voice.

"It was a brilliant plan. You're amazing. I'm truly sorry I didn't listen, and that you gave up your grandfather's painting, but I appreciate it," he replied, feeling even worse.

Meline nodded and they grew quiet as they drove toward the small airport where he had a private jet waiting. He concentrated on the road, keeping one eye out for cars that might be following them. Once they arrived, Roc grabbed the crate and followed Meline up the stairs of the plane.

"We're almost gassed up, if you'd like to take your seats." The pilot gestured toward the cabin.

"We have one more joining us, if you could just wait for a minute," he informed the pilot.

"Of course, sir." The man nodded.

Roc took a seat next to Meline and looked out the window. He watched the ground crew finish fueling up then leave. He kept darting his wary gaze up and down the tarmac. Meline had come through for him. Her plan didn't attract attention, and they came and went from the museum like any run of the mill delivery. But he couldn't help being suspicious of how well it went. Roc replayed the encounter he had with the cop outside the museum, and the expressions worn by the guard and curator. It all felt too easy.

A shadow near the hull of the plane captured his attention.

Finally. He watched his sire sneak into the baggage hold.

"I just got a text. We'll be going alone," Roc called to the pilot sitting in the cockpit.

"All right. We're cleared for take-off."

Roc sat on the edge of his seat as they taxied down the runway and didn't relax till they lifted off the ground. He cast a concerned glance at Meline when she released an audible sigh. Despite her bravado, this whole ordeal was wearing on her. She shouldn't have to shoulder the burden of evading his foes. On top of it, he'd hurt her.

I'm truly sorry, angel.

"I should check on my sire," he said after the plane leveled off.

She nodded then leaned her head against the window. He got up, grabbed the crate and headed toward the rear hold.

"The sigil is calling to me. Let me see it," Petronus said before he got one foot through the door.

"Here." Roc passed his sire the crate. Of course the sigil

was his sire's first concern. "I'm going to assume we weren't followed, since you didn't knock on the door."

"No." Petronus waved him off as he cracked open the lid then paused, a relieved expression crossing his stern face.

Roc couldn't recall seeing his sire look so happy before, maybe once, when he was young.

"Your Earthian did good." Petronus reverently lifted the butterfly out of the box.

"She did." Roc nodded.

Petronus' claw extended, and he gingerly pried the wings off the sigil. It seemed like a shame to ruin a beautiful piece of art, but it couldn't be avoided. Hopefully Meline wouldn't be hurt by this. The instant his sire held the sigil in his hand, a crimson light filled the cargo hold and a series of symbols shimmered over the surface of the odd blood-red stone.

"I need to compare this to a map," Petronus said as he read the Khargal script.

Roc pulled out the burner phone and brought up the map app then widened the view so his sire could see the entire continent.

"The coordinates are leading us here." Petronus pointed to Mount Nirvana on the map.

"That's in the Northwest territories, almost near Alaska."

Of course the pick-up location is in the middle of nowhere. Why wouldn't it be? Roc groaned.

"We need to hurry. It shows pick-up is less than a rotation away. Divert this vessel immediately." Petronus almost looked panicked.

"Shit! That soon?! It'll take most of that time just to get close. Can you shut off the self-destruct feature on that thing just in case we don't make it?"

Petronus swiped his finger over the sigil.

"It is off. Do not get your tail in a twist, Rochelle." His sire smirked at him.

"Oh, I'm sorry that an exploding alien device makes me nervous," he retorted. Petronus was unbelievable.

"Exploding?" Petronus snorted. "It does not explode."

"You always said the sigil was dangerous and would self-destruct if it was left behind."

"Yes. The Earthians are growing advanced and cannot have this. This technology is dangerous in their hands. They are not ready for it yet. And yes, it does self-destruct if left behind after we ascend, but it does not explode." Petronus shook his head as he laughed.

"You're a real piece of work," Roc growled. Yet again, his sire's lack of communication had left him in the dark. "I have no interest in going to Duras, so you're real lucky I did think it was going to explode. That's the only reason I tried so hard to find it, since your grumpy ass refused to rouse, no matter how many times I went to that damn dig site."

Petronus' brow furrowed, and he was silent for a moment.

"I am sorry. There is a lot I should have taken the time to tell you. I wish things had been different."

Roc's eyes widened hearing his sire's sincere apology. His shock doubled when Petronus gripped his shoulder. Strangely, he found it comforting.

"Why? Why did you retreat into the *duramna*?" he asked, trying to keep years of hurt from tingeing his voice.

"Your dam died, you left, and then Nicolas was sighted with me." Petronus' face contorted as old memories assailed him. "The religious zealots thought Nic was cavorting with the devil. I could not let him suffer and I was tired. We made up a story and put on a big show of him defeating then entombing me in stone. It was the only way."

"Oh." Roc nodded.

A host of emotions filled him. On one hand he was relieved Nicolas hadn't turned on his family, but on the other, he'd had everything wrong all these centuries. Yes, his sire retreated into the *duramna*, weary from life on Earth, but he had good reasons. Rather than being angry, the whole situation was devastatingly sad.

"Come to Duras with me. I understand you are enamored with Meline, but I do not want to lose you again. I have lost too many loved ones." Petronus squeezed his shoulder.

Roc's brow furrowed as his sire threw him for another loop. How long had he waited to hear him say those words? This was too much all at once.

"I have to go divert the plane." Roc gripped his sire's arm, returning the unexpected affectionate gesture, then left the luggage hold.

On his way to the cockpit he found Meline fast asleep. She'd been up all night and was exhausted. He couldn't blame her, this had been a non-stop adventure and he was weary to the bone. Everything his sire revealed and the events of the last few days were hitting him hard.

His life used to be so clear. All he had to decide was what to steal. But the moment he met Meline everything changed. She filled his shadowy world with light. And what did he do in return? He brought her danger and broke her heart. Was she right? Was he too afraid of losing her to hold on?

He clenched his fists in frustration.

That might be part of his problem, but the attempts on her life were very real. He'd been alone all this time for a reason;

he wasn't human, and never would be. He didn't want to let Meline down, but as long as he was in her life she'd be at risk. It didn't matter how much he wished it wasn't so.

Roc hung his head as he walked toward the cockpit. This was an impossible situation.

MELINE

"We're here" Roc rubbed her arm.

"Where's here?" Meline blinked in disbelief as she stared out the airplane window. It was dark but she was certain she saw snow-covered mountains beyond the runway.

"The middle of nowhere Canada. My sire learned the pick-up location was some remote peak in the Northwest territories."

"Northwest Canada! How long was I asleep?" She gaped at him.

"Eight hours. We just landed in a little place called Fort Laird, but we're still a hundred miles south of our destination."

Meline glanced out the window again, shocked she'd slept through the entire flight. Obviously, it had been uneventful. She'd been exhausted but there's no way she'd sleep through Nightshade ambushing the plane. Once they got off the ground that would've been near impossible. The asshole claimed to have connections, but she doubted he could scramble a fighter jet to shoot them out of the sky. Her shoulders eased. It was a relief to be half a continent away from that psychopath. And they actually succeeded retrieving the relic.

Her eyes widened when she caught Petronus sneaking out of the belly of the plane. She was glad there weren't that many spotlights and only a handful of bundled-up staff milling around the small airport. Petronus looked around then leapt into the sky, disappearing into the harsh arctic night.

"It would be a little hard for him to hide in the tiny puddle jumpers that venture north in these parts. It's cold, but not impossible for our kind to fly in this weather," Roc commented as he glanced out the window over her shoulder.

"He's going all alone?" She frowned. Petronus was a crusty character but he was Roc's dad, and despite being able to withstand the weather it didn't seem safe or right.

"No."

"Oh. You're going with him," Meline whispered, her heart suddenly in her throat, her eyes burning as tears formed.

So, this is goodbye. But this time it was for good.

Meline turned back toward the window, so he couldn't see her devastation. She should be happy for Roc. He was reunited with his only family and they were going back home where they wouldn't have to worry about people like Nightshade, except she couldn't muster a smile. Maybe it was foolish, but as long as he was here on Earth, a glimmer of hope lived inside her. But this—this was all so final.

Roc cupped her chin and gently tried to turn her to face him. She resisted. The last image she wanted him to have was of her ugly crying.

"Meline."

The pain in his voice had her relenting. Her breath stuttered out seeing his serious silver eyes.

"I've had a lot of time to think. I probably should go to Duras with my sire, we're apparently not that different," Roc laughed morosely. "Over the last few centuries I let myself grow hard as the rock we shift into. I found solace in things 'cause the thought of getting close to someone only to lose them to danger, illness or time…" Roc shook his head as he rubbed his chest.

He didn't need to finish that statement. She understood his pain only too well having lost her family. Tears streamed down her cheeks.

"I know the life I can offer you isn't what you deserve." Roc's brow furrowed as his voice grew thick. "But, angel, you make my life worth living, and are the only reason I can think of to stay. I love you so much."

She couldn't reach him fast enough. Meline threw her arms around Roc's neck and slammed her lips against his, pouring all the love she felt for him into her kiss. Her elation was magnified by the shear devastation she'd felt only a moment ago. Her heart was going to burst out of her chest.

"So, does this mean I'm forgiven and should stay?" he laughed, while clutching her so close it was almost hard to breathe.

"Yes!" She peppered his face with kisses as happy tears spilled from her eyes.

"Eh hmm," someone coughed and they both turned to see the pilot standing in the doorway of the cockpit. "I found a pilot heading up to the lodge at Glacier Lake, if you're still interested in reaching Nahanni National Park tonight. Apparently, it's the last run of the day." The man pointed outside to a tiny craft that actually had a propeller on its nose.

"Well, we better get going. I should see my father off," Roc said with an appreciative nod to the pilot as he opened the cabin door.

"Wait. You can't go out there like that," the pilot exclaimed, staring at her fall jacket and bare legs.

"Oh yeah, I guess I'm not dressed right for this weather." She frowned, shivering as a gust of wind and swirling snow invaded the airplane cabin.

"We didn't really think this through," Roc added, smirking at the blustery weather.

No, they hadn't, but it's not like they knew where the sigil was going to lead them.

"Here." The pilot kindly tugged off his coat.

"I can't take your jacket." She looked down at the offering.

"It's okay, it's old." The man thrust the jacket into her hand. "Sorry I don't have one for you."

"That's all right. Thank you. I really appreciate this." Roc helped her pull on the second layer before they headed down the steps.

It was cold as they hustled across the tarmac, especially on her legs, but they were only going a dozen yards to the waiting plane.

"Wait," she chattered, halting Roc as they neared the small craft. She reached up and fixed the hat threatening to blow off and reveal the remnants of his horns. "We can't expose that little surprise."

"Thanks, angel." He grinned, and they continued on.

"You the ones going up to Glacier Lake?" the pilot who looked like he never shaved a day in his life greeted them.

"Yes." Roc knocked snow off her as they ducked into the cramped cabin.

"Hey." Meline nodded to the two men in the back, dressed like park rangers, as she took one of the two remaining seats behind the pilot.

This was the smallest plane she'd ever been in. There was no way Petronus would've been able to hide in here. The cargo storage behind the four passenger seats made the trunk space in her car look lavish. Poor Roc could barely fit beside her. She felt bad as he hunched in the seat and his head still brushed the ceiling.

"You know it's just as cold, maybe colder, where we're going, right?" one of the rangers asked with a scornful cock of his brow.

"I've got gear for sale if you've got cash," the shaggy pilot interjected.

Meline had a feeling the man made a small fortune off ill-equipped tourists. He probably saw dollar signs the second they approached his plane.

"Sold!" Roc said without batting an eye as he got out his wallet. "How does a grand sound for a coat for me, and enough to cover my girlfriend from head to toe?"

"You got it." The pilot licked his lips greedily as he took the handful of bills.

"I bet people like us keep you in business," she commented to the rangers, attempting to make small talk as the pilot exited.

The pair nodded, but didn't reply. Instead they stared dubiously at them like they were morons. She could only imagine what kind of trouble ignorant tourists got into up here in God's country.

Meline shivered when the pilot got back in toting a large bundle that he handed off to Roc.

"I'm glad I stopped at the ATM before our little adventure this morning," he whispered as he helped her shimmy into the coat and snow pants.

"Me, too. Thanks." She beamed at Roc, then cozied against his side as he wrapped an arm around her.

"Can we get going?" one of the rangers piped up.

"I'm going," the gruff pilot rumbled as he started up the engine and taxied down the runway.

Anxiety thrummed with every beat of her heart as they took off, shocked they didn't skid all over the icy tarmac as they built up speed. It was dark once they got in the air, but surprisingly the snow on the ground glowed in the moonlight. The plane stayed low, skimming the harsh landscape, and it seemed like the pilot was following a river cutting through the trees heading toward the nearby snowy peaks.

That must be how they find their way around up here.

"I learned a little something about Nicolas while you were sleeping," Roc spoke in hushed tones.

"Really?" She turned away from the chilly wonder to focus on him.

As Meline stared at his ruggedly handsome face, she could hardly believe the twist of fate that brought them together. Never in her wildest dreams had she imagined her boring little vacation would drop love in her lap, much less someone so unique. Her heart swelled, and she sighed happily.

"Apparently the harsh stuff in the journal was all a ruse to throw off the church and keep Nicolas safe." Roc paused and took a second look at her. His eyes crinkled up as he grinned. "Your head is elsewhere, isn't it?"

"Yes, but that's nice to know." A flicker of green caught her attention over his shoulder. "Oh. Are those the northern lights?"

"Yes, ma'am. You picked a good time of year to come see them," the pilot replied over his shoulder.

"They're gorgeous."

"I can think of something lovelier," Roc whispered suggestively into her ear.

"Stop," she giggled and elbowed him gently, then cast a glance at the rangers.

Oh my god, they're staring. It was so embarrassing the way they smirked at her. She could almost hear the pair telling them to 'get a room.'

Meline shoved down her embarrassment. She was too giddy to really care what the grumpy rangers thought. They were probably just sour they had to go back to work, and their job was in the deep freeze.

She glanced back out at the glorious sight and nearly squealed in shock. Silhouetted against the wavering green lights was a giant winged creature. The dark shadow of Petronus looked like something straight out of the Jurassic era.

Oh fuck! Think fast before anyone sees.

"You know what I have planned when we get to the lodge?" she whispered loud enough the others could hear as she licked the shell of Roc's ear.

He pulled back and cast her a shocked questioning glance.

"Petronus," she mouthed and overtly glanced toward the window.

Roc closed his eyes in frustration for a moment.

"No, what?" he husked, playing along.

"Well, I won't be needing all these layers, 'cause we won't be going out much," she purred into his ear.

"My angel is wicked."

Meline didn't need to cast a surreptitious glance at the others to know her little act had their attention. She could hear their heavy breathing and something else, something subtler, like rapid heartbeats. Even Roc's had kicked up in tempo. It was so strange that she was able to hear all that.

"He's gone," Roc mouthed after glancing out the window, drawing her attention back to their dilemma.

That was close. She sighed in relief.

"But I wouldn't mind if you continued telling me all that you have planned," he whispered into her ear, too quiet for anyone to hear.

"Oh. That's for me to know and you to find out," she giggled.

When she squeezed his thigh, she felt something thick jump beneath her palm. Her mouth parted in surprise as her gaze flew to his. She knew he was turned on but didn't realize how much.

"That's my tail," Roc whispered in her ear as he twitched it again. "I think what you're looking for is over here." He moved her hand to his other thigh, and she felt a thick, warm bulge through his pants.

"Oh my god, you're awful." She laughed and smacked his knee.

"Yeah, but you like it," he chuckled.

"Oh, look, we're getting close to the mountains," she redirected the ornery beast.

"I bet my father would love seeing this."

Meline repressed a snort at the unexpected reference to the man who instigated the rowdy banter.

"Your father would be nothing but trouble if he were up here with us. But I'm starting to question who's the bigger pain in the ass."

"Who, me?!" Roc's eyes widened and his mouth gaped in mock innocence.

She shook her head. From the moment she met Roc her life had been anything but dull.

The sudden gust of wind behind them caught her by surprise. She glanced back, and her eyes widened just as the second ranger jumped out of the plane. She had no idea they had to leap out in the middle of nowhere for their jobs. If she did, she wouldn't have been so critical earlier.

"What the fuck?!" the pilot barked, and she realized this wasn't normal.

Her gaze swiveled to Roc and panic struck seeing the dark expression on his face.

❧ 18 ❧

ROC

The two rangers had been grim from the moment they got onto the Cessna. He should've suspected something was wrong.

"Oh God," Meline screeched and scrambled to put her seatbelt on as the suicide door beside her flew open.

He gripped her jacket to keep her from falling as he leaned over and reached for the red door handle.

The sudden explosion in the engine rocked the plane.

"Fuck!" the pilot yelled as smoke and fire burst from the nose of the aircraft.

Roc looked in horror at the rapidly approaching mountainside the stalled Cessna was diving toward. He couldn't get his coat off fast enough in the cramped cabin. There wasn't enough time. Swiftly he grabbed Meline, but only got a grip on her thick coat before leaping out the open door.

"Roc!" she screamed, the arctic wind battering them as they free fell. It threatened to tear her from his grasp.

"Grab onto me!" he yelled over the deafening torrent.

236

He tugged Meline closer, but her oversized coat was slipping. He clawed at his jacket, desperate to release his straining wings while struggling to hold on to her. He only bought the damn thing to keep up appearances. He couldn't even free his tail.

"I'm trying." Meline's clasping fingers grabbed ahold of his pant leg.

The explosion as the plane struck the mountain sent a hot shockwave reverberating through the air, and Meline lost her grasp on his leg.

"Fuck," Roc growled.

He let go of his jacket and used both hands to tug her against him.

"I'm good." She tackled his waist with a death grip that was surprisingly strong.

Roc glanced down at the rapidly approaching treetops. He grit his jaw in determination and shred the remains of his jacket, letting his wings burst free. They rustled the upper most branches of the towering pines as he churned the air, bringing their downward descent to a halt.

"Oh God," Meline sighed in relief when they started to climb again.

"You can say that again."

His heart was pounding so hard in his ears that he didn't hear the steady drone of the helicopter blades until it was too late. Suddenly something tangled in his wings. Meline's eyes widened as they started falling again. Roc desperately tried to envelop her in his pinions, but the net had them completely ensnared. Meline was vulnerable.

He clutched her close, his palm cradling the back of her head as they hit the forest canopy. Roc twist, trying to angle himself as they struck the branches, snapping several limbs as they fell. He fought the temptation to harden his *duramna*. If he could wrap his wings around Meline, shelling would protect her, but that wasn't an option. He couldn't risk wounding her if they landed wrong.

Roc tried to grab the first big limb, but it gave way. His back slammed into the next thick bough forcing the air from his chest. He pitched forward and had to release Meline entirely to shove off the trunk before crushing her.

"No!" he roared as she lost her hold on him and fell.

"Roc!" she screamed then went quiet when she hit a branch.

He watched in abject horror as her limp body tumbled the rest of the way to the ground, landing amidst the brush. The second he hit the ground he raced over and picked his way through the thick undergrowth to find her face down in the snow.

"Please be okay," he prayed. "Angel," his voice broke as he gently turned her over then saw blood in the snow. There was a nasty gash on her forehead.

Roc panicked. He couldn't hear her heartbeat through all the thick layers and the thundering of his own. His hands shook as he unzipped her coat. Just as he was about to feel for a pulse, the snow crunched behind him and he froze. Through the thick brush, he watched a man in all white creeping slowly between the trees. He didn't need to see the face beneath the ski mask to know Nightshade was behind this.

It was dark, but the moonlight cast enough light that the armed man quickly located the branches he'd broken during the fall, and was about to find his footprints leading to Meline.

He couldn't allow that. Roc hardened his *duramna* as rage burned through his veins.

This ends today.

He burst out of the brush, launching directly for the mercenary. Before the man could get off a shot he was on him. Roc wrenched the bastard's gun away and tossed it.

"Where is that asshole?" he snarled.

The man refused to answer. Roc gripped the fucker's head and twisted without a second thought. But the crunching sound of his neck breaking wasn't nearly satisfying enough. His angel lay battered in the snow. Every last one of these psychopaths would pay.

A sharp pain struck his back. Roc glanced down to see what looked like a harpoon protruding through his shoulder. He roared and spun on his assailant. Roc started tugging the chain attached to the harpoon, reeling the mercenary in. Five more men stepped into the small clearing and leveled their rifles at him. Among them, the two park rangers.

"No! I want him alive. Secure that chain to a tree."

Roc recognized the voice muffled by a ski mask. His gaze swiveled toward Nightshade.

"You want me? Come and get me yourself!" he bellowed, his voice so deep it brought snow cascading down from the branches above.

The mercenary holding the chain couldn't pull hard enough. Roc ignored the stabbing pain radiating down his arm as he stormed toward the megalomaniac, dragging his would-be captor behind him. Someone else grabbed the net tangled in his wings. The butt of a gun struck the back of his head. Roc staggered but nothing would distract him from his goal.

Nightshade's eyes widened. He knew death was coming and nothing would deter it.

"Shoot him!" Nightshade yelled.

The bastard on his back swiftly retreated as the men on either side of Nightshade raised their weapons. Roc paused, though not because of the threat they posed. He started laughing. Nightshade held his hand up to halt the mercenaries before they opened fire.

"Obviously you see the futility of resisting. At this range even you are no match for semi-automatic weapons," Nightshade smugly boasted.

"Hardly," Roc laughed like a mad man, then nodded to the trees.

Petronus leapt down behind the two gunmen. Nightshade spun in time to witness his sire lunge, wings extended. It was a gruesome, satisfying sight, watching the way his sire stabbed the two lackeys in the back, the talons on his wingtips bursting out the front of their chests. Their blood sprayed everywhere, staining the pristine snow as they dropped to the ground. Nightshade took off running when Petronus grabbed one of their guns.

"Fuck!" the mercenary who'd been on his back yelled.

It was a dumb move. Petronus swung toward the fool and opened fire, killing the man instantly. Roc felt the pressure on the harpoon in his shoulder go lax and heard his assailant take off. Petronus took aim.

"No. I've got this," Roc said as he snapped off the protruding end of the harpoon.

He took aim and launched the barb. It hit its mark, spearing straight through the final mercenary, pinning him to a nearby tree.

"Very nice aim." Petronus glanced around in satisfaction at the dead gunmen.

"You have to go after Nightshade, before he reaches the helicopter. I refuse to let that fucker get away. I need to get Meline. She's hurt." His face twisted into a grim frown.

Lar, please let her be okay, he begged the Khargal deity he never saw cause to worship before today.

"I am sorry. I kept my distance when I realized you spotted me from the craft. By the time I saw what was going on I was too far away to help." Petronus' brow furrowed. "Let me help you."

Petronus carefully pulled the rest of the harpoon from Roc's shoulder. Even without the barbed tip it stung like a bitch.

"Thank you, sire," Roc said as Petronus untangled the net from his wings.

"It does not look bad. Clean through."

"I'm fine." Roc flexed his arms and wings. "But Meline's not." He rushed back to the tangle of undergrowth at the edge of the clearing. "Please, go kill that asshole."

Roc wanted to see Nightshade's life as it fled his body. But he needed to see to Meline first. She meant far more to him than vengeance.

"He will not get far. This is more important." Petronus helped him pull back the brush.

Roc was stunned for a moment by his sire's consideration then returned to his task of clearing the growth.

"She's gone!" Roc looked around in confusion.

MELINE

Meline came to. She batted away the brush and sat up. Her ears were ringing, making it hard to get her bearings. It was taxing crawling through the snow, out of the undergrowth. She was so dizzy she had to pause and steady herself against a pine tree. There was something crusty when she felt the sore spot on her forehead. She pulled her hand away and stared at the dried blood.

Roc!

The memory of falling flashed through her mind. Mostly it was the horror on Roc's face she recalled. Meline pulled herself off the ground and staggered forward, looking left and right for evidence of where he landed. She grabbed ahold of a tree as another round of dizziness hit her. Meline growled in frustration. She needed to find Roc. The double vision and the ringing in her ears weren't helping.

Meline pushed on, despite being disoriented, grabbing the trees she passed to keep from falling down. Every step she took she grew more worried and determined to find Roc. She knew she wasn't well when she crossed Roc's path and instead of one set of footprints she saw several. Meline blinked to clear her vision and rubbed her ears to get rid of the annoying popping, but it persisted.

I hit my head good. She wasn't sure how many more knocks she could take before something rattled loose in her brain.

She followed Roc's tracks, eager to find him. He had to be frantic, desperately looking for her, like she was him. As it was, he blamed himself for every little thing that happened to her. She couldn't let him worry. Meline reached the river and stopped dead in her tracks as she stared at the helicopter sitting on the bank.

Shit! The rest of what happened to them flooded back like a nightmare. *Roc!*

Meline whirled around and gaped at the tracks she'd followed. She hadn't been seeing things. Those weren't Roc's footprints in the show. Her breath sped up as she realized what the loud popping had been. It was gunfire. How had she not recognized that?

I have to do something. But what?

Her first instinct was to race back the way she came. The people after them had obviously been shooting for a reason. She couldn't leave Roc to defend himself.

What exactly are you going to do? You're unarmed.

She warily looked around, seeing no one guarding the helicopter, Meline raced toward it. She opened the door and climbed into the back, looking for a weapon.

"Dammit. Surely you brought more guns." But all she found was camping gear.

Rustling in the tree line captured her attention. She peered out the helicopter window then quickly ducked back down behind the pilot's seat when she saw who was emerging from the woods.

Nightshade! Shit. Shit. Shit!

Frantically she grabbed a sleeping bag, unrolled it, and pulled it over her, then piled several packs on top. She'd barely covered her head when Nightshade flung open the helicopter door. It was dark but not nearly dark enough. She repressed a startled sound when she heard him toss in his rifle then climb into the pilot's seat. Meline forced her breathing to slow as she huddled beneath the pile of gear. Her heartbeat was pounding a mile a minute, but she heard Nightshade flip several switches.

Oh crap! He's going to take off with me stowed in the back.

"What the fuck?" Nightshade cursed.

He slammed the door as he got back out of the helicopter. Meline poked her head up and saw the harried man throw open the engine hatch. Obviously, something was wrong. Her gaze flew to the rifle in the front seat. Now was her chance, while Nightshade was preoccupied. Ever so carefully, she rose and reached for the rifle, keeping a nervous eye on the window.

Her fingers grazed the cold metal when Nightshade abruptly stopped fiddling with the engine and turned toward the woods. She ducked back down and hid again before he opened the door.

"I don't care how valuable those monsters are. I'm not about to sacrifice myself for anything or anyone," Nightshade muttered as he rustled around the front seat.

He cocked the gun, chambering a bullet. The sound was so close she started to tremble, wondering if her hiding spot had been discovered. But when he didn't yank the sleeping bag back, she gathered her courage and slowly lifted the edge to peer out. She breathed a sigh of relief to find Nightshade standing in the open door, his back facing her. He was pointing the rifle at the woods. That could only mean one thing.

Anger filled her as she thought about what the evil man had done to her family and planned to do to the man she loved. Her gaze drifted to a hunting knife strapped to the side of a backpack. There was movement in the tree line and Nightshade took aim.

You will not hurt my man!

ROC

P anic filled him as Meline's tracks merged with the others.

"They are going toward the flying vehicle," Petronus noted as he studied the snow.

"It doesn't look like she struggled." Roc tried to make sense of the footprints.

"Maybe the vile Earthian did not capture her."

Roc was relieved Meline was up and moving. It didn't make sense after the way she fell. He thought for certain she was horribly injured. He even feared she'd broken her neck. He'd been unbelievably relieved to see her tracks leading away from the clearing. Except now she was wandering straight into danger.

"We have to go before that fucker hurts her or takes off with her."

Roc lifted off the ground, darting between the trees. He heard the rush of water as he neared the river.

"Rochelle, no." Petronus snagged his tail, hauling him out of the air, just before they emerged from the woods. "I disabled the vehicle; they are not going anywhere. Now, we must be smart, or he will hurt her."

Roc nodded. His sire was right. He gingerly approached the tree line then ducked behind a large trunk when he saw

Nightshade aiming the rifle into the woods. Petronus took up a similar position nearby. Roc panned the river bank.

Where are you, angel?

His eyes widened when he saw the moonlight reflect off something inside the helicopter. Faster than should've been possible, Meline leapt onto Nightshade's back and plunged the knife into his neck with a feral scream. Blood sprayed everywhere as she severed the unsuspecting man's carotid. Nightshade's eyes widened, and his mouth bobbed open, making gurgling sounds as he dropped his rifle. Relentlessly, Meline gripped Nightshade's hair and drove the knife deeper.

Roc recovered from the stunning sight of his female exacting her revenge on the man and swooped in.

"Angel?" he asked in concern, seeing the way she still had a death grip on Nightshade, even though the man was no longer a threat. He had no clue how such a little thing could possibly hold up all that dead weight.

It took a moment for Meline to focus on him, her rage shifting to relief then horror.

"Roc!" She dropped the body and started hyperventilating as she looked from him to her bloody hands.

"It's okay." He quickly pulled her to him. "You're okay!"

It wasn't the dead fucker's blood that concerned him. He turned Meline's head and examined her wound. The nasty gash on her forehead wasn't nearly as gruesome as he remembered. In fact, it looked like little more than an unpleasant cut. He didn't know how it was possible but wasn't about to question it. Amazed and relieved, he enveloped her with his wings.

"We need to get out of here. This area is remote, but those Earthians tracked us somehow. There could be more," Petronus interjected, pulling Roc from his momentary respite.

Sacrament! he cursed, reminded of the frigid wasteland and potential danger that still lurked nearby.

"Too bad you sabotaged their helicopter." Roc frowned. "I don't like the idea of flying with Meline in this weather." She was starting to shake so hard in his arms that he was becoming concerned.

"I'm okay. Not cold." Her voice was muffled inside the cocoon of his wings, but he still heard her teeth clack together.

"You're coming down from an adrenaline high."

"We can bundle her up in one of these sacks." Petronus pulled a sleeping bag out of the helicopter.

"That should work." Roc took the downy bundle and helped Meline into it.

He made sure she was secure before lifting off into the air, heading north with Petronus soaring by his side.

 19

ROC

"Is that a dwelling in that clearing by the stream?" Petronus shouted into the wind.

A surge of hope filled Roc till he glanced down. He couldn't see through the steam rising from the small hot spring at the edge of the river. The trees surrounding the clearing acted like a bowl, preventing the wind from driving away the mist.

"Let's get a closer look," he agreed.

If he was going to build a cabin in the middle of nowhere, near a hot spring would be a prime location. And it couldn't come soon enough. Roc was worried, very worried about Meline. He foolishly thought they left their worries behind them in New York, however, the last leg of this journey was proving just as treacherous. She survived falling, and escaped an ambush by gunmen, but if they didn't find shelter, hypothermia would do her in.

"Let me make sure it is not inhabited." Petronus nodded to him.

Petronus dove through the cloud of vapor while Roc held back with his precious bundled cargo in his arms.

"That's a heated pool, isn't it?" Meline asked as he headed for a large pine tree a safe distance away.

"It is."

"You think I can bathe in it?" The desperate tone in her voice made his gut twist.

Meline was still shivering despite the layers sheltering her from the elements, but at least she was speaking. Her silence as they flew had worried him. He landed on a thick branch, leaned against the trunk and pulled her against his body.

"I'll add a mountain of snow if it's too hot. Or fan it with my wings," he teased, though in all seriousness, he'd move heaven and Earth to give her whatever she wanted.

Roc's brow furrowed as he looked at the tiny bit of Meline's face poking out from the cinched-up sleeping bag. Usually she would've laughed or given him a smile when he made such boasts. Instead, she didn't even look him in the eyes.

"I'm sorry for all of this. What you did back there..." He was supposed to protect her, not the other way around.

"I'm not your sweet angel," she sobbed, her face contorting as she burst, tears welling up in her eyes and spilling down her cheeks.

"No, no, no. You are still sweet, angel." He leaned in and kissed away her tears, hoping his lips weren't too cold.

"I'm not. I stabbed him, killed him, and I'm not even sorry," she hiccupped. "Oh God, I probably killed those men in the car wreck, too, didn't I?" Her trembling turned into full body shudders.

Shit! Say something to make this better. But he didn't

know if he could. The look of horror in Meline's eyes broke his heart. This was exactly what he feared life with him would be like.

Before he could come up with something to soothe her, Petronus swooped in.

"The cabin is empty," his sire reported. "I started a fire inside."

Roc sighed in relief. At least they had that going for them.

"Is she okay?" Petronus mouthed and frowned as he cast Meline a sideways glance.

Roc shook his head no, gripped Meline tight and followed Petronus. They landed outside the one-story log cabin and went inside.

"Good." Roc nodded, seeing the large stack of dry firewood piled near the fireplace. They could hole up here till he found a way to get back to civilization.

"It is already getting warm." Petronus added another log to the fire.

"Here you go. Relax." Roc sat Meline in a chair by the fireplace, kneeled in front of her and loosened the tie around the sleeping bag. He frowned seeing the frozen tears stuck in her eyelashes. "Everything will be okay soon."

"Rochelle, it is time. I will wait outside."

Roc's frown deepened as he watched his sire leave the cabin. He hadn't thought saying goodbye to Petronus would affect him this way, but the sudden hollow feeling in the pit of his stomach was hitting him hard.

"Will you be okay? I need to say goodbye and tell him I'm not going."

Meline nodded. Her sad expression reflected the way he felt. He kissed her forehead and stood.

Roc found his sire outside staring at the nearby snowy peak and the wavering northern lights. He stepped beside him and took in the majestic sight.

"I never imagined I would miss this place," Petronus whispered after a minute.

"I'm going to miss this, too," Roc replied, though he wasn't talking about the impressive landscape. "Sire, I'm not going with you."

"I know." Petronus wrapped one wing around him and pulled him closer.

Roc looked at his sire's soft expression and realized Petronus was also saying he'd miss him.

"Rochelle, do not make the same mistakes I did. Nothing in life is ever perfect. I foolishly wallowed in my misery, not truly appreciating what I had until it was too late and my precious Theresa was gone. And I lost you in the process."

"Mum knew you loved her. Remember how she would grin when you'd huff and puff?" Roc smiled at the happy memory.

"I do." Petronus face took on a wistful expression. "And I remember the way she used to look at you. She never cared that you were different. It is the same way that female in there looks at you."

"I love her. I never realized I could love anyone so much. It almost hurts. I don't know how I'm going to manage." Roc frowned. "She's going to be gone in the blink of an eye if I don't get her killed first." The thought of watching Meline grow old and die was crippling.

"No, your *Hondassa* is strong, a fighter to rival any Khargal female. She has proven that these last few days. Kiss Meline often. Mate her often and you will have a long life together. If I had taken my own advice Theresa might still be with us."

Roc's eyes widened as what his sire meant sank in. Suddenly the memory of Petronus desperately kissing his mum as she died made sense.

"I'm changing her, aren't I?" Roc exclaimed.

He'd noticed the way she was stronger, healed faster, could smell and see better, but had brushed it aside with all the chaos. An indescribable sense of relief filled him.

"Yes. I really did you a disservice not explaining things." Petronus shook his head in regret. "That needy feeling, the way your gums itch and you salivate, that is the mating hormone, the *dassa*. The more she has, the longer she will live and resist the diseases Earthians succumb to."

"I can do that." Roc grinned.

"I am sure you can," Petronus chuckled then grew serious. "I should be going."

Roc wrapped his arms around his sire. "You don't have to go."

"I love you, *mon fils*..." Petronus replied, sounding torn.

"But you miss your home and the clan you left behind," Roc added for him. "I understand. You deserve to find happiness."

"Thank you. I wish I could have both," Petronus' voice wavered with emotion.

"Maybe you could come back for a visit." Roc smiled hopefully, though he had a feeling that wouldn't be possible.

"I would like that. Now, go take care of your *Hondassa*." Petronus squeezed him one last time then stepped back and lifted into the air.

"I love you," Roc blurted before he missed the chance.

"I never regretted having you in my life. No matter the distance, I carry you always." Petronus smiled, letting his tail drift down to ruffle Roc's hair, the way he used to do when he was young.

"Goodbye," Roc whispered as he watched his sire disappear.

MELINE

As she stared into the fire, Meline replayed all the horrific things she'd done over the last few days. She was a monster. That's what they called people who had no remorse when they killed.

No. That awful man killed my parents and was going to hurt Roc. She refused to regret protecting the man she loved.

And yet it came so easily. She flexed her fingers inside the sleeping bag. She could still feel the way the knife felt in her hand as she plunged it into the fucker's neck.

The road to hell is paved with good intention. Was this how psychopaths justified one murderous act after another?

Meline shook her head. Roc needed to know she could hold her own. He'd get sick of her real fast if she lost her shit whenever things got serious.

You told him you could handle this, so pull it together.

It was getting warm in the cozy little cabin. She peeled the sleeping bag off and noticed the dried blood all over her hands.

"Aw God. I need wash." She blanched at the gruesome sight.

Meline went over to the small sink and turned on the faucet, but nothing came out. No doubt the owner shut off the plumbing to keep it from freezing.

"Dammit."

There was a curtain partitioning off the corner. She pulled it aside to reveal the indoor version of an outhouse.

Nope. I'd rather go squat in the snow.

Meline looked around the cabin. Besides the kitchen, which was little more than a non-functional sink, a wood burning stove, and an island that doubled as a table, there was a narrow bed with a trunk at the foot of it and the two chairs by the fireplace.

"Beggars can't be choosers, but this is a far cry from the lake-side lodge we talked about earlier. A shower would be nice, except the water wouldn't work in it either."

She gave up her search. It looked like the only way she was going to wash up was out in the hot spring.

There was a gust of cold air as the door opened.

"Are you okay?" Roc asked quietly, his voice filled with concern.

"There's no running water to wash this blood off."

Meline glanced up from her filthy hands to see Roc wearing the saddest expression she'd ever seen.

Oh my god, I'm the most selfish bitch ever. He just said goodbye to his dad.

"I'm doing better now. Are you okay?" She hurried around the island and wrapped her arms around him.

"He's gone—again," he whispered and pressed his lips against the top of her head, kissing her crown.

"I'm sorry." Meline squeezed him tighter. She hurt for him.

It was amazing how he made her feel better just by being near. Hopefully she did the same for him. Roc pulled her hands up and frowned at all the blood.

"Let's get this off you. If you think you can brave the cold to get to the spring?"

"I think so." She nodded.

"I'm sorry. I never meant for you…" His brow furrowed.

Meline shook her head to silence him.

"None of that. I'm okay, really. It just freaked me out that I killed him and didn't even blink an eye. But I'd do it again to protect you," she insisted.

"It's my job to protect and care for you." Roc shook his head as he turned her hands over in his larger ones.

"But I'm your angel, what good am I if I can't watch over you?" Meline smiled up at him.

"Yeah you are." He grinned and leaned in to kiss her.

"No way. I'm dirty!" She danced away and ran for the cabin door.

With a giggle she pulled off her coat, tossing it into the snow as she headed for the steamy pool. A hungry growl hot on her heels had her yanking her dress over her head as she ran faster. She reached the spring, tugged off her shoes and dipped her toe in. The water was nice and warm. Meline stripped out of the snow pants, taking her panties with them, and waded in.

She turned to find Roc stalking toward her in only a pair of boxers, a trail a clothing littering the snow behind him. Roc's wings rustled in the wind. She soaked in the impressive sight, glad he didn't put them away. She loved every bit of him, from his broad shoulders and muscular chest, down to those ripped abs and corded thighs. His tail flicked behind him, like a predator on the hunt. Her gaze darted to his hips and she sucked in a deep breath seeing the way his cock tented his boxers.

"I was about to kiss you and you ran. That's unacceptable, wicked little angel," Roc rumbled, his voice so deep she was surprised it didn't melt the surrounding snow the way it did her insides.

The serious expression on Roc's rugged face and the way his silver eyes flashed in the moonlight said he meant business. She retreated into the heated pool, keeping her eyes glued to her intense lover. The water was warm, yet the sight of him mixed with the sensual rebuke made her shiver.

"You're just sore I beat you," she gave a slight laugh, unable to hide the nervous giddy sensation he incited.

"No. I warned you never to run from me, with good reason."

Roc stopped at the edge of the pool. His heated gaze raked over her as he hooked his boxers and lowered them. Her heart started pounding harder as she stared at how hard and thick his cock was. The ridges beneath his broad crown made her pussy ache with need as she recalled how they felt sliding into her. Meline stifled a startled sound when the beast of a cock got closer as Roc stepped into the hot spring. It was crazy how she gravitated toward him but wanted to flee all in the same breath.

"From now on, you will let me kiss you whenever and wherever I want," he informed her.

Her mouth dropped open at the demand. Not that she disagreed but that was a little presumptuous.

"Is that so?" She arched her brows at him.

"Yes." Roc's tail lashed out and wrapped around her waist.

"And you'll let me stick my cock in you whenever and wherever I want." His tail tugged her against his firm body, his arousal grinding into her stomach to punctuate his illicit edict.

"Hold up there, buddy." Meline pressed her palms against his chest. "I draw the line at your monster cock going wherever you want!"

Roc cupped her ass cheeks with both hands and spread them. She jumped when the tip of his tail slid along her crack, teasing her puckered opening.

"You don't mean that. I've seen the way you orgasm when I play with your tight little ass." He cast her a sardonic smirk as he pressed the tip of his tail into her trembling ass. Her mouth dropped open at how audacious he was as he wiggled the appendage.

Two could play at this game. She reached down and gripped his cock with one hand and cupped his balls with the other. Roc groaned and widened his stance as she stroked his length while massaging the firm pair of globes between his thighs. She gasped and nearly forgot what she was doing when Roc's tail pressed deeper into her ass. Her pussy spasmed and a flood of moisture mixed with the hot water. Meline shook her head, denying the pleasure. Her hand drifted from his balls to the pucker of his ass. Roc's thighs tightened as she pushed one finger in.

"Meline, fuck, okay," he barked when she wiggled her fingertip.

"You want to play with my ass. I think this is only fair. I'll strap on a cock and take you from behind as I jack you off," she threatened while kissing his bare chest.

She stroked his cock faster as her finger delved deeper into his quivering puckered opening. She reached a sensitive spot deep inside and Roc shuddered, his cock jerking in her hand.

"Sacrament! I give." Roc grabbed her hands, forcing her to pull out and release his cock, as his tail retreated from her own ass.

"Oh," she pouted in disappointment. "Things were just getting good. So, does this mean no strap-on?" Meline asked, her lips twisting into an evil grin.

Roc smirked at her, then his expression softened as he stroked her back.

"I was serious about us making love as much as possible, but there's a good reason, not just me being a randy pervert."

"Is that so?" She traced his washboard abs, waiting for him to continue.

"I'm in love with you and want you in my life for as long as possible."

"I love you so much, Roc." Meline wrapped her arms around his waist and hugged him tight. So, this was where he was going. Roc was still worried about losing her. "You know, handsome, there's no guarantees in life. But if we worry about tomorrow all the time, we'll miss today."

"I know." He nodded. "But the more I love you, the longer you'll live. You'll heal faster and resist illness."

"That's what's been happening!" She gaped in shock and felt her forehead where the gash had been. It wasn't completely healed but it was certainly much better. "And this is because we have sex?"

"Yes and no. There's a gland in my mouth. I guess the hormone spreads through my bloodstream. It never responded to anyone, then I met you."

"Oh." She smiled at the notion she was special to him. She knew she was, but this somehow confirmed it.

"I didn't know it until my sire told me, but you're my mate, my *Hondassa*."

"Roc?" She stared up at him. Was he telling her what she thought he was?

Roc knelt in the pool. He was so tall the water still barely came to his chest. She started to hyperventilate as he took both her hands in his large palms. Behind him, the iridescent northern lights were an undulating curtain banding the sky, with the stars dancing like little diamonds. It presented an amazing backdrop for what she felt coming.

"You've been mine from the moment I heard you say such wildly silly things in your sleep, and you know I love you, but will you do me the honor of being mine?"

"Yes!" Meline cried as she wrapped her arms around his neck. "You didn't even have to ask!"

"Oh, yes I did. The sex on demand thing didn't work out so well for me, I wasn't about to screw this part up," he chuckled, then planted his lips against hers.

She sank into the warm water, and he shifted so she was straddling his lap as they kissed. The tingling sensation his kiss evoked was all the more pleasurable because she now knew what it meant. The idea they were going to spend a long, long life together filled her with unspeakable joy. Her tongue explored his mouth, stroking his canines, then retreated to nibble his lips.

"Mmm," Roc groaned into her mouth, his hands roaming her body, squeezing her hips, stroking her sides, caressing her breasts.

She wanted to be closer to him, as close as two people

possibly could be. Meline ground her hips against Roc, rubbing her pussy over his stiff cock trapped between them. Each time her clit struck the ridges on his engorged shaft, a spike of pleasure coursed through her, making her stomach do little crunches. Roc broke their kiss as his tail coiled around her waist and lifted her up.

"Do I have your permission to make you scream?" he rasped against her lips, his voice thick with desire.

Meline barely nodded when Roc swiftly tugged her down. His cock drove deep into her pussy, stretching her slick walls. He swallowed the keen that burst from her lips. The ridges lining his girth abraded her sensitive flesh as he steadily pulled her down, impaling her on his length. It was such sweet torment. Meline gripped his wings, her nails digging in as he buried the last inch inside her, shoving at the recesses of her quaking channel.

"Yes," Roc groaned as she trembled with ecstasy.

She threw her head back when Roc rotated his hips. His lower stomach grazed her clit and the head of his pulsing cock lit up the nerves lining her channel.

"Roc."

Her voice was part moan, part cry when he latched onto one of her nipples and sucked deep, giving it just a little nip, the sensation going straight through her. Meline spasmed, squeezing his cock. Roc jerked inside her.

"Fuck," he growled, his hot breath teasing her nipple.

With bruising strength, Roc gripped her hips tighter and started thrusting as he resumed tormenting her other nipple. Her fingers speared into his hair, holding on for dear life as his pace increased. Roc's lusty deep growls vibrated her nipple, making her reel from the resulting bliss. She panted, moaned and cried out as the pleasure swelled. His cock hammered in and out of her slick pussy, forcing past her rhythmically clenching muscles.

"Yes, fuck me harder." She tugged his hair as she writhed.

Roc snarled and turned feral. He pulled nearly all the way out and stabbed back in, grinding against her clit as he went wild. Her whole body shuddered, her legs squeezing his waist as her overheated body started coming apart at the seams. Suddenly his tail was working its way into her ass. The feeling of it sliding over the ring of nerves had her quaking harder.

"Roc," she screamed into his damp hair as the orgasm shot through her.

Roc burst. His pulsing cock flooded her channel with the liquid hormone that was unadulterated passion. Her pussy milked him of every last drop, but he didn't let up.

"More. Not enough." Roc attacked her mouth. He was an insatiable, lust-driven animal.

Roc spread her cheeks wider and his tail started fucking her ass in earnest. It pistoned in and out, pressing deeper than ever before, while his cock abused her needy pussy. She contorted in his grip, her orgasm raging on, building into maelstrom. He rumbled in warning as she struggled in his grasp, fighting the impending eclipse. His mouth found her shoulder and bit down to keep her still. Meline convulsed at the delicious bite of pain, her heels digging into his clenching ass.

Her eyes flew wide when she felt a gust of cool air. She looked around in awe and discovered they were midair. She was so hot the arctic breeze felt good against her skin. This was a first, then again everything with Roc was a first. The way he turned her inside out and possessed her with such abandon made her feel alive in a way she never imagined possible.

He said he knew she was special that first night he broke into her hotel. It was the same for her. When she saw him in the bookstore, the daunting knight coming to her rescue, she knew then there was something different about Roc. It had nothing to do with him being a gargoyle, no, this was different. It was like something inside her woke up and sat at attention, finally having found the one.

20

ROC

"I love you," Meline breathlessly chanted, ecstasy making her contort in his arms.

He never imagined three little words would mean so much. There wasn't a single thing in any of his vaults that could buy something so precious.

"You are my whole world," he mouthed against her shoulder, holding her tight as they made love high above the steamy pool.

Abruptly Meline stilled. This was the part he liked the most. The calm before the storm. Roc thrust harder and faster, her shallow staccato breaths and subtle trembling spurring him on. With each press, his tail undulated in her ass. His little angel was made for pleasure, loving every wicked thing he did to her, and it made him insanely hot.

He groaned into her shoulder when she grew painfully tight around his cock. He curled his hips, forcing his way deeper into her slick pussy. Then abruptly, like a clap of thunder, Meline burst with a ragged keen. The spasms that wracked her pussy and spread through her whole body were glorious. She was so unbelievably beautiful when she flew apart in his arms.

His shaft swelled, and his balls tightened up, as her silky heat gripped him with wave after mind-altering wave. He roared in ecstasy as the nirvana burned through him. His cock jerked uncontrollably, again bathing her sweet pussy with his release. For the first time in his life he hoped it took root.

"Don't move. Please, Roc, don't move," she begged while convulsions continued to assail her.

"I'm trying," he panted as he landed back in the warm pool.

They sat for a long while in silence, holding each other and catching their breath.

"This is really beautiful." Meline nodded to the flickering green lights rolling over the snowy mountains. "I never imagined seeing such a sight, much less making love to an awesome guy in a place like this."

"I'm going to take you to see so many wonderful places, Paris, Rome..." He squeezed her tighter, his wings folding around her back, careful not to obstruct her view.

"Roc?" He heard the question in her voice.

"What is it?"

"I lost my family and I know how hard that is. But you still have your dad. Are you sure you're okay with him leaving?"

He looked into her hazel brown eyes and saw how sad she was for him.

"I asked him to stay, but he wouldn't be happy here. It's okay, you are my family now," he reassured her.

"I know, but have you thought for just a moment about

going with your dad? You wouldn't have to hide or worry about being hunted."

"No! There's no way I'd leave you." Roc shook his head adamantly. "I can't believe you're even suggesting it."

He pulled away from Meline, suddenly frustrated and hurt.

"No, no, no." She wrapped her arms around his neck before he could get far. "What if—well—what if I went with you?"

His gaze shot to hers. She was serious. Taking her to Duras was something he'd never considered.

"I've always wanted to travel, and if you're not being hunted then I would be safer, too," she quickly added.

Meline presented a convincing argument, knowing full well her safety meant everything to him.

"Petronus did say Duras welcomed other species," he said thoughtfully.

"Then it's settled." Meline hopped up, scrambled out of the pool and started dressing.

"Are you sure about this?" Roc followed her and threw on his clothes.

"Yes, and we better hurry!"

Roc was still stunned by the time they got her bundled up and they lifted into the air. He would do anything for her and she truly looked excited at the prospect of seeing a new world. She was braver than he was. As he flew north, he couldn't help wonder if they were jumping from the frying pan into the fire.

"The GPS says we should be there," Meline hollered, her mouth obstructed by the sleeping bag.

He panned the slopes then paused, seeing a recognizable

shape sitting on a rocky outcropping. He swooped in and set down several yards behind the figure staring into the distance.

"Most of the others have already gone. You better get going, time is almost up." Petronus waved him off without bothering to turn around. His sire thought he was someone else.

Why is he just waiting here?

The answer came to him as he noticed the way his sire's wings hung at his back, his tail lax, not even a single twitch. Petronus looked conflicted, alone and profoundly sad. His sire was always the biggest, baddest, unmovable piece of stone he'd ever known, and yet over the last few days he'd learned differently. The uncertainty about whether this was the right decision instantly fled.

Roc glanced down at Meline to confirm she was still okay with this. She smiled then nodded toward Petronus.

"You think there's room on that ship for two more?" he asked.

Petronus spun around. "Rochelle!"

"Yeah." He grinned.

"What about your *Hondassa*?" Petronus looked at Meline in concern.

"I'm going, too." Meline nodded inside her fluffy bundle.

"If that's allowed." Roc was suddenly nervous.

"Well, none of the other Earthians were rejected." Petronus looked around the mountainside, as if confirming there were no other humans wandering about.

The comment about other humans intrigued him, but Meline was the only one he cared about.

"And she'll be treated well on Duras?" He had to ask the important question.

"We are not a closed society." Petronus nodded.

"Then let's do this," Meline chimed in eagerly, making Roc laugh.

"One more thing." He frowned, recalling his old friend.

"Yes?" Petronus looked suddenly nervous, thinking perhaps he changed his mind.

"Is there's any way I can get a message to John? Everything will easily transfer to him if not, but I don't want him to worry and I'd like to say goodbye."

"Oh yeah. I'm going to miss John and Jen. Maybe I can send her a message, too." Meline snuggled into him, her eyes suddenly misting.

"I think we can find a way." Petronus nodded.

"Okay. I'm ready if you are." Meline cast him a brave smile.

"You never cease to amaze me." He squeezed her against him.

MELINE

"Hold onto me," Petronus said, and Roc gripped his wing, while tightening his arm around her.

I can't believe this. Meline was so excited as she watched Petronus swipe his hand across the jeweled surface of the sigil.

The blustering snow and rocky mountainside flickered, and her stomach felt like it was doing somersaults. She bit her lip to keep from retching. Her eyes widened when everything came into focus again, her nausea instantly forgotten.

She stared at the inside of the spaceship, mouth hanging open in amazement. It looked like metal and stone had grown into a ship, if that was somehow possible. Her neck craned up to take in the vaulted ceiling. The rock, or was it metal, spidered across the walls looking like the veins of a leaf, but was probably conduit or something. Her gaze darted to the Khargal who stepped away from a group of others.

"I think that's Traver. Looks like he's captain of this rescue mission." Petronus stepped forward and greeted the Khargal in a language she didn't understand.

"Don't worry. This is new for me, too." Roc set her down and peeled off the sleeping bag.

"I'm not worried, more excited than anything. It's wild to think I once dreamt of seeing the world and now I'm going to see worlds." She smiled up at him, barely able to contain herself.

"So, it looks like I'm keeping my promise to show you exotic places after all." Roc hugged her against him.

"It does, but you know, none of that really matters." She stroked his chest, feeling how strong his heartbeat was.

"Why is that, angel?" His liquid silver eyes held her gaze as he cradled the back of her head.

"I don't really care where we go, or what we see." She leaned in and brushed her lips against his. "As long as I have you by my side, my love, my Roc."

And she was right, everything else faded away as Roc enveloped her in his wings and kissed her.

The End

Thank you, for reading *Hard as Rock*, Khargals of Duras. Learn what happens to the other Khargals by reading Regine Abel's *Heart of Stone.*

Her winged savior was no angel.

When death nearly claims Brianna at the tender age of eight, a being that shouldn't exist saves her. Twenty years later, she becomes an architect specialized in historic buildings, still searching for evidence that the one who saved her—the one who haunts her increasingly wild dreams—truly exists. When a mystery man hires her for a major project in the catacombs of an old church turned exclusive, gothic nightclub, Brianna believes she may have her chance at long last.

Alkor has grown weary of this era. Forced to hide in plain sight, forbidden from ever claiming the only woman to have stirred his mating instincts, he considers going back into hibernation rather than pining for her from afar. But the sudden activation of the beacon changes everything. Rescue is on the way! With his only means of reaching the rendezvous point trapped in the catacombs, Alkor hires Brianna to help recover his treasure. However, his lost sigil isn't the only thing he intends to take back home with him.

Time is running out, and the evil forces conspiring to capture him will stop at nothing to achieve their goal, even using Brianna. Did Alkor save his true mate only to lose her now that they might have a chance at a future together?

https://www.amazon.com/Heart-Stone-Khargals-Duras-Regine-ebook/dp/B07NMK6K6K/

GLOSSARY

At-Ukris: aerial Duras animal. Looks like a cross between an eagle and an octopus roughly the size of a whale

Bansial: the Durassian word for sticky

Canikin: the Durassian word for lady parts

Dam: mother

Dassa: mating fluid

Duramna: stone form

Duras: Khargal home planet

Durassian: the Khargal language

Earthian: what Khargals call humans

Fa: the Durassian word for Mrs.

Grack: the Durassian expletive for fuck

Guurlk: Khargal liquor

Hondassa: Mate

Kher: Khargal term for siblings

Khargal: what gargoyles call themselves

Lar: the Durassian word for god

Macero: the Durassian expletive for hell

Maztek: Duras animal similar to an earth whale

Rose Syndicate: clandestine organization that is pursuing gargoyles and their technology

Sartek: a random predatory animal on Duras

Sigil: the device used for contacting the rescue beacon and teleporting to the rescue ship

Sire: father

Tanem: the Durassian word for temporary companion taken before a true mate

Want more sexy Khargals? Check out all the books in the series! You don't want to miss a single one!

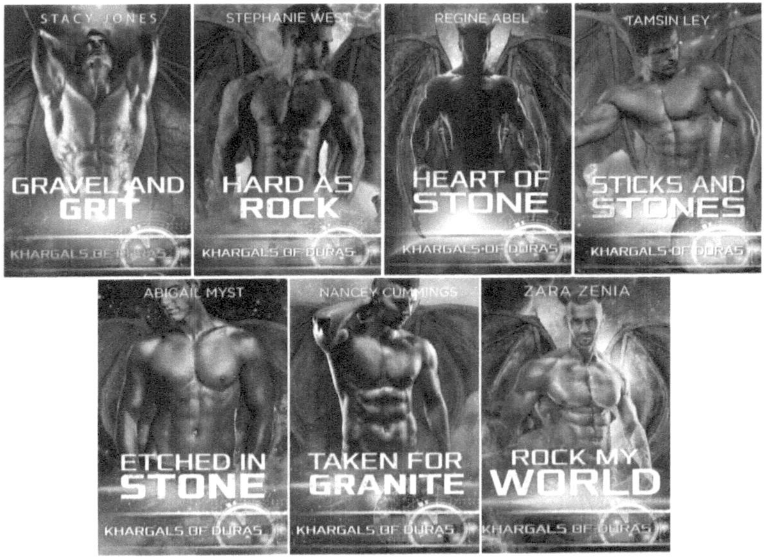

https://nanceycummings.com/khargals-of-duras/

ACKNOWLEDGMENTS

I'd like to thank all my fellow authors who made writing this series a wonderful experience I won't soon forget, and look forward to working with you in the future.

Thank you to my wonderful husband, the love of my life, who puts up with my nonsense. He was the inspiration behind the sleep talking scene. Frustratingly, I never got him to tell me what the stealth frog was doing with sliced pickles.

And bless my grandpa who lovingly ate my grandma's cherry pies for decades without saying a word about not liking them.

If you've already consumed the entire Khargals of Duras series, check out my Cadi Warriors, the Fated Mate series, *Viper's Hope* (Anguis Defenders Book 1) and more at:

http://amazon.com/author/stephaniewest

Or follow me on Facebook, my blog, or newsletter, where I announce new releases.

Facebook
https://www.facebook.com/StephanieWestAuthor/

Website
https://stephaniewestauthor.com/

Newsletter
http://eepurl.com/c1UTNb

CADI WARRIORS SERIES

The Warrior's Pet (Cadi Warriors Book 1)
https://books2read.com/u/brGokM

Giselle didn't know how long she lay near catatonic, willing the terrible headache to go away. She sat up as one of the reptilian aliens entered. Giselle backed up and looked around, realizing she was alone in a gilded cage.

"What's going on?" she stammered.

"If you're wise you'll keep quiet. Pets don't speak on this planet," the creature admonished.

A pet? Giselle's eyes widened. She hadn't misheard.

Her cage was moved into a large tent. There were hundreds of aliens gathered for the auction, and these creatures were the largest yet. Their flesh was red like some kind of demon might be, with hair a uniform dark black. From what Giselle could see, their eyes were a stone-cold obsidian hue. Giselle noticed the fearsome creatures had long tails that rose out from what looked like chainmail kilts. Giselle shrunk back when she saw the creatures also had sharp fangs.

How in the hell could she get out of this, and if she did, how could she possibly survive on an alien planet?

Kagan beheld his pet. Nothing like her kind had ever set foot on Cadi. Kagan wondered where in the universe her unique species hailed from.

Giselle refused to behave and even enjoyed his attempts to rebuke her, reveling in the rough handling a male usually refrained from with females. Giselle was brave instead of meek, standing up for herself in a sea of foreigners.

Kagan had at first insisted that Giselle understand her place in Cadi society. But something more valuable than precious metal or jewels would be lost if Giselle were forced into the role everyone thought she belonged.

Can Giselle find acceptance and love on an alien planet, or will she always be nothing more than a warrior's pet?

Warriors' Providence (Cadi Warriors Book 2)
https://books2read.com/u/mZP5ol

Warrior's Paradox (Cadi Warriors Book 3)
https://books2read.com/u/bWzZgW

Warrior's Pain (Cadi Warriors Book 4)
https://books2read.com/u/3kr0KN

Warrior's Purpose (Cadi Warriors Book 5)
https://books2read.com/u/bP50Vr

Warrior's Plight (Cadi Warriors Book 6)
https://books2read.com/u/m0MrnV

ANGUIS DEFENDERS SERIES

Viper's Hope (Anguis Defenders Book 1)
https://books2read.com/u/3J80rv

Hope covered her ringing ears as she stared wide-eyed at the molten rock strafing across the sky. It got larger and brighter with the smoke trail parting the horizon. The sudden eruption of water out at sea was cataclysmic when the meteor struck. The wave of water that barreled toward San Francisco a moment later was small at first, then grew in size. Hope watched aghast as the water pushed aside massive buildings. She couldn't begin to fathom the level of devastation in front of her.

As if the tragedy she'd witnessed wasn't enough, something lurked in the trees outside her campsite. She watched as a portion of the tree separated from the trunk. The colors morphed into a bronzed, earthy tan figure of a man. The camouflaged man was at least seven foot tall with well-built legs and a massive broad chest. He swayed hypnotically as he walked with the sleekness of predator. His facial features were not human, yet not altogether frightening. He was an alien, a giant freaking alien, and he was abducting her!

Before the scourge of the universe struck, Viper never aspired to do more than rule his people, but his entire life had changed in the blink of an eye. The tragedy galvanized him with a single-minded purpose, to see to it he defended the Anguis and any other race unfortunate enough to cross paths with the plague, and wipe it from existence.

Finding his mate was the farthest thing from Viper's mind as he attempted to rescue the humans off the doomed planet. With his own planet in turmoil over aiding so many other species and the universe at risk from the catastrophic plague, Viper never expected to find Hope.

Caution - This book contains a rough scene where our heroine is chained and taken by our hero. If you have triggers, this book isn't for you. However, fear not, in the end, Hope finds the experience mind-blowing.

FATED MATE SERIES

***Nameless Fate* (Fated Mate Book 1)**
https://books2read.com/u/bMQrWB

Harper might get an uncanny gut feeling every now and then, but that didn't mean she believed in portents, and certainly not the kind that got her abducted. As Harper gripped the bars of her cage in the alien prison, it sunk in that she seriously had been kidnapped from Earth, to become the fated consort of some alien prince. This wasn't some elaborate prank, or government experiment. True to form, Harper pissed off the tyrannical king with her refusal. Now she found herself at the mercy of convicts, locked away and forgotten in the bowels of a mountain.

Harper's gaze fell on a shadowy beast of a man, sitting casually on the rundown catwalk. The imposing man looked like he ruled the prison. He was the color of midnight, and his eyes were that eerie arctic blue that was nearly colorless. Harper shivered as he regarded her.

All Nameless knew was the Hold, with its misery and struggle. He never wanted to keep a female, surviving was hard enough, but that was before the Pink Pearl dropped into his world. Nameless had never seen anything like the stunning, exotic little creature. Not only was she the catalyst for strange dreams and revelations about his past, but she made him feel. He had to have her.

Harper wanted free of the alien prison, and she wanted to go home, except Nameless wasn't prepared or willing to let her go, even if she hated him because of it. He owned every part of her, and bound her to him, in ways that could never be undone, collar or no collar. In her wildest dreams, Harper never imagined the twists destiny could take, or that she would find soul-deep satisfaction with such a nameless fate.

Follow Harper and Nameless as they struggle to get free of the Hold, and seek their revenge on the despot responsible for putting them there.

Note: This book contains erotic scenes where the dominant hero bends the heroine to his will. What pisses her off the most, is that she likes it.

Fated to Fall **(Fated Mate Book 2)**
https://books2read.com/u/mVBZzP

ABOUT THE AUTHOR

About Stephanie West

As a child, I had difficulty learning to read, so anything I took an interest in was deemed acceptable. I have always enjoyed fairy tales, mythology, science fiction, and action. However, romance inspired me most of all, love being the greatest adventure. As I read, my mind wanders, spinning its own tales. So, after encouragement from friends, I figured I'd share my ramblings with the world, and my life as a part-time science fiction and paranormal romance author began.

All my tales feature strong, gutsy and sometimes gifted heroines overcoming difficult odds, a lot of action, and steamy scenes that don't fade to black. Generally, the romantic adventures I tell are about one hero and heroine, but occasionally a girl needs more. Although I've been called dark and told my stories push boundaries, they always end happily ever after. I try to use my tales as a way to share the various escapades, comedies, and tragedies that have peppered my life, from archaeology in the hot sun to riding on a Harley with a dark stranger. It is my greatest hope you finish each story inspired to make your dreams come true no matter how impossible they may seem.

Thank you for going on this journey with me and here's to the imagination and a little daydream.